Neither of us said much on the way to the barbecue place. In the nine years that I'd been with Richard, Bea and I hadn't spent much time together. For the most part, I thought she was this nice old lady. The most time we'd spent together was Christmas dinner a few years back. Nothing was the way that I had wanted it to be. I was spending my first Christmas away from home in my baby's father's mother's house. My parent's home was filled with Christmas decorations and people laughing, fighting, and cutting the general fool. Meanwhile, I was hundreds of miles away, in a house where the only decoration was a tree that could best be described as the model for that horrible little tree in the Charlie Brown Christmas Special. Add to that, Richard got called in to work. He drove back to Atlanta, leaving me with his mother and her senile aunt. I barely knew either of them. To be fair, Virginia had a lot going on.

PEACE BE STILL

COLETTE HAYWOOD

Genesis Press Inc.

Black Coral

An imprint of Genesis Press Inc.
Publishing Company

Genesis Press, Inc.
P.O. Box 101
Columbus, MS 39703

ISBN: 1-58571-129-2
Manufactured in the United States of America

First Edition

Visit us at www.genesis-press.com
or call at 1-888-Indigo-1

DEDICATION

Wow! There are so many people for me to thank. Thanks Baby, you mean everything to me. Thank you Camille, Charlotte and Brian. I love you and hope that you are as proud of me as I am of you, this just goes to show that YOU CAN DO IT! Never give up!

Mom, Dad, thanks for the head start, I don't say it often enough but I love you guys! Last but not least, my family and friends. There are too many of you to name but you are all a blessing to me. I say with both honesty and sincerity that I am truly blessed to have each and every one of you in my life. From the bottom of my heart thank you for making me rich!

CHAPTER ONE
RACHAEL

I watched Richard walk out of the gas station, the sun beating down on the milky brown skin of his shiny baldhead. He got into the car and handed me a Snickers.

"Thanks." I accepted his peace offering, turned off the air conditioner, and rolled down the window, despite the stifling heat. It was mid September, but in south Georgia, it was as hot as any day in the middle of July. I took in a deep breath of the humid air then took a bite of the candy.

"Are we driving all the way to Albany in silence?" Richard asked and pulled onto the highway. "Or are you going to talk to me."

I rolled the window up and turned the air back on. "I'm not, not talking to you. I just don't have anything to say."

"Rachael, it's only nine months."

It took nine months to grow a baby. I should know, I'd grown three. "If it's only for nine months, me and the kids can stay with my parents in Michigan."

The muscles in his face tensed. "We already went over this. I'm not about to be separated from my kids like that. If you stay at my mother's, at least I'll be able to see them on weekends. Besides, your parents didn't offer, my mother did. I am a man. I'm not about to go and ask another man to take care of my family." He momentarily took his hand off of the steering wheel and motioned to himself with his thumb. "That's my job."

The idea of living with my mother-in-law didn't suit me. I remembered the horror stories from my own mother about her and Dad living with Grandma. Living with family is hard, even if you get along. People need their space. "Everything is always centered around what you want," I countered.

"That's not fair," Richard fumed. "Everything that I do, I do for you."

The car behind us blew the horn, and Richard realized that he'd slowed down on the on ramp to the expressway. He pushed on the gas and merged into traffic.

I looked into the backseat of the car. I hated arguing in front of the kids. Thank goodness, they were still sleeping. "Keep your voice down," I hissed. "You'll wake the kids.

"Sorry," Richard said, lowering his voice. It was important to the both of us that we put the kids first no matter what. "But what haven't I done for you?"

"What about school?" I asked. Ever since I dropped out of college with our first daughter, Sherril, I'd planned to go back.

"What about it? I was the one who paid for the last classes you took," he said, trying to remain calm.

I started for a minute then stared at Richard. "If you remember correctly, I had to put my plans on hold because you decided to start your recording studio."

"I've always been up front with you about the fact that I wanted to have my own business."

"You being upfront don't get our bills paid."

"Was that what you were thinking when you decided to attend cosmetology school instead of finishing your degree?"

"No it wasn't. I only went to cosmetology school because you told me too."

"I can't make you do anything."

"Well you strongly encouraged it."

"That's because I thought you would like it. You didn't seem act like you wanted to go back to college, and you were always doing hair anyway." He harrumphed. "It's not like you were getting straight A's."

I cut my eyes at Richard. "The bottom line is, I'm always the one putting what I want to do on hold so that you can do your thing."

Richard sighed. "We can go back and forth like this all day and not get anywhere. Both of us have made mistakes, and both of us have to make sacrifices. Do you think I want to be away from my family?"

"No, I'm not saying that but I…"

"I want my kids to grow up in a house with a yard. We already have the baby sleeping in the room with us. Why do that if we don't have to? We both decided that we could save money for a house by taking Momma up on her offer. I know it won't be easy, but why turn down this opportunity? When I move into the studio, we can save the nine hundred dollars we spend in rent plus the money from utilities. Besides, with you all gone, I can get a second job and save even more money. Think about it, that's at least twelve hundred dollars a month. That gives us an eighteen thousand dollar minimum at the end of nine months."

I looked at Richard skeptically. "What do you mean minimum?"

"I'm not counting the money that I generate from the studio.

Think about it, we can bank that money. All of the money I make at my job will go straight to the bank, minus expenses."

I couldn't argue with his reasoning, but my greatest fears were coming to pass. I was twenty-eight, married with three kids, and going to stay with my mother-in-law. I'd be stuck in a place where I had no friends and absolutely nothing to do but devote myself to the kids. Taking care of five-year-old Sherril, three-year-old Virginia, and six-month-old Elliot was an important job. However, it couldn't be my everything. I'd go nuts! Instead of falling apart, I kept reminding myself that this was in fact a blessing. A lot of couples would kill for the same opportunity.

Virginia's house seemed larger than I remembered. Virginia had dinner waiting for us. She welcomed me with a hug when I came in the door.

"Hey, Momma." Richard kissed her on the cheek then took the baby upstairs to change his diaper.

"Grandma!" Sherril and Little Virginia squealed in unison.

Virginia bent down to give them a hug. "Hey darlins."

With the exception of her blonde hair, Little Virginia looked just like a younger version of her grandmother. They both had delicate features and fair skin.

"Grandma, may I have a cup of coffee?" Sherril asked. With her caramel complexion and big brown eyes, she looked more like her father. They also shared similar dispositions. Both were quiet and reserved. Like her father, Richard, Sherrill preferred to sit back and observe a situation as opposed to jumping into the fray.

"Of course, baby. I have your coffee waiting for you at your place at the table." Virginia turned to me and winked. What Sherril thought was coffee was really milk with maybe a quarter of a teaspoon of Café International.

I thought that was sweet, but could only muster a weak smile.

Sherril giggled, grabbed my hand and dragged me into the dining room where Virginia's sister, Bea, was putting the finishing touches on the table.

"Hey, Sherril," Bea greeted, swooped down to grab Sherril in a hug then pulled her up so that she had to stand on the tips of her toes.

"I can't breathe," Sherril gasped.

Bea laughed and let her go. Sherril ran over to the Strawberry Shortcake place setting and took a seat. "Grandma, is this pink plate mine?" she called to Virginia in the kitchen.

"Only if you like it," Virginia called back.

Little Virginia grew timid from the excitement and hid behind my legs. "Hey, Bea," I said and picked up my daughter. "Aren't you going to say hello to Aunt Bea?" I asked Little Virginia.

Bea walked over to me. "I hope you have a nickname for this baby. We can't have two Virginia's on the premises."

I laughed. "I hadn't thought about that. Why don't you give her one now?" I tried my best to be cordial on the outside, but on the inside, I felt like crap. My husband was due to leave in a little more than an hour.

Bea looked at Little Virginia long and hard. "She looks just like Virginia. We should call her two."

5

"We are not going to call my baby two," Richard said from the kitchen.

"Boy, you been in this house five minutes and didn't speak to me. Now you want to come in and start ordering folks around. You not to old for me to spank your behind."

Richard entered the room laughing and went over to Bea to give her a kiss "How you doin', Aunt Bea?" He stood with one arm around her shoulder and held the baby in the other.

"I don't know, I guess I'll make it."

Virginia entered the room, carrying a large pot. "You know Bea, there is always something going on with her." She sat the pot in the middle of the table.

Bea rolled her eyes at Virginia. "Well. Every body is not perfect like you."

"So, what are we calling my little name sake?" She didn't bother giving Bea the time of day. Instead, she walked over to me and leaned down to pat Virginia on the cheek. Virginia turned her face into my chest, peeked out, and turned back quickly when she saw us looking at her.

"We'll call her Vee," Bea decided.

Richard had to leave immediately after dinner so that he could get back to work. The two of us went outside to unload the car.

"Remember, baby, it's only nine months," he said as he took a heavy suitcase out of my hands.

I nodded my head. "Okay," I whispered, choking back tears.

He put down the suitcase and pulled me toward him. "I'll try to come down every weekend."

I lay my head on his chest and let the tears fall. He would be busy working and running a business. He wouldn't have the time to come down every weekend.

"Are you crying?" he asked.

I nodded.

"Baby, please don't cry, you know what that does to me."

I nodded again. "I'm sorry. But, I like living with my husband."

"You are so stupid," he said and kissed me on the lips. "Ugh." He drew back and wiped his mouth. "I just got some of your snot in my mouth."

We both laughed and turned around to meet the kids who were following Virginia out of the house. "I told the girls that they could help me wash the dishes after they said goodbye to their father."

Little kids love to play with water, and mine were no exception. Washing dishes was a combination of two things that they loved: bubbles and water. I wished that my life were that simple.

Richard knelt down to the girl's level. "Come and give me a hug."

Little Virginia, or Vee, didn't understand what was happening. She fell into Richard's arms and razzed him on the cheek. To her, that was the funniest thing in the world.

Richard returned the favor.

"You're leaving now?"

Richard nodded.

Sherril backed up and shook her head. She was still young enough to think that he wouldn't leave just because she refused to say goodbye.

Richard reached out and pulled her too him. "I love you," he said quietly.

Sherril hung on to his neck, crying.

"Come on, baby, the sooner you let me leave, the sooner you can help Grandma wash the dishes."

Sherril wasn't having it. Richard looked to me for help. I bent down and picked Sherril up.

"I want my daddy! I want my daddy!" Sherril cried, flinging her legs and arms.

Richard couldn't take it. Quickly, he stood up. "I'll call you as soon as I get back," he said, looking at me anxiously.

"Goodbye, baby. I love you." Leaving my suitcase outside, I turned and walked into the house without waiting for him to pull off. The sooner I got Sherril inside, the easier it would be on all of us.

During the first few days of my stay with Virginia, we tiptoed around each other. Her house was so quiet. Even with my three kids it was abnormally quiet. Part of that was because the house was so big, not that I'd grown up in a small house. But my parents' house was a ranch. Virginia lived in a large, three-story, five bedroom, three and a half bath home.

You could tell that it had been built in the early sixties from the winding wrought iron staircase and the granite tiles in the foyer and kitchen. And the patio, actually it was styled more in the fashion of a lanai, ran from the dining room all the way to the living room. It was definitely a beautiful home. All of the living room furniture was covered in beautiful silks and linen. Virginia wasn't one to scrimp on style.

Every room in the house was full of pictures of days gone by. In the living room, Virginia dedicated her curio cabinet to pictures of her parents and their respective families. Included in the cabinet was a book that once belonged to her maternal grandfather; it was full of famous signatures of people he'd had the good fortune to meet during his lifetime. Most of the people I didn't recognize, but I was shocked to find the signatures of Ralph Waldo Emerson, Mary McCloud Bethune, and Booker T. Washington. I was even more shocked to read that these people regarded him as a friend and not just some stranger whose book they'd signed. There was also a framed copy of the first meeting of Negro bankers, which eventually became the Negro Banker's Association, dated September 15, 1926, in the Knights of Pythias Hall in Philadelphia.

One of Virginia's aunts married a professor who became a dean at Fisk University. Beatrice, for whom Bea was named, and her husband circulated and were among the "Talented Tenth." Upon her death, she bequeathed the majority of her belongings to Virginia. In which case, Virginia had original paintings from Aaron Douglas, signed first editions text from Langston Hughes, W.E.B. du Bois, Arna Bontemps, and the list goes on.

It was almost like living in a library. I spent a great deal of time chasing behind Little Virginia, pulling her off of the top of the baby grand and stopping her from climbing on top of coffee tables to get to the books and pictures. Finally, I pulled two side chairs into the doorway to block her entrance. Unfortunately, I still had to deal with her banging on the door to the hall clock. I was constantly erasing her prints from the glass.

On the other hand, none of it fazed Virginia in the least. In the softest voice, she would simply admonish them, "Mind out now, mind out."

She had been around these things most of her life and met half of the people, so they were just regular folk to her. She had gotten more excited about a front page article about her son, Edward, in the paper detailing a big case against a police officer charged with excessive force that he'd won. She called all of her family and friends to make sure that they'd seen it.

When it came time to brag about her own accomplishments, she simply brushed them off. I had to almost beg her to tell me about the picture in which she and Richard, Sr. posed with Martin Luther King, Jr.

While Virginia and I walked around each other on eggshells, Bea and I hit it off like gangbusters. The two of us clicked. I enjoyed her sense of humor. Bea and I had just come into the house after running a few errands when the phone rang. It was the principal at Sherril's school.

"Mrs. Anderson, this is Mrs. Abbott, the principal at Glen Lake Baptist School. We have some information we need to discuss about Sherril."

My stomach dropped. "What is it, is she sick, has she been hurt?" I asked anxiously. Only two weeks of living in a little hick town otherwise known as Albany and already there's a problem!

"I assure you that she is fine physically," she continued calmly. "It's just that, well, there has been a rumor going around at school."

What in the world, the girl is only five, what type of rumor could there be? Sherril had only been in school for a day and a half. "What's going on?"

"We really need to speak in person."

Her emphasis on the word "really" had my heart racing. "Okay, I'll be there in five minutes."

I found Bea in the kitchen pouring Vee some juice. "Bea, do you mind putting the kids down for their naps while I run up to the school?"

"No, no, go ahead. What is going on?"

I shrugged my shoulders. "I don't know, they won't tell me."

I was in such a rush to get to the school, I didn't remember to thank her until I got to the door leading to the garage. "Thanks Bea," I called on my way out of the door. It only took a short time to get there; the school was less than three miles from the house. Still, I was going crazy trying to figure out what in the world this woman could be talking about. I'd butted heads with Mrs. Flowers, the assistant principal, when I insisted that Sherril be put in the first grade.

I'm from Michigan where the cut off for children starting school is December 1st. In Georgia, the cut off was September of the school year. Since Sherril's birthday was October 26th, she was supposed to sit out a year before starting school. That made absolutely no sense to me. By the time Sherril turned four, she knew her ABC's, her colors, and how to count to twenty. It took some searching, but I found a school that would place her according to her development, which tests showed was first grade. When I tried to enroll her in the first grade, Mrs. Flowers insisted, "Our program is more rigorous than others. In which case, she really would not be ready for the first grade." Once I showed her Sherril's test scores, she reluctantly agreed to put her in the first grade.

If it were 1860, Mrs. Abbott would have been wearing a hoop skirt, sipping a mint julep, while lounging on the veranda. She was a modern day southern belle. Her outfit looked like something straight out of Laura & Ashley, every inch of it was coordinated. She wore a navy sweater with bold fuchsia flowers all over it. The skirt was the same navy background as the sweater, with matching flowers in a smaller print. Of course, her stockings and shoes were navy. The coup de grace was the little flower clip on her shoes; it was the exact same flower found on the rest of her ensemble. As for her makeup, it was flawless. Her lipstick was a matching fuchsia, with coordinating shades of pink blush and eye shadow.

While shaking hands with her, I was struck by the amount of jewelry she wore. She wore a ring on every finger, and not just any old rings either. I'm not sure how many carats she had total, but my guess would be a carat and a half, not to mention the gold chains she wore around her neck. Thank God I didn't laugh aloud when I looked at her ears. She had on little flower earrings that were, of course, the same flower as everything else. Unbelievable!

Mrs. Abbott rose from her seat and gestured toward one of the two chairs in front of her desk. "Hello, Mrs. Anderson, please have a seat. I'm so sorry that our first meeting has to be under these," she paused, "circumstances. I'm sure that you were alarmed by my phone call, but these matters are best handled in person."

Nodding hello, I took a seat across from her, wishing that she would get the hell on with it. She leaned toward me and whispered, "Well, it has come to my attention," she paused, looking around to make sure no one else could hear her, "that Sherril has been using the word," she quickly looked around again then at me, "penis."

Surely, I thought, this couldn't be the reason this woman called me to the school. I sat dumbfounded as she continued. Apparently, Sherril's teacher overheard her using the word penis. According to the teacher, this was the second time she used the word. Under the "circumstances," she felt compelled to tell Mrs. Abbot. What the hell did she mean by circumstances? Saying the word penis twice constituted a circumstance? I tried to remain calm, thinking that there was more to the story. All the same, I felt my face grow hot.

Mrs. Abbott shifted in her chair nervously. "Mrs. Anderson, I am compelled by Georgia law to investigate any report that there might be some goings on. In which case, I called Sherril to my office to ask her if anything had occurred that she felt she might need to tell someone. She informed us that yesterday afternoon when she and her cousin were playing with their kitten, a man came out of the woods. According to her, he took his penis out of his pants and slapped them with it. Next, he threatened that if they told anyone, he would kill the kitten. She said that his name is Herbert Shirley. Do you know anyone by that name?"

Yeah, this woman was definitely unbelievable. To be fair, I knew that people in her position had to take instances of physical and mental abuse very seriously, and yes, they did have to investigate all reports. On the other hand, they received training for what to look for. Talk about ridiculous. The girl had used the word penis twice for Christ sake! They pulled her into the office for that. I'm positive that once she got into the office with this woman, a story was coaxed out of Sherril. I wanted to grab the woman by the shoulders and shake her little hairspray helmet head for all that it was worth for scaring me. Instead, I spoke calmly, "Mrs. Abbott, I appreciate your concern. However, I can assure you that nothing has happened. We've only been here a few weeks. In fact, Sherril has been within my reach since we've been here."

"Mm hmm, well, why would she make up such a story? Is she familiar with the word penis? Does anyone in your home go around saying that word?"

This woman positively took the cake. "Of course she knows the word penis. It is the correct name for a part of the human anatomy. She does have a father and a baby brother. So yes, in all honesty, the word has come up."

Mrs. Abbott sat looking stupid. "Well," she stammered, "I'm not sure that Mrs. Bramble heard the entire conversation. But, there is still the matter of Mr. Herbert Shirley."

Herbert Shirley, I thought, Herbert Shirley, that name did sound very familiar. Then it came to me! That was the name of a character in one of Sherril's books. I rose in my chair and said firmly, "Mrs. Abbott, I can assure you that the entire story is made up. Herbert Shirley is a nursery rhyme character. But, if it will make you feel more comfortable, we can both talk to Sherril."

An aide was sent to bring Sherril to the office while Mrs. Abbott and I waited. Mrs. Abbott proceeded to tell me that she ran a Christian school, which meant that the school families were very serious about keeping their children away from certain influences. She pleasantly explained it would be extremely helpful if I teach Sherril that certain body parts were not to be spoken about while at school.

Virginia introduced me to Glen Lake. It was an exclusive Christian Academy. Sherril's father, Richard, had gone there as a child. Virginia said that the school was started as a response to desegregation, and she enrolled Richard in an attempt to desegregate.

My Mother's wit took over when Sherril entered the room. She looked so pitiful. She'd been caught in a lie! She'd never been in so much trouble. I wasn't mad at her though. Sherril was just giving Mrs. Abbott what she thought the lady wanted. "Sherril." I turned to her and asked, "Could you please tell me about Mr. Herbert Shirley?"

She ran into my arms crying so hard she could barely respond. "He is for pretend."

Mrs. Abbott's face turned red as she stared at the two of us, me stroking Sherril's hair, in an attempt to soothe her.

"Sherril," I spoke once she calmed down.

"Yes." She rubbed her swollen eyes.

"Remember when we talked about saying things for pretend like they are true?"

She nodded and fell against my chest.

"Well this is one of those times. Why would you make up something like that?"

"Because I want my daddy," she wailed.

Mrs. Abbott was speechless. She quickly apologized for the confusion and gave me the, "Let's work together" speech.

My poor baby, I didn't know what to say to her on the way

home. I was feeling a combination of things: anger, embarrassment and sadness. Whew! It was only two o'clock, and, already, I wanted the day to end. I shoved my own emotions aside and focused my attention on Sherril. I reached for her hand. "You know that you can talk to me about anything right? You don't have to make up stories."

Sherril's face turned crimson. "Yes, ma'am," she stammered and began crying again.

I stroked Sherril with my right hand and kept the left on the steering wheel. "I miss Daddy, too."

"You do," she whimpered.

"I tell you what," I continued bravely. "I'll help you when you're feeling sad and missing Daddy, and you can help me."

Sherril stopped crying and looked at me with one eyebrow raised. "How can I help you?"

I shrugged my shoulders and turned onto our street, using both hands to steer. "Well, how about hugs, don't they make you feel better?"

"Yes." She beamed. "And I can sing to you, too!"

I pulled into the driveway, turned off the car and winked at Sherril. "That's a great idea. And I can help you write Daddy a letter, or call him whenever you want to talk."

Sherril's face wrinkled with worry. "But I don't know how to spell that much."

I put my hand to my chin and pretended to be deep in thought. "No," I said slowly, "but you're learning how in your new school. How about this, I will help you write the words you don't know?"

Sherril's eyes sparkled. "Yes, and then Daddy will be proud of how smart I am when I write him my own letter."

Kids are much more resilient than adults. Sherril went bouncing out of the car and into the house, yet I still felt like shit.

I gave Sherril a snack and sent her upstairs to join her napping siblings. Bea was in the den fussing about the remote control.

Although she and Virginia were sisters, they were opposite in almost every way. Bea was a handsome woman, tall and dark. Though also attractive; her sister, on the other hand, was a small woman of average height, with a fair complexion. The only thing the two sisters had in common was the texture of their hair, which was soft and fine. It had probably been long and black as young girls. At this stage of the game, Virginia had hers colored black, and Bea's was mostly gray. While Bea was loud and gregarious, every thing about Virginia was delicate and ladylike; she was truly a Black American Princess.

"I don't know why this thing won't work." Bea banged the remote on the end table next to the recliner she was sitting in.

"Shh," I said and held my finger up to my lips. "The kids are asleep," I whispered.

"Sorry," Bea whispered. "But I'm missing my story."

"I think it needs new batteries." I walked over to the television and turned to Bea. "What channel?"

"Six."

I turned to channel six then took a seat on the couch across from Bea. I hadn't watched a soap opera since Erica Cane was married to somebody back when I was in college. Taking a magazine off of the coffee table, I started flipping through the pages.

"You won't believe what happened at the school," I said,

looking up from the pages of the magazine.

"What?" Bea finally asked when her soap broke to a commercial.

"She said that some pretend man slapped her with his penis."

The color drained from Bea's face. "I hope you took it seriously."

"Of course I did. We called Sherril into the office, and she explained that she made it up."

"You have to investigate when children tell you things like that."

"Bea, I did. Sherril said that she made the whole thing up."

"Well you never know…" Bea said and took a sip out of her glass.

I could see that she was becoming more and more upset. She seemed to be in some sort of daze. Without thinking, I blurted out, "What's wrong with you?" I shook her arm.

All this did was prompt her to cry. Lord now what? This was turning out to be one helluva day! I refilled her a glass of water, giving her time to compose herself. Bea gulped the cold water like a woman in the desert, barely pausing long enough to catch her breath. Placing her glass on the table beside her, she rocked back and forth as I rubbed her back. The silence in the room hung as heavy as a pair of old time drapes. Finally, I sat down beside Bea on the couch and softly called her name, "Bea."

Bea sighed heavily and looked up at me with the saddest eyes I'd ever seen.

CHAPTER TWO
BEA

"I know that you think I'm a crazy old lady, but I'm not. It's just that a lot has happened to me in my life," I said.

Rachael shook her head. "Now don't. Everybody has problems. Look at my day so far."

Well, the girl had that much right. "I watch you with your children, and I can see that you are a good mother. So I guess you know that you have to pay attention to children when they say things because you never know. Maybe if I had been close to my mother, I would have never been hurt like I was. Did you know that I had a baby when I was fifteen?"

"No," Rachael answered. "I had no idea."

I concentrated on drinking the last few drops of water in my glass. Of course she didn't know, even Virginia didn't know. After all these years, it was still hard for me to talk about. "It ain't something that anybody talks about. It still happened; I remember it like yesterday. I was a lot like Sherril when I was a little girl, always running, jumping, falling, fighting you name it. Anything to do with sitting still I didn't want to be bothered with. I suited Mother all wrong. As far as she was concerned, I needed to learn how to act and behave more like Virginia."

Rachael patted my hand. "That's nothing. I used to feel the same way about my dad and my sister."

Staring at the glass in my hand, I went on. "I used to have

more fun playing with my little brother R. Thomas than Virginia, even my best friend was a boy. Like I said, I didn't have any time for prissy little girls. My best friend was Roscoe, the housekeeper's son. In the summer, she brought him to work with her everyday. Mother would pay him to do odd jobs. Girl, we used to have a good time playing together after he finished his work. One day, we were playing on the swing out back. You know how kids are, once they get tired playing the old way, they make up something new. We were trying to see how high we could make the swing go if we stood in it pumping together. We were pumping that swing higher and higher, back and forth when Virginia came out and saw us. She always was bossy, just loved to tell somebody what to do. She stood with her hands on her hips calling, 'Bea, get out of that swing!'"

I looked up from my glass and into Rachael's eyes. I could see that she was confused, but I didn't care. I needed to tell this story my way and in my time. "I stuck my tongue out at her, and she went running to tell Mother. Mother had a fit. I promise you, she tried to beat me to death. She made Daddy have a talk with me when he got home. Things are so different now. When I was a child, we didn't know anything about sex. Today, everywhere you go it's sex, sex, sex. Kids can't help but know things. When I was a child, sex was frowned on. Decent people didn't talk about those things. Daddy sat me down and explained to me that there were some things that good boys and girls did not do. Boys and girls standing face to face pumping up and down in the swing was one of those things. He said, 'I know that you didn't mean anything by it, but some people like to see the ugly side of things. This means girls have to be especially careful about what they do.

A bad reputation is easy to find and hard to lose.'"

Rachael chuckled. "Believe me, the same holds true today as far as reputations go. Things haven't changed that much."

I nodded my head. She had a point there, but still. "For all of that, they still didn't tell me nothing about what sex was. As a teenager, I was still more comfortable with boys than I was with girls. We weren't rich like people said, but my daddy was a good provider. Girls were always getting jealous about dumb mess, like the kind of clothes you wore and that type of foolishness. I never had that problem with boys. The summer I turned fourteen, Daddy hired a bricklayer from down around Macon to come and do some work around the house. While he worked, I used to talk to him about things like baseball and fishing. He was a nice look-ing man with paper bag brown skin, dimples and the straightest, whitest teeth. He looked like a young Sidney Portier. It didn't take me long to get a crush on him. You know, puppy love." I chuckled nervously and shifted my bottom. "He was only eight-een but already he had a wife and a baby on the way. I used to dream about what it would be like to be married to him. Even though I used to flirt with him, I ain't never led him on. I did lit-tle girl stuff, like offer him cold drinks. I carried on something awful, all the time telling him how great he was. That must have had an affect on him."

"What is wrong with that?" Rachael asked, hunching her shoulders. "Everybody had a crush on somebody at some point or another."

I could barely look at Rachael I felt so ashamed. It's amazing how something that happened over forty years ago could still make me feel so filthy. "I can tell you what is wrong with that,"

I murmured with my head lowered, recalling the pains of the past.

I looked out of the stained glass window of the backroom upstairs and into the backyard. I'd never been to England, but I would guess that with its fountain, statues, and any and every variety of flowers, Mother's courtyard could easily match anything over there. We were having some brickwork done, and the man doing the work was mighty good looking.

"Miss Cathy, I'd be happy to hang these clothes out for you," I said, walking up to the cleaning lady who was out on the back porch feeding clothes through the wringing machine.

Miss Cathy stopped her work and looked up at me. "Since when did you get so helpful? You must be up to something."

"No ma'am," I said, picking up the basket. "I just thought I'd help you out since Roscoe is at home sick."

Miss Cathy returned to her work. "Well, make sure you hang them thangs up so they don't fall. Ain't no sense in me havin' to run behind you and do the same work twice."

"Yes, ma'am, I'll be careful," I said with a raised voice so that Vincent, the man who was doing brick work for Daddy, could hear me coming.

It was a perfect day for the new sundress that I was wearing. The sun was shining bright, and the sky was full of soft white clouds. I made my way to the clothesline, humming loudly.

"Hey, Miz Lady. How you doin' today?" Vincent called.

I blushed. That man was some kind of fine. Mother wouldn't allow him to work in our yard with no shirt on, but that didn't stop his muscles from bulging through his thin shirt. "I'm fine."

"Yeah well, it would take a blind man not to see that," he joked.

My stomach fluttered. The sun shone brighter, the breeze blew sweeter, and I decided that I must be in love. No one had ever dared speak to me like that before. I felt naughty, but I liked it.

Vincent put down the brick he held in his hand and walked over to me. I pretended not to notice, but my heart was jumping. He stood in front of me staring. "Is that a new dress you got on?"

I looked into his eyes. He held my gaze, daring me to look away. My face flushed. "This old thing?" I asked.

"You'd look good in anything," Vincent said, as he stepped closer to me.

"Bea," Miss Cathy called.

I spun around. "Yes, ma'am," I answered quickly.

"You okay back there ain't you? I hope Vincent not givin' you any trouble."

"No ma'am," I stammered, turning to look at Vincent. He winked. I smiled bashfully and dropped my head.

"Well, I'm headin' home. Your momma will be here in a little bit. She gone down to the office with R. Thomas," she said, referring to the bank my daddy owned. "You gone be okay right?"

"Yes ma'am." I nodded, looked up at Vincent, and smiled.

Vincent smiled back.

"I'll be fine. You tell Roscoe I hope he feelin' better," I said to Miss Cathy.

"I'll do that." She hesitated before closing the back door. "Take care now."

"Yes, ma'am," I answered and reached into the basket.

A short while later I heard the side door bang shut and Miss Cathy's footsteps crunch down the gravel driveway as I continued hanging clothes.

"Here, let me help you," Vincent said. He wiped his dirty hands on his pants. Before I could stop him, he reached into the basket of clothes. I looked up when I felt his hand touching mine. We were both holding a pair of women's underwear. "These aren't yours are they," he asked in a husky voice.

I gasped, and dropped the pair of underwear like they carried measles. I wanted to melt right there on the spot. "I think I need some more clothes pins," I stammered and backed away. I turned and ran toward the garage. I heard footsteps coming up behind me and quickly turned around. Vincent bumped into me. We both lost our footing and began to fall against the garage door. Vincent grabbed me around the waist to break our fall and together we stumbled inside the garage. I stood as still as a statue as he caught his footing.

"You don't have to be sacred," he said softly, taking the loose strands of my hair in his hands.

I could smell the tobacco on his breath. "I'm not," I lied, stepping back. I took my hair from his hand and put it behind my ear.

"Your hair is as soft and fine as silk. A girl as good looking as you, with all this pretty hair," he said, running his hands through my hair. "Haven't you been kissed before?"

I looked down. "Kissed?" I hadn't even been touched, at least not in a man woman way.

He took my chin in his hands and lowered his mouth to

mine. I closed my eyes. So this is what a kiss feels like, I thought. I let myself enjoy it. I felt so grown up, like Lena Horne in the movies. I never even saw Daddy kiss Mother like what I was doing. I let my body relax against Vincent's.

He held me closer and started pressing his body into mine. Vincent moved one of his hands down the front of my body and stopped at my privates. I opened my eyes and tried to push him away from me, but he held me tighter.

I screamed, but his mouth covered mine, so all of my screaming was in vain.

"Don't worry," he muttered, "ain't nobody home."

I panicked. The smell of tobacco that I found enticing just minutes ago, sickened me to my stomach. He wrestled me to the ground, and my back hit the cold concrete. Pain shot through my shoulder blades. My head fell between the bags of lime and cow manure that the gardener used for fertilizer. As I struggled to get Vincent off of me, a cloud of dust rose from the bag of fertilizer and filled my nose, causing me to gasp for air.

"See there, you bought as excited as me, but we gone get to it," he said, taking my hands and holding them up over my head. He started kissing me on my neck, and chest. I felt him tugging at my underwear. I shut my eyes tight and turned my head into the bag of cow manure. My nose flooded with the smell of shit, but anything was better than looking at him.

Your body can't be prepared for something that it doesn't want. It felt like I was being ripped apart by a butter knife, I wouldn't want my worst enemies to feel that kind of pain. Every part of my body came alive with what was being done to me, the grit on the floor felt like boulders to my skin. I took my mind someplace else, trying to pretend like my head wasn't buried in a bag of cow shit while Vincent buried himself inside of me.

When he finished, Vincent got up and pulled up his pants. He walked over to a wheelbarrow where he kept a stash of beer. "You want one?" he asked and held out the brown bottle.

I pulled my dress down, not bothering to try and straighten out my underwear. Instead, I watched him like a mouse cornered by a cat, waiting for my get away.

"Whew, girl," he said, wiping his brow with the bottle. "You's a wildcat. I'm 'bout worn out. I don't know how I'm gonna get the rest of my work done. You know we gone have to keep this between us?"

My throat constricted, I didn't have the voice for words. He didn't have to worry 'bout me telling nobody, I was too ashamed of my part in it. When I finally found the courage to stand, I thought my legs would come out from under me. I made the painful walk back to the house and crawled up the porch steps. Somehow, I made it up the stairs and into the bathroom. I took a washcloth and washed the scum of him off of my tender privates. That wasn't enough. I still felt dirty. I filled the tub with water so hot it scorched my skin when I sunk into the water. I willed myself to sit in the tub despite the water's temperature.

"Hail Mary, full of grace, the Lord is with thee, blessed art thou amongst women and blessed is the fruit of thy womb, Jesus. Holy Mary Mother of God, pray for us sinners now and at the hour of our death," I prayed while scrubbing myself with a piece of lye soap that Miss Cathy kept in the bathroom to treat emergency stains on clothes.

Mother came to my room to check on me when she got

home. "It's a little early for bed. The sun hasn't even gone down yet. Are you feeling okay?"

"No ma'am. My stomach is upset," I lied.

I stayed in bed for three days before Mother finally made me get up and go to school. As soon as I got home from school, I went straight to my room and hid out. Vincent hadn't finished with his work. The sound of him singing and working like everything in the world was normal drove me near bout out of mind. He was a constant reminder of my transgression.

When my period didn't come, I wasn't even scared. Matter of fact, I was relieved. Normally, when my time came I'd have to stay home from school the cramps would be so bad. That must be how Mother realized that something was wrong. She took me to the doctor without telling me why.

Lying on top of the cold steel table, I suffered the second humiliation as Dr. Barnes poked and prodded me. He finished my exam and instructed me to get dressed and meet him in his office.

Mother was waiting with Dr. Barnes when I entered his office.

"Have a seat, Beatrice," she ordered.

I hurried to take the seat beside her.

"My exam indicates that you are about six weeks pregnant."

"But I…"

"Sit down, Bea!" Mother hissed.

Slowly, I took my seat. "Please, Lord, don't let me be pregnant," I prayed silently over and over, trying to bargain with God. "It was only my first time, and I promise not to do it again."

"There are several different ways that we can handle this," Dr. Barnes said, like I was a car that needed a tune up.

"I think that the first suggestion is best," Mother answered unmoved.

The two of them were talking as if I weren't even in the room.

When we got home, Mother ordered me to my room. I was in my room praying the rosary when I heard her talking to Daddy about my condition.

"I can't believe she went and did this to herself," Mother ranted.

"You act as if the child acted alone," I heard Daddy answer.

"What difference does that make?" Mother fumed.

"Well…maybe she can get married. My mother was married by the time she was Bea's age."

"That was a different time, and those were under different circumstances. Bea is not ready for this and you know it, she is a child herself."

"So you want to just up and send her away?"

"I don't see that we have a choice," Mother cried. "We can't have people thinking she's damaged."

"Is that what you're worried about?" Daddy raved. "Your precious reputation!"

"I am not even going to dignify that with an answer. You know as well as I do how a girl fares once her reputation is ruined. Besides, we still have Virginia to think about. Don't think that this won't affect her as well."

"What are you talking about? Virginia is at Fisk," Daddy argued.

"If the word ever got out…"

"But this child is our grandchild, our own flesh and blood." Daddy sighed.

"That is why we need to make sure the child goes to a good home, with a mother and a father that are in a position to take care of it."

"All right, do what you have to do," Daddy said, surrendering to Mother's wishes.

The shame I felt burned through me whenever anyone looked at me—even R. Thomas. He could sense that something was wrong and begged me to talk to him. But, I didn't dare. Nobody ever did ask me who the father was. The next morning, Mother had Miss Cathy pack my bags. I was sent to live with a friend of Mother's in Macon. Sister Cantrell was a nice lady, a true friend who could keep a family secret. Sister Cantrell took real good care of me, which wasn't hard to do. I didn't do anything but cry and sleep.

"Bea," Rachael said with a voice full of emotion, jarring me out of my painful past to present. "I am so sorry. I can't begin to imagine what that must have been like for you." She came over to my recliner and hugged me.

I closed my eyes and cried. "You already know what having a baby is like; I don't need to tell you about the birth. The only part I care to remember was when I saw my baby. Knowing I wasn't going to keep him, they wouldn't let me hold him. I wasn't even supposed to see him, but I caught sight of his face when the nurse picked him up. The doctor stepped in to block my view, but I will never forget watching the top of his head as they carried him out the room. He had a pretty little head, full of the curliest, jet-black hair. To this day, that is the most I know of my little baby boy."

Rachael winced and drew back to look at me. "You didn't get a chance to meet the adoptive parents?"

"No," I answered sadly and wiped my tears with a bit of paper towel. "Back in them days, we didn't have what you call open adoptions. I wouldn't be surprised if Mother just handed the baby over to somebody."

"Oh, Bea," Rachael proclaimed in surprise, "why would you say that?"

I shrugged my shoulders. "That is the way we did it back then. Colored people especially. In those days we didn't have to fool with lawyers and paper work. If you said a baby was yours, people believed you. Mother saw to it that I didn't take part in any of the adoption arrangements. If there were any papers to sign, I didn't do it. We told everyone that I had been at an all girls' Catholic school. No one suspected a thing. Virginia was already gone. She left for college when she was only sixteen."

"So what happened when you came back home?"

"Nothing. Mother warned me not to say anything about where I'd been. I wasn't even allowed to tell my own brother and sister. I didn't want to talk about it anyway. You know, I loved that baby, even if I didn't get the chance to raise it. That's the kind of hurt you never get pass."

"You talk about what happened like you deserved it. You didn't deserve it, Bea. That man took advantage of you."

"You probably think I'm crazy, in here crying like an old fool."

Rachael squatted down by the recliner, her butt grazing the ground. "See, there you go again. No. I don't think that you're crazy. I think that you're in pain. I know what it's like to be a survivor of sexual abuse."

"What!" I gasped. I rose up in my chair so that I could get a good look at her. She said it like it was the most everyday thing in the world.

"Yeah," she said, rocking back and forth on the bottoms of her feet. "I was molested as a child."

"So what happened? What did you do?" I don't think that I could ever talk about what happened to me that calmly.

"It was my uncle, so I kept it a secret. Of course I felt bad about it when it was happening, but I don't think I really processed it until I got married and had kids."

"What happened then?"

"I don't know... I had all of this anger, and I didn't really know where it was coming from. I was finding any excuse to argue, and the arguments would get out of hand. We were fighting about something one day, I can't even remember what it was, and I picked up Sherrill's Little Tikes chair and slammed Richard across the back with it. That was it for him. He told me that I had to get help or we couldn't be together."

"So you went to therapy?" People these days talk about therapy the same as they do going to church. They act like it is everyday normal. I still wasn't used to that. The way I was raised, therapy was reserved for people who were almost out of their mind. If you did go to therapy, you best keep quiet about it.

"Yeah, and it helped a lot. I learned that all that time I'd been blaming myself for being molested. When I realized that I was a victim and not responsible for what happened, I was able to become a survivor."

"What is a survivor?"

"A survivor is a person who has been victimized, but they decide that they don't want to let what someone else did to them define their life."

"You talkin' in circles now," I said disgusted. How could you not let abuse affect your life?

"No I'm not. But you won't understand what I'm saying until you're ready to heal."

CHAPTER THREE
BEA

Later that night, I was outside sitting on the porch smoking a cigarette, drinking a nice cold glass of ice water and going through a box of old pictures when Rachael drove up.

"I didn't know you were coming by," I said as she approached the porch.

"I thought you might like some company." Rachael smiled.

"Have a seat." I motioned to the wicker chair to the right of me.

Rachael sat down. "Here." She sorted through her purse. "I bought snacks." She took a bag of chips and two drinks out of her purse, twisted the top off of one of the drinks then handed it to me.

"Oh," I said, looking at the bottle, "you on that flavored water kick, too?"

"No. But, it's what we have at the house. I keep trying to tell Virginia that it isn't really water since it has as much sugar and other stuff as a regular soda."

"Virginia never liked water, but Mother swore by it. She always told us that there was nothing better for pretty skin." I poured the water out of my glass and replaced it with the flavored drink that Rachael gave me.

"You have pretty flowers," Rachael said, looking out at the scrabble mess of my flower beds. "They smell wonderful."

"They do, don't they?" I inhaled the sweet scent. My house was nothing like Virginia's. I lived in your average brick ranch style home, with two bedrooms and two bathrooms. My house was built in the sixties. The kitchen floor was linoleum and the bathrooms were tiled in that awful avocado green. Looking at the color of puke now, I don't know what I was thinking then.

My porch and yard were my pride and joy. The porch ran the length of the front of the house, and I had wicker furniture placed here and there so that I could enjoy looking out at my flowerbeds. Normally, I took pride in tending them. If I do say so myself—and I know I'm prejudice—I had the prettiest caladiums, impatiens, and coleus in the neighborhood. But I hadn't tended them in a while, and they were growing out of control.

Now my moonflowers were something special. I loved the way the big white petals of the moonflowers bloom at night. And their perfume is heavenly. With the right amount of sun, they love to climb, and mine were doing a fine job crawling up the porch rails.

"So what are you doing?" Rachael asked as she leaned back and propped her legs up on the porch railing.

I'm glad it was dark. The white paint was peeling off of the porch railing. I glanced at the shutter behind Rachael's chair. I had the original shutters and most of the wood trim replaced with vinyl two years ago. I was meaning to do the same to the porch, but never quite got around to it.

"I'm just going through some old photos. Talking to you dredged up some old memories."

"Are you okay?" She turned her head to look at me closely.

"Oh, I'm making it." I opened the bag of chips and took a

handful. Them folks that do those potato chip commercials are right, you can't eat just one. I enjoyed Rachael's company. Sometimes, I got jealous watching Rachael take care of her children. I know it was silly, a woman my age being jealous of a young girl, but I missed having all of the things that she had. I'm an old fashioned woman. Gloria Steinem, the lady with the big blond hair, would have had a fit if she'd ever talked to me. Not that I'm saying a woman's place in this world is in the house, but if you have to have a place in this world, a house ain't a bad one, depending on who in it with you. Even now, I'd kill to have a good husband and children of my own. That's 'bout all I ever wanted out of life.

Richard and Rachael made some pretty babies. The oldest, Sherril, looked just like her daddy, and I'm proud to say that she took after my side of the family. She had a straight nose like my daddy and a copper tone skin. Too bad her hair was nappy; she got that from her daddy, too. Not that there's anything wrong with nappy, but with all that hair she had, Rachael had one heck of a good time combing it.

Now that second baby they got, Vee. I could tell she'd be a handful with her tiny little high yellow self. When I was watching her, all she wanted to do was climb and get some place high. It didn't matter what she climbed: the stairs, the bookcase and just about all the other furniture in Virginia's house. I thought she would break her little neck for sure. My fussing didn't stop her at all. She laughed, shook her finger at me and fussed right back. She was so cute I couldn't be mad for long. Sherril looked like her daddy. She had his disposition too. She was a mild mannered child who only spoke when she had something to say.

The baby was a cute little thing too. Funny how all of Rachael's babies came out different. His hair was just as soft and curly. And he had the longest eyelashes. They were the perfect compliment to his big doe eyes. Shame to waste eyelashes like that on a boy. I'm proud to say that those lashes were another feature handed down from my side of the family. Mother had that same soft, fine hair and long, pretty lashes.

Rachael reached into my box of pictures. "Oh look, these are three of the prettiest babies I've ever seen. They look like little black china dolls. Who are they?"

The lamp from inside my front room shone through the window. I held the picture up to the light. In the picture, three young girls were dressed in their Sunday finest. They sat in a row like stair steps. The last girl was just old enough to sit up by herself. "That is Mother and her two sisters."

"Which one is your mother?"

"She is the one sitting in the middle. The biggest girl is Aunt Lena, and the younger one is Aunt Cecelia."

"I never hear Richard talk about them, were you all close?"

"Oh no. Mother's sisters didn't have the time, or the patience, to be bothered with anybody's children. Maybe they wasn't used to the noise children keep up or the fact that they like to run around and get dirty. Aunt Lena was just plain ole mean."

"I think I remember Richard saying that. But what did she do that was so mean?"

"She didn't spank us or anything, but she always had a mouthful to say about you. I wouldn't even want to count the times I overheard her telling Mother about what R. Thomas and me should and should not be doing. You can best believe that whatever she wanted was the complete opposite of what we wanted."

Rachael reached into the bag of chips. "I had an aunt like that," she said and popped a chip into her mouth. "She was sanctified, and she could never get past the idea that my mother let us wear pants."

I laughed. "People have the strangest notions. Since we didn't have our own children, R. Thomas and I swore that we would be good aunts and uncles to all of our nieces and nephews. I was bound and set to be a good aunt, not like the aunts I had. Daddy's sister treated us fine, but we didn't fool with her that much. She and Mother didn't care for each other."

"What about your Aunt Cecelia?"

"Oh her, she was mean, too. She sent me a bracelet once. She attached a nice little note that read, 'Dear Bea, I found this bracelet on the street, and it reminded me of you.' Ha! I threw that thing in the trash. When Mother found out, she got upset and called me ungrateful. 'Well, Bea, at least she thought about you.' Maybe she did, but she didn't think much. Even as a child it seemed to me that she could have done more than send me some trash she found on the street. The stamp she used to send it was worth more than that little tarnished piece of bracelet. Mother's sister was married to a professor up in Boston, and they didn't have any children, so it wasn't like she couldn't afford to buy me a nice gift. I wasn't expecting anything, but why send junk? Humph, maybe that's what she thought I deserved."

Rachael reached into the box for another picture. "If Sherril had done that, I would have said the same thing. Who's this?" She held the picture out under the light so I could see.

It was a headshot of a very distinguished looking black man. "That was my mother's father."

"So what was he like?"

"I don't know. He died way before I was born. He was a Music Professor at Albany State."

Rachael continued going through the box, stopping to ask questions as she saw fit. "Who is this group of girls?"

"Let's see." I bent over to take a look. The picture was one of a group of about fifty girls standing on the steps outside of a large brick building. They all looked like they were in their late to early teens, and they each had on a long skirt, dark stockings, ankle boots, and a white blouse. A dark-skinned older woman stood in the middle of the group. She wore a floor length high-necked dress. I scanned the photograph, and my eye stopped at Mother's smile. Aunt Lena stood on the row above her, and Aunt Cecelia was the last person on the last row. "That is a picture of Mother and her sisters at Haines Institute in Augusta. Oh my goodness," I said, holding the picture closer to the light. "The woman in the middle must be Miss Lucy Laney. Mother always liked to brag that she learned from none other then Lucy Laney herself."

"Who is Lucy Laney?" Rachael asked, leaning into the light to see the picture up close.

My jaw dropped. I was so disgusted I had to put the picture down. "How could you not know Miss Lucy Laney? She was only the most important educator in all of Georgia."

"I'm sorry," Rachael said, holding her hands up in defense. "I'm from Michigan, remember?"

I didn't care. I was on a roll. I swear, they don't teach these kids nothin' no more. "It was Lucy Laney that gave Mary

McCloud Bethune her start. Girl, pour me some more water out of that bottle. You are about to get yourself hurt."

Rachael laughed and poured some of that flavored water in my glass. "I'm sorry. I didn't mean to get you all flustered." She raised her hands in mock indignation.

I took a sip from my glass. "It's important to know your history."

"So educate me." Rachael sat back and munched on chips, waiting to be educated.

"Well," I said, thinking back to the beginning of what I knew about Miss Laney. "She was born a slave. But I think it was her master's sister that taught her to read. Miss Laney's father was a minister, and somehow he got his freedom, and he was working to buy his family's freedom when the Civil War broke out. Anyway, Miss Laney went on to go to Atlanta University. After teaching for a few years in Macon and Savannah, she started Haines Institute. At Haines, the students learned Latin, Greek, Algebra, and music. She also taught them every day things like cooking, sewing, carpentry, and laundering. They were taught just as good as any white children."

"Wow, and to think I never heard of her," Rachael said, clearly impressed.

I took another look at the picture then placed it back in the box. "My mother had an education better than most white women. Seems like all of that learning came natural to Virginia and R. Thomas. Me, I had to work at it. All children need plenty of hugs and praise, but Mother wasn't that kind, at least not with me. Nothing I did was right for her. I sat wrong. I spoke wrong. I crossed my legs wrong. On top of all of that, I looked completely wrong. Times have definitely changed. I remember when James Brown made that song, "Say It Loud, I'm Black and I'm Proud." You couldn't go anywhere around black folks and not hear that song. People started wearing afros and dashikis—or whatever you call them African shirts. Folks weren't singing them kind of songs when I was comin' up. No. In my day, black wasn't beautiful and brown wasn't hip. Beautiful didn't start unless you could pass the paper bag test. I failed that test just as sure as I failed every other test I ever took. Mother may have loved me, but she spent her entire life trying to make up for the fact that she thought I was ugly."

"That must have been rough," Rachael said, snuggling down in her chair trying to get comfortable. "Show me a picture of your father."

I rummaged through the box, looking for a picture of Daddy. I found one of Daddy and Mother sitting on a blanket separated by a picnic basket. I handed the picture to Rachael.

"Oh," she cooed. "He was handsome. I see where Richard gets his facial features."

"Yes, he was good looking." I pulled another picture of Daddy from the box and stared at it. My daddy was a dark man, tall and full-bodied. I don't mind saying that Richard wasn't the only one that took after him. I got my looks from him, too. A few months ago, one of Virginia's grand children was selling this calendar of the different tribes and countries over in Africa. I used to think that Africans were a bunch of people running around in animal skins, jumping up and down like they did in the Tarzan movies. Not the Africans in that calendar, some of them were good looking. One man from Ethiopia looked just like my daddy: straight nose, thin lips, and that dark, smooth, pretty kind of black skin.

"What are you thinking?" Rachael asked.

"Oh, I was just thinking about how funny the whole color thing can be. When I was coming up, a dark-skinned man might not have it as easy as he would if he was light-skinned, but he could still get by. Not so for a woman." I shook my head. "Nobody said life was fair, if they did, they must have been a newborn. It's no big secret that pretty women have it easier in life. I got the short end of the stick in the looks department."

"I think you're beautiful," Rachael said softly.

I felt my face flush from the sincerity in her voice. I wasn't used to getting compliments. "I don't know about all of that. For a dark-skinned woman like me, it was harder to find a decent job or a good husband. People use any reason to act all high-class and siddity. I'm blessed to come from a good family with high expectations. Still, Mother and her friends couldn't hide the fact that they thought it was a shame I was so dark."

"That's really sad." Rachael sighed.

"I heard them say, 'Too bad she's so dark with all that long pretty hair,' so many times that I prayed God would make me lighter skinned so Mother would like me more. My mother was as fair skinned as a black woman could be. People swore that her and her sisters were the prettiest women in Southwest Georgia; and if you ask me, Mother was the prettiest. Her own mother was more white than black. That's how she and her sisters got that long, straight hair and fair skin. Once she and her friends were all claiming who their white relations were. When it was Mother's turn, she looked at them like she was bored, tired, or disgusted, take your pick, and said, 'Well, the rumor is that my grandfather is the Lieutenant Governor of Georgia, but ain't no sense claiming him, because he sure don't claim me!'"

"Really," Rachael said surprised. "I'd never heard that before."

"I was shocked, too. Mostly because I'd never heard my mother say the word ain't. I wanted to please her. She only wanted what was best for me. Too bad we could never agree on what that was. Mother said pretty is, as pretty does. To her line of thinking, I might not be able to change my looks, but I could damn sure make up for it in grace and style. The problem was, I didn't have any grace or style. Oil and water came together better than Mother and me. The only thing that I could do to her satisfaction was cook and clean. Since she died, I've spent a lot of time thinking about how things could have been different if she and I were closer. Maybe then I would have been able to tell her about what happened. But those were the times."

"But you were close to your father right?"

Thinking about Daddy perked me right up. "Oh, honey, yeah. I was as close as close can be with him. I was crazy about Daddy, and he was crazy about me. I got jealous if he gave Virginia or R. Thomas too much attention. Seems so silly now, but when Virginia went off to college, I wanted her to stay gone. Daddy made such a fuss over her when she came home. 'My first daughter only sixteen and already away at college,' he'd say. With her gone, I was Daddy's one and only little girl. I used to ask him, 'Daddy, why does she have to come back here? Can't she just stay gone?'"

Rachael laughed. "You are so silly."

"Yeah," I said, nodding in agreement, "but that's what I asked him. 'Come on now, Bea,' he'd say laughing. 'You know she lives here, too. She my daughter, just like you my daughter.' Daddy was the only person besides R. Thomas who truly understood me. I tried to be like Virginia and R. Thomas, they did good in school. The more I tried, the dumber I felt. I didn't like to read, couldn't stand math, and didn't have much use for test taking. Mother and I used to go back down around and under when it came to school."

"Some people have books smarts, and some people have street smarts. Everybody wasn't meant for college," Rachael said, stretching.

"Yeah." I nodded. "That's the same thing my daddy said. It didn't bother Daddy he never even made it to the eighth grade. He understood that book sense wasn't everything. He used to say, 'Folks go to school to get their Ph.D., then come to me to get their j-o-b!'"

Rachel leaned over to the box and pulled out another picture. I could tell she was tired and appreciated her coming to check on me. "Oh, here's R. Thomas," she said. "Whew, there sure are some fine men in this family."

"You ought to quit." I laughed and snatched the picture from her. "Yeah," I said, looking at R. Thomas sitting in the drawing room with his German Shepard, Heidi, at his feet. "He was good looking. Truth be told, R. Thomas was the smartest out of the three of us. I know people thought he was always talking a bunch of foolishness with his sickness and all, but even though he was rambling saying the same things over and over, he made good sense. He was a genius. That boy could draw, he could paint, and he played the piano. I don't know what it was about Daddy's death that caused him to go over the edge. Daddy did dote on him though, so did Mother."

"I only knew him when he was sick, tell me about him."

"What you want to know for?" Talking about myself was one thing, but I didn't much care to put R. Thomas's business in the street.

"I don't know." Rachael shrugged. "I'm just curios."

"Curious my tail. That's just the refined way of saying nosey."

Rachel popped her lips. "I'm a part of this family now, too, even if it is through marriage."

I rolled my eyes at her. "Well, you are right about that. Let's see," I said, thinking. "At the time Daddy died, R. Thomas was going to Columbia University in New York City. I think that Mother was even prouder than Daddy. R. Thomas was studying music just like her father did. I didn't know my grandfather, but from the picture, you can see that R. Thomas looked just like him: tall, dark, and handsome!"

"You got that right," Rachael agreed. "I bet the women wouldn't leave him alone."

"Huh, you would have thought that he would have had a steady string of girlfriends, but he didn't, and I'm probably the only one that knows why."

"Tell me," Rachael commanded, leaning toward me with interest.

"Yeah," I sighed with an added curl of the lip. "You nosey. Well, anyway, R. Thomas was in love with one of the graduate students in the music program. She was a Jewish refugee from the big war. R. Thomas bragged to me about her parents playing all of the big halls in Europe."

"I guess they came here to escape the Holocaust," Rachael butt in.

"Are you going to let me tell the story or not?" I snapped.

"Sorry, go ahead."

"All right, where was I? Oh yeah, the girl's parents…It's so sad her parents got killed in one of those concentration camps, but she made it here. The whole thing was doomed from the beginning. Wasn't no way he could have brought that girl home. White and Jewish. Maybe nowadays, but not back then. She left him for a Jewish professor at Fisk, another refugee. It made perfect sense to do what she did. Course that didn't help R.Thomas's heart none. I still have the letter he wrote, crying about their breakup. When I left for Boston, we promised to write each other once a week. I shoulda known something was wrong when he started sending me twenty letters at a time, all written on the same day. But I thought he was heart broken and kept his confidence like he kept mine. That's why we trusted each other."

Rachael yawned. "I wish I'd known him when he was better."

"He was something," I said, smiling sadly.

"It's getting late, Bea." Rachael gathered the mess we made together and put it in the bag she brought. "I need to get back. I'm sure the baby will want to nurse soon. Are you going to be all right?"

"Oh, honey, I'll be fine," I said, dismissing her with the wave of my hand. "You get back to those children of yours."

"You sure." She hesitated before getting up.

"I'm fine," I assured her. "You go on."

"All right." she headed toward the car. "You call me if you need to talk."

I watched her pull out of the driveway as I collected my empty glass and the box of photos. Rachael gave one final wave before driving down the street. I waved back and turned to go inside. After all of that reminiscing, I wasn't the least bit tired. I went on inside the kitchen and put the box of photos on the table. The table was covered with junk mail and other papers. I was going to have to clean that mess up. I dropped my glass into the sink with the other dirty dishes. Wasn't no sense in being all out nasty, so I filled the sink with warm water and added a few drops of dish liquid and a capful of ammonia. The dishes could soak until the morning. I got the pictures from the table and went on back to my bedroom. I wasn't tired, but that didn't mean that I was in the mood to clean either.

I walked the length of the hallway, side stepping the basket of dirty laundry that I'd also meant to wash earlier. That dirty laundry wasn't going anywhere. Once in my bedroom, I put the box of pictures on the bed, took off my clothes, and laid them across the footboard of the bed. A long hot bath was what I needed. Maybe it would help to ease my mind.

There wasn't a thing masterly about the bathroom inside my bedroom, but it was mine, and it suited my needs. I ran myself a bath, adding more than enough Epsom salt to the hot water and a drop or two of lavender oil to cap it off. I soaked for a good half hour before deciding to get out. I hate the part of getting old where you can't move around like you used to. Not that I was ever a big mover or anything, but still. I had to grab hold to the wall, which was slippery because it was the same avocado green ceramic tile as the floor. The porcelain sides of the tub were also slippery. I had to sit back down in the water twice before I was able to get myself out of that tub.

I grabbed my bathrobe off of the hook on the back of the door and slid into my bedroom slippers. I like to go straight from the tub into a pair of slippers. Ain't nothing worse than getting into a bed full of grit.

Instead of drying off, I climbed into the bed still damp from my bath. Even though it was early October, the nights had only cooled down to about seventy degrees. At my size, seventy degrees is plenty warm. Despite the bath, I was still wound as tight as a cuckoo clock. My nerves were on edge. I took a cigarette from the bedside table, lit it and reached for the box of pictures.

Virginia swears that one of these days Im'ma fall asleep while smoking a cigarette and set myself on fire. I used to fuss at R. Thomas the same way. Now I'm the one burning holes in the mattress.

I pulled out a picture of myself. I was sitting at a typewriter. I remember when Daddy took that picture; it was my first day at secretarial school. Daddy accepted that I wasn't college material. When I finished high school, he sent me to secretarial school so that I could get a job down at his bank. I made up my mind to do well in that school. That way Daddy would help me find my son. Mother thought that not talking about it would make me forget about him, but it didn't. Finally, I got up enough nerve to go to Daddy and ask him to help me get my son back. Ooh! I was so happy when he agreed. Daddy said that my flesh and blood was his flesh and blood. He wanted to see me happy. My daddy was a good man. He felt how hurt I was when I had to give up my son, even though we never talked about it.

A tear fell on the picture. I placed it back in the box and pushed the box aside. The photos in that box held nothing but bad memories for me. Even the happy ones drew me to a sad place in my heart.

By the time I graduated from high school, my son was three years old. I didn't have a clue where he was, or what he looked like, but I named him Joseph anyway. I went into a state of mourning every year on his birthday. I was in Daddy's office over the garage crying my heart out when Daddy found me.

"Good God, Bea! You near bought scared me to death. What in the world is wrong with you?"

"Today is the day, Daddy," I moaned.

Daddy came over to the couch and sat beside me. I fell onto his shoulder.

He held me in his arms. I was crying so hard my tears soaked through his shirt. When I finally stopped crying, I looked up and there were tears in Daddy's eyes.

"I know it's hard baby, but…"

"Daddy, can't you help me find him?"

Daddy looked tired. Not the everyday I need to go to sleep tired, but bone tired. He drew me to him. "It's not that easy, Bea. There are considerations."

"But, Daddy, it's my son that we are talking about." I got up from the sofa and paced back and forth, wringing my hands. "What if it was me? Wouldn't you want to find me?" I sniffed.

"Of course I would," Daddy said, massaging his temple. "But what about the people who have been looking after him all this time? Have you thought about how they might feel?"

"He is my son," I said with authority. Of course I thought

about the other people, but I had to put that out of my mind. A child needed to be with his mother, his real mother. "Daddy." I knelt down on my knees in front of him. "I'm grown now. I know that Mother is afraid people will talk, but I don't care."

"Do you really think that you can go through all of that?"

"Yes, sir," I answered softly, laying my head on his knee. "I've been thinking about it. I could go to secretarial school…"

"Your mother was planning to send you to college with your Aunt Cecelia."

I lifted my head. "Come on, Daddy, you know as well as I do that I'm not college material."

"Well," Daddy sighed, "you could get a job as a secretary at the bank."

I saw a glimmer of hope. Daddy was weakening.

"I promise, Daddy, I'll be the best worker you ever had."

"You just concentrate on getting through that secretarial school, I'll do the rest."

"Oh, Daddy," I cried. "Thank you." I jumped up and threw my arms around him. "I won't let you down, I promise." I started crying again. Only this time, they were tears of joy.

I spent the next few months working hard at secretarial school, dreaming of the day that I would be reunited with my son. Things were really going my way. Daddy had it all arranged. He gave me one of his houses, it only had two bedrooms, but that was all that I needed. I was scheduled to finish secretarial school on a Friday and begin working at the bank the following Monday. I woke up the Saturday morning before I was to start work and scrambled to my knees. I was in a panic because I'd forgotten to say my prayers. The last thing I needed was to fall from grace.

"O my God, relying on your infinite goodness and promises, I hope to obtain pardon of my sins, the help of your grace, and life everlasting, through the merits of Jesus Christ, my Lord and Redeemer." I went downstairs after getting dressed and joined Mother and R. Thomas in the kitchen. Mother was putting a pan of biscuits in the oven. She looked up when I entered the room.

"I hope that you made your bed. Miss Cathy won't have the time to clean up behind you. We have baking to do for the church's mission dinner."

"I'm sure she did," Miss Cathy said, winking at me behind Mother's back. I could always count on her to be my ally.

The clock in the hall chimed. "Oh no, I'm going to be late," Mother said as she yanked off her apron. "Come on R. Thomas. If I'm not there to supervise, they'll have that church basement looking like a barnyard affair."

R. Thomas rolled his eyes behind Mother's back and went to the mudroom to get the keys.

Miss Cathy and I laughed.

I went over to the icebox to get the butter. I scooped a pat of the homemade butter onto a dish and sat it in the middle of the table. "Honey or jam?" I asked Miss Cathy.

"Honey." She took the pan of golden-brown buttermilk biscuits out of the oven then set the pan on the table, making sure it rested on a towel so that it wouldn't scorch the tablecloth.

I reached out for a biscuit, and Miss Cathy slapped my hand away. "Chile, you know that's too hot.

"I like it that way." I reached for a hot biscuit. She was right, it was too hot. I dropped the biscuit onto my plate and blew on my fingers.

Miss Cathy laughed. "You always did have to learn the hard way. So what are you up to this fine morning?"

"I'm going shopping for my new job." I sat up a little bit straighter.

Miss Cathy smiled. "You doing good, baby. I'm so proud of you."

"Thank you," I said, frowning. The moment the words left her lips, I realized that Mother hadn't said a word about my new job. Now of course I knew that I was going to work for Daddy, but, I'd worked hard to come out at the top of my class.

"Don't worry, baby, your Mother is proud of you, too."

I shook my head. "No she isn't. If she was, she would have said."

"Oh, baby, you and your momma never did know how to talk to one another. She just worries about you is all."

I started tearing up. "Uh, uh," I said, stuffing a biscuit in my mouth. "I don't think that woman can stand me."

"Now you wait a minute." Miss Cathy waggled her finger in my face. "I ain't gone stand by and listen to you sass your momma. You show some respect."

"Yes'm," I mumbled.

"She and I done had plenty of talks about you, and she love you as much as any other child."

Well she sure don't act like it, I thought.

I didn't start for home until late that evening. When I pulled onto our block, I was surprised to see so many cars. They were parked up and down the street and all over the yard. I had to park my car around the corner. I struggled up the street with my bags when I saw Daddy's secretary leaving the house in tears. Something wasn't right. A panic washed over me. I dropped my bags and went running into the house past several faceless people. "Daddy, Daddy!" I screamed at the top of my lungs.

Some one grabbed me. I saw R. Thomas pacing back and forth, muttering to himself. Mother was crying hysterically on the sofa. Miss Cathy entered the room. Tears were streaming down her face. She carried a shot glass and a bottle of whiskey that Daddy drank from every New Year's eve. I struggled to go to her, but they wouldn't let me go.

"Where is my daddy!" I screamed.

Miss Cathy set the bottle on the étagère, rushed over to me, and took me in her arms. "He's gone, baby," she whispered in my ear.

My world turned to black.

I woke up the next morning not knowing how I got up to my room, undressed and into bed. For a minute, I forgot the night before, but the many voices of the people filling the house floated up to me, and the memory came crashing down. Terror gripped my soul, and I started screaming. "I want my daddy! I want my daddy!"

Miss Cathy came rushing into my room wearing the same dress that she'd had on the night before. I felt like the air was being sucked out of me. I couldn't breathe. I started gasping for air.

She took my face in her hands. "Breathe," she commanded.

I inhaled, and slowly, my breath returned. "Why?" I cried.

"Oh, baby." She rocked me back and forth. "Only God knows."

I spent the next two days half alive. I couldn't eat or sleep. All I could do was cry, and say thank you to the black and white people who came by to pay their respects. Even the poor brought food. With their last bits of sugar, they created all types of pies and cakes. Miss Cathy started giving away whole meals.

Two weeks went by after Daddy's funeral, and I waited for Mother to come to me with news about my son. I'm sure Daddy, told her something. Mother continued pretending that I'd never even had a child. I decided to take matters into my own hands.

I parked in front of the Sweet Shoppe across the street from the bank. Mr. Barnes, the security guard, was the last one to leave. He was so old and moved so slow, it seemed like it took him forever to lockup. My body got the shivers when I entered the building with Daddy's keys. It was the first time that I'd been there since Daddy died. Memories of Daddy sitting behind his desk, laughing as I rushed in to his office, came flooding back.

My heart stopped at the sight of the Daddy's picture hanging by the front door. I touched his lips, and reached up to kiss him, saying a silent prayer, "Almighty God, through the death of your Son on the cross, you have overcome death for us. Through his burial and resurrection from the dead, you have made the grave a holy place and restored us to eternal life. We pray for those who died believing in Jesus and are buried with him in the hope of rising again. God of the living and the dead, may those who faithfully believed in you on earth praise you for ever in the joy of heaven. We ask this through Christ our Lord. Amen."

I peeled myself away from Daddy's portrait and slowly made my way toward his office. The walk to his office seemed to stretch out for miles. I said the prayer of intercession before turning the knob and opening the door. I felt Daddy in that room. He'd spent so much time there. I heard a scratching sound and nearly jumped out of my skin. "Hello," I called out.

No one answered. I soon realized the noise was coming from the blinds hitting against the opened window. Then I realized that this was the place where Daddy died. He was sitting at his desk when he had a heart attack, and in the commotion, they'd overlooked the open window. I had to take a seat.

I sat down at Daddy's desk and inhaled. Daddy didn't believe in wearing cologne. Instead, he'd claimed, "All I need is clean." My nose filled with the scent of him, lye soap and tobacco. Daddy's cigar lay in the ashtray. I reached out to touch it. The fountain pen that I'd given him lay on top of a bunch of papers that he must have been in the process of reviewing and signing. I placed it in my purse.

I breathed in and out several times before beginning my search. First I went through the papers sitting on a neat stack in the middle of the desk. It was all bank business. *Just stay calm,* I thought. I opened the first drawer. The papers were all stacked neatly, but none of them had anything to do with my son. I took another breath and went through the second drawer. Nothing. By the time I started searching the file cabinet, I was in tears. There was nothing there that would give me a clue about my son. I wasn't ready to give up and go home. Leaving that office felt too much like giving up. I slouched onto the couch and cried.

"Baby, what in the world are you doing here?" Mrs. Daniels, Daddy's secretary, asked as she gently shook me awake.

My mouth felt pasty, and I had a crook in my neck from sleeping with my head on the arm of the sofa. "I was looking for something."

"Well tell me what. I do all of the filing, so I guess I would know if it was here."

I took a deep breath. The way I figured it, I didn't have much left to lose. "My father was looking for a little boy."

Miss Daniels dropped to the sofa. "I don't know anything about that," she stammered.

"You do, you have to know. Nothing gets by you in this office," I insisted.

Miss Daniels folded her hands together in a tent. "Your mother…"

"Beatrice!" Mother suddenly appeared in the doorway. "It's time for us to go home now."

I pushed past Mother and ran to my car. Sister Cantrell had come to town for Daddy's funeral and had decided to stay a bit to visit with family and friends. She was staying at her sister's house. I did a u-turn in the middle of the street, heading for Miss Cantrell.

Sister Cantrell opened the door before I even knocked. "Come on in" she said, stepping to the side to let me pass.

I breathed a heavy sigh and entered the sitting room. The smells of breakfast filled the room, and from where I was standing, I could see Miss Cantrell's sister's family seated around the kitchen table.

Sister Cantrell closed the kitchen door.

"You know where my son is," I pointed to her.

Miss Cantrell walked over to me and gently led me over to an arm chair. "Sit down, baby."

I sank into the chair. "Tell me where my son is," I pleaded.

"Oh, darling," she sighed. "This has been such a hard time for you. But you don't want to make things worse."

"Worse?" I asked in a hoarse whisper. "How could I make things worse?"

"Don't you think your son loves his family?"

"I am his family," I cried.

"Think about your son," she explained. "Children need both parents. Good Lord, child, think about you! What respectable kind of man is going to want to be with someone who's been damaged?"

I was confused. Maybe she was right. It had already been over two years since my son was born. I didn't know what kind of family he had. For them to go through the trouble of adopting him, it stands to reason that they had to love and want him. Did I have a right to take him away just because he was mine? My poor baby didn't even know that I was on this earth. Maybe things were better off left alone.

I dragged myself home and shut myself up in my room.

Of course Virginia was home for the funeral. She'd graduated college by then and was going to graduate school in Boston. Everyone in the house was so caught up grieving, we barely took notice of one another.

I was lying in my bed trying not to think when Virginia came into the room.

"It's going to be okay, Bea," she said, sitting on my bed. "We just need time."

"That's easy for you to say. You have a life in Boston, miles away from here."

Virginia's face brightened. "You can come with me."

"How?" I asked, sighing. "What would I do in Boston?"

"We could find a job for you in the hospital where I work," Virginia said, thinking aloud.

"I don't know, Virginia. That's way up north. It's cold and I … I have a job here."

"You can get used to the cold. Besides, you would love my apartment. We could finish decorating it together. Please come," she begged. "I need you to come. I want to be with my family. I've been away from home since I was sixteen. We barely even know each other anymore."

I looked around my room. The doll that Daddy bought me for my ninth birthday was sitting on the dresser. The flowers that he gave me the day I finished secretarial school sat dead on my dressing table. The bags of clothes that I bought right before Daddy died were sitting at the foot of my bed, untouched. Looking at the bags, I knew that there was no way that I could go to work in the bank. I had to get away.

"When do we leave?" I asked, getting up from the bed to get my suitcase.

The next morning, I had to apologize to Rachael for keeping her waiting when she came to pick me up for my doctor's appointment. Usually, I try to be on time, cause I hate to be kept waiting. Most people would have been fussing, cussing, and blowing the horn, but not her. She came on in the house, carrying the baby and holding Vee's hand.

"Bea, this really is some nice furniture." She looked around the room. "How long have you had it?"

"I've been around this furniture most of my life. Most of this furniture comes from the house downtown. Once we settled Mother's estate, Virginia and I divided everything between ourselves and tagged it. Wasn't no use in letting the stuff waste away in the house when I could use it, so I brought it here."

Rachael ran her hand along the top of one of the end tables, walked across the room, and sat in the chair next to the window, holding the baby in her lap. Vee stood leaning against her mother's knees. Rachael leaned over and started examining the fabric of my drapes. Pulling on the drapery cord she asked, "Why do you have it so dark in here? You aren't a vampire. Girl, let there be light."

The sunlight coming in through the large picture window was so bright it hurt my eyes. "Nobody told you to mess with my window," I snapped, yanking the draperies closed. I hadn't meant to sound so nasty, but I didn't need her snooping around trying to mind my business.

Vee started wiggling around.

"Where is the bathroom?" Rachael asked, getting up from her chair.

Before I could offer to take Vee, Rachael grabbed Vee's hand and with the baby on her hip she rushed to the back of the house. Didn't they teach those girls up north any manners? When you were a guest in someone else's home, you were supposed to sit your behind down and stay put unless invited to do otherwise. My house was a mess. I used to be such a good housekeeper, but the last thing I felt like doing was cleaning a damn house. Even though I didn't care to clean it, I still had enough pride to care what people thought about it. I was rushing so fast to catch her I tripped over the torn up linoleum. Damn I wish I had the money to get that fixed.

"It's way too dark in here," she said and flicked on the light. "This light doesn't help much either. What in the world made you put a yellow light in this bathroom?" she asked. Still holding the baby on her hip, Rachael bent down and tried to pull Vee's pants down with her one free hand. By this time, Vee was a shaking and wiggling so hard she could barely stand "Hold on baby," she said to Vee. With one hard tug, Rachael was able to pull her pants down. She sat Vee on the toilet in the nick of time and turned to me. "You can barely see the toilet seat."

"I don't need no uninvited person talking about my house. If you don't like it, you can just invite yourself on out!" I didn't care if she was my nephew's wife; nobody was going to make me feel bad in my own home. I stumped into the kitchen to check and make sure that the side door was locked.

Rachael followed me into the kitchen and took a seat at my kitchen table. She pushed aside the mess I had on the table, set her diaper bag down, reached inside and pulled out a blanket. I stood by the door watching as she draped the blanket over her shoulder and nursed the baby. Once she had the baby settled, she offered Vee a cookie.

How rude, I thought, *the least she can do is apologize.*

"Whatever!" she said, half-laughing. "Aren't you ready yet? We need to go ahead and leave. I have to pick Sherril up from school at 2:45."

Driving down the street, I tried to change my mood. Ever since I first went to Dr. Evans about my hands, he started having me take all kinds of test. The fact that I had carpal tunnel was bad enough. But a series of test showed that I had high blood pressure and the beginning of congenital heart failure. So, he said that I needed to exercise and try and lose weight. After all that, he still wasn't satisfied. He also wanted me to take tests for my mind.

Rachael looked at the directions that Virginia had given her. "When Virginia said that you were going to a therapist office. I assumed that you were finally going to get some help to start your healing."

"I don't know about all of that," I said, shaking my head. "But I told Dr. Evans that I hadn't been feeling like myself ever since Mother and R. Thomas died. So he wants me to see a therapist and take some tests. All these tests he got me taking, the next thing you know, he'll be testing me for sugar."

"You know what they say, better safe than sorry."

I sighed. Over the years of working at Daddy's typing, my hands had developed some pain. I used to be able to handle it by taking a few aspirin. After a while, that wasn't working so well, and I started using AsperCreme. Finally, when the AsperCreme didn't work, I took to rubbing them down with Ben Gay. That's when I went in to see Dr. Evans. Once he diagnosed me with carpal tunnel, he and Virginia helped me file the paperwork for disability.

Rachael took her eyes off the road to look at me. "I hope that you finally get the help that you need. You've been carrying this burden for too long."

The lady that was giving the test was one of those debutantes in waiting types. You know the kind; the south is full of 'em. She had her a cutesy little haircut, picture perfect makeup, and just the right amount of jewelry. The woman had probably never cursed a day in her life, and my guess would be that she only got into the field of medicine because she wanted to marry a doctor. Her walls were covered with her diploma and pictures of her in different bridesmaid dresses. For all practical purposes, her wall was a big wedding advertisement.

She welcomed me into her office with a phony smile and a limp handshake. "So I understand that you have been having some trouble coping lately." She blinked her eyelashes and smiled so hard I thought she was trying out for a beauty contest.

"Right," I said, sounding like a halfwit. I was busy looking at those lashes, wondering how much mascara she went through in a month.

"Okay! Well now, I just have a few simple tests that we need to do and then we'll be finished. Okay!" She clapped her hands together like we were in school.

"Uh, huh." I nodded.

"Do you know what today is?"

"Wednesday."

"And what day of the week is that?"

"Huh?"

"The second day, the fourth day?"

"Oh, the fourth day," I stuttered. I'd never been any good at test, but the questions that this lady was asking me were too damn stupid!

"What comes before Wednesday?"

"Tuesday."

"After Wednesday?"

"Thursday. What kind of stupid test is this?"

"Oh don't worry, honey," she said, fluttering those lashes again. "These are just the normal questions we have to ask. Okay, so where were we?" She seemed almost excited. "What did you eat for breakfast today?"

"A donut and some coffee." I sighed.

"Is breakfast a morning or an afternoon meal?"

"Humph, morning!"

"What time is considered morning?"

I couldn't help myself, I blurted out, "Look, I could have stayed at home in my bed if all you were going to do was ask me these stupid questions!"

"I know it seems tedious, Mrs. Walker," she said, talking to me like I was a child. "But these are questions that I have to ask for the test. Just bear with me. Okay."

"Okay," I agreed grumpily. *You are confusing old and sick with dumb and stupid,* I thought. By the time we finished, I was bone tired. I wanted to go home, get up in my bed, and try to catch the rest of my stories.

CHAPTER FOUR
RACHAEL

Bea came out of the doctor's office stomping and pouting. Thank God she was getting help. My heart went out to her. I could see that she had some serious problems. After all that she'd been through, she deserved a break. My own problems weren't half as bad as hers, but I half felt like I needed to join her.

So far, Richard still hadn't been able to come and visit. Between the studio and his job, he didn't have the time. Talking on the phone was something, but it wasn't enough. I felt myself sinking into a depression. I was sick of problems. For six years mine had been snowballing—pregnancies, babies, marriage, and most of all, money. I swear, as soon as you figure out one crisis, another one comes along to knock you right back off kilter. I kept reminding myself to try and take things day by day. Every weekend Richard spent working brought us closer to our goal. Lord knows I could be in a funky mood all by myself. I really wanted to help Bea, but until she was ready, how could I? I decided to take the both of us somewhere where we could relax.

"Bea, why don't we go down to the Riverfront? I hear that it's pedestrian friendly, and we could use the exercise."

"No!" she said, popping her lips. "I don't want to go down to no Riverfront, too many gnats down at that Riverfront. Besides, I don't want to have nothing to do with no exercise."

"Listen, Bea, I'm just asking a question. Now what do you

want to do? Cause I can just as easily drop you off at home. I don't know what's wrong with you, but next time you need to ask that therapist for some drugs. People can't even ask you a simple question."

"Well I'm sick and tired of damn questions. The lady in that damn office asked me enough of 'em already. Besides, I know you been talking to Virginia. She the one that told you to try and get me to exercise. Could I please get all of y'all to stay out of my business!"

"You know you really need to get over yourself," I said, dismissing her with the wave of my hand. "The last thing on my mind is your business." It didn't take me long to learn that Bea needed to be handled with a firm hand. Otherwise, she would complain, moan, and pout you to death.

"I'm hungry, let's stop and get some barbecue," she said, still pouting like a petulant child.

"Humph!" I smiled. "I guess you call yourself apologizing. Which way do we go to get the barbecue?"

Neither of us said much on the way to the barbecue place. In the nine years that I'd been with Richard, Bea and I hadn't spent much time together. For the most part, I thought she was this nice old lady. The most time we'd spent together was Christmas dinner a few years back. Nothing was the way that I had wanted it to be. I was spending my first Christmas away from home in my baby's father's mother's house. My parent's home was filled with Christmas decorations and people laughing, fighting, and cutting the general fool. Meanwhile, I was hundreds of miles away, in a house where the only decoration was a tree that could best be described as the model for that horrible little tree in the

Charlie Brown Christmas Special. Add to that, Richard got called in to work. He drove back to Atlanta, leaving me with his mother and her senile aunt. I barely knew either of them. To be fair, Virginia had a lot going on.

I'd just found out that instead of sweet potato pie, we were having mincemeat. Mincemeat, I'd never even heard of that. As far as I knew, it was a chopped up meat pie. There I sat on the verge of tears, imagining the dessert table back at home spilling over with Mom's lemon crème pies, sweet potato pies, and Aunt Rosetta's German chocolate cake, not to mention all of the other foods that were part of our traditional Christmas dinners. I knew that it would be a horrible Christmas dinner that year. Bea and R. Thomas prevented that from happening. That was a year before R. Thomas died, and thanks to the two of them, I had a ball. They talked and joked, and joked and talked. We had a little party that night. The only thing missing was the alcohol. We were having such a good time, even Virginia joined in on the fun.

It was a year later when I saw Bea again. This time she was in absolutely no mood to be funny. The occasion was R. Thomas's funeral, and Bea was falling apart. Her mother had just died eight weeks earlier, but that was no surprise. At the time of her death, Henrietta was ninety-seven years old. She'd been confined to her bed for the better part of six years and at a rate of steady decline for at least fifteen. R. Thomas was a different case. Everyone was too involved in Henrietta's passing to notice the steady hacking cough that R. Thomas had. By the time the doctor called it to Virginia's attention, it was too late. He'd been a chronic smoker for years and had developed both throat cancer and heart disease. When the family learned of his illness, we were more frightened of the throat cancer. Everyone was shocked to get the news that R. Thomas died in his sleep due to a heart attack.

After the funeral, Bea upset the family by insisting that somehow the hospital was responsible for R. Thomas's death. I wasn't comfortable enough with the family at the time to ask specific questions as to what she was talking about. I do know that she upset everyone when she went and hired a lawyer and insisted that an autopsy be performed. To the best of my knowledge, that whole episode held up the settling of R. Thomas's will for some time. I should have seen then that Bea was given to bouts of high drama.

The restaurant Bea chose was a shack. The building was so lopsided it seemed to be searching for something to lean against. I found myself constantly amazed at the amount of ram shackle buildings that this city contained. The amazing thing wasn't that there were dilapidated buildings, but that they seemed to be everywhere. In my travels around the city, I noticed little shacks sitting right next to nice properties. As a matter of fact, Big Tim's Honky Tonk was right across the street from the doctor's office. Now that was funny. The place was as clean on the inside as it was raggedy on the outside. Even the cardboard patching on the ceilings managed to be filth free .

We sat down and began to eat our food off of the paper bags that we were given for plates. Talk about ambiance. Atmosphere aside, the barbecue was really good. I found myself imitating Bea as I dipped my bread into my sauce. "Girl, a little food sure does make you happy. Look at you. Dancing and singing in your chair like a little kid at a birthday party. Are you sure you're the same person I picked up from the doctor's office?"

"Chile, don't pay no attention to me. I got a lot on me right now. How are you and Virginia getting along?"

"In the short time that I've been here, she's barely said anything at all."

"The two of y'all don't get along?"

"It's not that. She doesn't talk much. How was your therapy session?"

"Nerve wracking. I feel so foolish talking about it."

"Okay then, don't talk about it. I only asked because it's obvious that there's something going on with you. Sometimes talking gives you clarity."

"Girl, I done already told you more about myself than I should have," Bea said, looking off into space.

I rolled my eyes, not that I was intentionally trying to be insensitive, but I couldn't imagine what could be worse than what she'd already told me. "Says who? Did somebody issue you a gag order? If you want to share something about yourself, then share."

"I never thought about it like that, but you're right. You should become a therapist. You making way more sense than that woman I just talked to."

"Okay," I said, raising my eyebrows. Apparently I was going to have to drag the conversation out of her. "Is it because of the rape?"

"No." Bea snarled, her lip curling at the corner of her mouth.

"Okay." I threw my hands up in the air. "I'm not trying to get you all upset. It just seemed to me like you had something on your mind.

Bea sat back and massaged her temples. "Shoot, it's a heap of mess I'm in. I don't even know where to start. The whole thing is shameful."

She had my mind piqued. "Please stop saying that, and tell me what you are talking about," I said, sitting back in my chair.

Bea took a long swig of her lemonade then said very quietly, "I got fooled by a con man."

I thought I heard her, but I wasn't sure because she was talking so low. I was confused; did she say something about a con man? How in the world did she get involved with a con man? I didn't say a word. I was trying to keep my face blank because I could tell that Bea was looking at me trying to gauge my reaction. I was tired. Sitting in a restaurant with two babies wasn't the easiest thing. Looking at my watch, I realized that Sherril had to be picked up in a little less than an hour. "Okay, we're running out of time, so spill the beans. Who is this con man, and what did he do to you?"

"Well, you know my daddy used to own a bank. He also owned a lot of property. Mother got the property when he died since there wasn't any will."

I put my hand on hers to interrupt. "Your father was a serious business man without a will?"

Bea rolled her eyes at me and began wagging her finger in the air. "There you go again with all your damn questions. Are you gonna let me tell you or not?"

Taking my hand off hers, I helped Vee with her drink. "Sorry, go ahead." I made a mental note to myself not to interrupt her again.

"Where was I?" Bea asked, looking up at the ceiling like the answer was there. "Oh yeah, the property," she said, looking at me once more. "Well, since I've been out from the bank on disability, I been living off of the money I get from the rent I collect."

"How many houses do you have?"

She hunched her shoulders in answer. I could see that I wasn't about to get the total story, so I let her continue.

"I know my daddy is turning over in his grave at how I lost all of that property."

This one I couldn't let go. "Well, how did you lose it?" I leaned forward.

"Oh different ways," she said, waving her hand. "Some I lost through back taxes, some was condemned, and the rest I lost to this damn con man."

Again with the con man, I continued stroking her hand. "Well what did he do?"

Bea looked up at me with tears in her eyes. I was totally confused, we still hadn't arrived to the point where she'd been conned. I prodded her along while stroking her hand. "Finish telling me."

"It started when I needed some work done on my house. I asked around, and this lady at my church gave me the name of her handy man. She was a nice church going lady, so I trusted her. The man came out and fixed my washing machine, he did a good job..." She played with her straw, twirling it around in her lemonade, which was mostly ice at this point

Bea took a breath of courage and then continued, "You know, he was clean, on time, and didn't charge me much. I offered him some dinner. By and by, we got to talking. He was nice and friendly. You know, good company."

She gave another long pause.

"Mmm...yeah." I nodded my head.

"Get your mind out the gutter now. We was just friends, not boyfriend girlfriend like, but plain friends. He wasn't my type. He was too young for me for one, and he was short. Besides, he had gold teeth. He was too common for me in that way. With his empty pockets, ain't no way we was going to be anything but friends."

Bea took another deep breath. "Anyway, he saw that I was an old lady living by myself, so he started coming around fixing things for me. I would fix us something to eat whenever he came to work. After a while, he started coming by even when I didn't have no work for him. He even brought his son by. A few times, he brought a lady friend. It was almost like having the son I did-n't get to raise. All this was about the time R. Thomas had died, so I was glad to have the company."

"Well, that's understandable. Everybody knew how upset you were after R. Thomas died."

"Yeah, well now I feel like a fool. The whole time he was coming to my house, he was plotting against me. The low-down, dirty devil. I feel plain ignorant. He had his plan set from the start."

"Come on now, Bea, stop that. You said yourself how vul-nerable you were." The question was, what did the vulnerability lead to?

"I guess. Anyhow, we got to talking about my houses one day. I was telling him about the back taxes and how some of the hous-es were about to be condemned. I wasn't telling him cause I want-ed him to fix them; I needed somebody to talk to. That's when he asked me to take him around to have a look."

Bea took her tissue and blew her nose. She took that same tissue, full of snot, and ran it through her fingers. Finally, she picked up another napkin, wiped her hands, and continued. "I did. At first, he said that they weren't in that bad of shape and he could fix most of the wrong things. I didn't have money since I wasn't charging much for rent. Plus I'd already lost some of the houses."

"So what did you do?"

"Well you know everybody in town think our family got plenty of money. Folks can be so foolish. Can you believe that after Mother died, one fool lady even had the nerve to call me up and ask me for her clothes? Mother hadn't even been in the ground for a full week. I asked, 'Well, ma'am, did you attend the funeral?'"

"No," the lady answered.

"Did you come by the house?"

"No."

"Did you send flowers, a card, your condolences or anything?"

"No."

"I was outdone. As well as you please, I said, 'Then hell no you can't have any of her clothes!' I hung up the damn phone! Can you believe that woman had the nerve to call me right back and call me a bitch?"

"Yeah, I can believe it," I said, adjusting the baby in my lap so he could nurse. "But that's a whole nother conversation," I quipped. "Go on with what you were saying."

Bea squirmed in her seat and started playing with her straw

again. "I knew everyone would be real upset with me if they knew about this, but at the time it seemed like the right thing to do. When we finally settled Mother's will, we divided up everything in the house. Virginia and I put tags on everything. The blue tags were hers, and the red tags were mine. Eunique Johnson—that was his name—said I could just pay him by selling off some of my things. I needed the money, so I said okay fine. Just go in and pick out anything with the red tag."

My heart dropped in my chest the minute I heard her. Those things meant a great deal to my husband's family. I had only been inside the house once, it had long since been vacant by the time I met Richard. Even so, I could tell it was a grand place in its time.

Richard loved to tell the story of the house. His grandfather had it built from the ground up for his new bride when she refused to move into the house that he had shared with his previous wife. Henrietta Butler had perfect taste, and she married a man that could afford to indulge it.

Romulus Williams built his wife a three-story, five bedroom, two bathroom Victorian. The first floor consisted of the formal living and dining room, a kitchen, a music room and a recreation room. Of course, there was a cellar and Romulus was astute enough to build his own private apartment over the detached garage.

The new Mrs. Williams also had a love of gardening and animals. Wanting to keep her happy, her husband made sure that she had a goldfish pond, a dog run and enough space for a garden so beautiful that the white women from The Garden Society came to her for advice.

Needless to say, Henrietta took care furnishing her home. She went on a shopping spree with her sisters in New York City to decorate. The rooms were filled with Chippendales, highboys, marble top accent tables, and a mahogany dining room set that seated nine easily, complete with a buffet, a china cabinet, and a server.

Virginia and Richard, Sr. were married in that house. Richard had countless stories about the good times that they'd all spent there. During the period that the will was being probated, everyone agreed that the decline of the house was a shame, but no one had the means to do anything about it. Everyone was busy pursuing careers and raising families. My husband often referred to his dream of restoring the house to its former glory. I understood Bea's reluctance to admit what she'd done, because they would all be upset.

"Bea," I said gently, "if you needed money that bad, why didn't you tell someone?"

Bea's voice quavered. "Cause everybody was already mad at me for going to that lawyer over R. Thomas's death. Now what do you think they would have to say if I told them I was broke while I was doing it?" Bea started shredding her napkin. "I was trying to take care of everything by myself. At first, it was all working out fine. When we started running out of things of value, Eunique asked me to let him sell the things marked with blue tags. Now those were Virginia's things, and I'm not a thief, so I said no. That's when he convinced me to sell R. Thomas's old Cadillac. I did, but he said that it wasn't enough to pay for the materials and labor for the rest of the work that had to be done. Trying to get those properties back up to code was expensive, one house had to have the roof replaced, another one needed to be rewired. It was all a big mess. I told him I could take out a loan to cover the cost of everything. Eunique said that wouldn't be a good idea. He said that people like to cheat older woman like me. He said that the court was full of foreclosures on the houses of old people who couldn't pay back their loans. Well, I'd heard of that happening, too, so I believed him. When he suggested that I sign over the six houses, I didn't have any misgivings. The way he explained it, it all seemed like it made sense."

Puzzled I interrupted, "Bea, what kind of sense does that make?"

"Well," she stammered, "he said that whether I actually had it or not didn't matter, but that people thought that I had a lot of money because of my family. He heard how they talked about our family because he'd heard the gossip and rumors. He claimed that the word was out that some of my tenants were getting together to file a lawsuit, claiming they'd hurt themselves. You know one would say he broke his leg falling through the steps, another would claim he got a bad infection from stepping on a rusty nail. I believed him. It seemed like he told the truth about everything else that he'd said. I really thought that he was trying to help me out when he said I should sign my property over to him."

"Please, tell me you didn't!" I bolted up in my chair so fast I woke the baby. The only other patron besides us looked up from his newspaper. I shrunk down in my seat.

Tears rolled down Bea's face. "I done already told you that I thought of him like a son," she whispered, looking across at the man. "You don't know what it's like to be in this world by yourself. You have a husband and children, but who do I have to keep me company in my old age?"

I sat forward and whispered loudly, "Why do you keep saying that you're in this world all by yourself? You have your family. Did Virginia ever meet this Eunique Johnson? What did she think of him?"

"No!" Bea said loudly.

The cashier at the counter looked out beyond the counter. She eyed us suspiciously then returned to her conversation with the woman working the grill.

"Why," I whispered?"

"She doesn't know anything about him. Why you always want Virginia to be all up in my business? I know how to handle my own business."

I could see that Bea was upset, so I didn't say anymore. But it was obvious to me that she didn't have a clue about handling her own business.

Bea didn't have too much to say on the ride home. Hearing her story, I could understand why she was so upset. I wouldn't want Virginia all up in my business anymore than Bea did, so I could understand why she wouldn't want me to tell her. At the same time, Virginia was the type of woman who always came through in a crisis, even if she drove you crazy in the process. Then again, if I told her about Bea's situation, Bea wouldn't trust me with anything else, and I really enjoyed our growing friendship. No, telling Virginia wouldn't work.

"And don't tell that baldheaded husband of yours either," Bea commanded, finally breaking her silence as we pulled into her driveway.

I just sat there. She must have been reading my mind. I was thinking about telling Richard. "I won't," I stammered.

"Good. The first thing he'd do is go running to Virginia."

She was definitely right about that. Even so, there had to be something that I could do to help her out. Lord knows, if I was her age and something like that happened to me, I would want somebody to come to my aid. "Have you thought about calling legal aid?"

She shrugged. "I ain't telling them strangers all of my business."

I shook my head. Pride certainly does go before the fall. "Bea, they are professional. I'm sure that they heard a lot worse than that."

"Mind your own business," she said, struggling with the effort it took to pull herself out of the car.

I don't care what she says, I decided, watching her stump up the walkway. I could at least call the people at Legal Aid to see what steps she would need to take.

CHAPTER FIVE
BEA

Even though we'd talked about it in my last confession, I kept having thoughts of killing myself. I would prefer to kill Mr. Eunique Johnson. One thing is for sure, one of us had to go, and I'd rather it be him. All I needed was a gun.

It was on my mind so bad, I called my friend Red and asked him to let me use his gun.

"You want to borrow my what?" he asked.

"Your gun," I said, trying to sound casual like I always call my friends and ask to use their weapons.

"What in the hell do you need a gun for?"

"Well," I drawled out, searching for a quick lie. "You know my dog ran off, and I'm afraid to be in the house by myself."

"That dog has been gone for months. Don't you go nowhere, I'm coming over." Red disconnected.

I went to wait for him on the front porch. It took Red all of five minutes to get to my house. I watched him as he walked up to the front porch. Red had been my friend since primary school. The name Red was short for redbone, even though Red was more high yellow than red boned. He beat up plenty of boys who tried to call him yellow. He took it as them saying that he was a coward. Like me, Red was Catholic. He'd had a long career as a high school principal. I could tell he was coming from one of his volunteer jobs because he was dressed in a suit. He always was a snazzy dresser. I don't think a pair of jeans ever touched his behind.

Red sat down in the empty chair, and I handed him a glass of iced tea

"Your grass needs cutting," he said before drinking his tea.

I nodded. My yard was in terrible shape. Not only did the grass need cutting, but I needed to have the pine straw raked up, too. I had one big Georgia pine growing in my front yard, and if the straw wasn't raked once a week, it could easily get out of hand.

"Nice night isn't it?" I asked.

Red nodded.

"It's supposes to get up to around eighty degrees tomorrow."

Red took a long drag on his cigarette and exhaled slowly. "What is going on with you, girl?"

"What are you talking about?" I asked, poking my finger into my glass of iced tea and twirling the ice cubes around.

He put out his cigarette and lit another one. "Faye called me. She seemed pretty upset."

Faye was a friend of ours. I had called her and asked her to call Eunique for me. I couldn't call him myself because he had Caller I.D. I knew he was using it to screen my phone calls. Course Faye had to be real nosey about the whole thing.

"Who you got me calling?" Faye asked. "Does he have a wife or something? Why can't you just call him yourself?"

One hundred questions later, I was willing to make up anything to keep her out of my business. "No, he does not have a wife. He's been two-timing me with this young girl. I need to let him know I'm not the type of woman to be played with."

Now I was just making all of that up. But, she didn't know it. That's why her big mouth behind went running to tell Red her news. Faye was an attractive lady. She was the same age as me, but she didn't like growing old, not that any of us do. I think it bothered Faye that she wasn't a head turner anymore. It's no secret that misery loves company, Faye spent most of her time telling other folks business. She probably told half the town about my phone call. I guess it made sense for Red to put two and two together and think I wanted to shoot the man. He wasn't completely wrong; I did want to shoot the man, just not for that reason.

"So who is this man that you running behind?"

I shrugged my shoulders. Lying is hard 'cause you got to remember what you said to one person so you don't tell the next person a different thing.

"What happened to that fella who used to come around here, I can see from the yard that he ain't been helping you out lately."

I took a deep breath and turned my head.

I heard Red striking another match. That man was going to smoke himself to death if he kept it up. Even I restricted myself to one or two every now and then.

"I heard that the rent went up on that house you have over by the high school."

My head spun around. "Who told you that?"

"Secretary in the school office. Her sister lives in the house."

I sighed and the tears came rolling down my cheeks.

"How come that fella going around raising your rent, Bea?"

"I signed my properties over to him…" The whole story came flowing out. I thought that if I stopped, I wouldn't be able

79

to finish.

When I finished, Red inhaled. He lit another cigarette. "Have you talked to Edward?"

"No," I said, looking off into the yard.

"Tell him. Your nephew is one of the most respected attorneys in this city."

"I can't tell him. Virginia will think that…"

"Bea," Red said sternly. "The last thing that you need to think about is what Virginia is will think. In the end, she would rather you have your property."

They say that pride goes before the fall, but crawling to my family for help was too embarrassing. When I was selling off my stuff, trying to make the money to fix up my properties, Edward was trying to get me to join this corporation he and the rest of the family were putting together. They had some idea of putting all of the family's properties together and getting paid out of that.

I don't like the idea of people being all up in my business. Plus, I couldn't wait for them to get everything finalized before they started giving me my share from the rent. I needed my money right away. Still do.

I looked at the clock hanging over the doorway in the kitchen and was disgusted to see that it was already 7:00 P.M. Virginia was liable to go to her own funeral late. She's always late. Even when she was a little girl she was late. All of the children in school could make it there on time, but not Virginia.

I would ask Father, "Why do the rest of us have to be here

before the bell and she gets to come in late every time?"

He never did give me a satisfactory answer.

Confession starts at 7:00 P.M. I told her 6:30 P.M. Confession had started five minutes ago, yet she still hadn't shown up. By the time I got there, Father Donahue would have a long line. I wasn't about to confess to Father Carter. Besides, I was hungry and the smell of cooked cabbage with potted meat coming from the crock-pot was making my stomach growl. I took the lid off and tasted just a little bit because I didn't want to go into confession smelling like cabbage.

By the time Virginia came, I wouldn't have any choice but to see Father Carter. Not that Father Carter was bad; he was just too young. If you ask me, there's something wrong with giving confession to a priest who spends most of his time in jeans and a baseball cap. The young people liked it, but me, I'm old fashioned. Father Carter didn't even have the women cover their heads before entering the sanctuary. That's just not right.

When I was a schoolgirl, we were not allowed to go into the sanctuary without covering our heads. Humph. Nowadays, women even wear pants into the sanctuary! I know that Father Carter doesn't have anything to do with that, but it's still not right.

Father Donahue was more my style. Most of us older folks liked to go to him for confession. I felt more comfortable telling him my problems. He knew most all of my business anyway. When I first left my husband and came back to live with Mother, he was the one I confessed to. He might be the only person that understood why I never got a divorce. Nobody, not even my husband, Larry, was going to come between me, and my getting to heaven.

I put the lid back on the crock-pot, cleaned up the drippings of cabbage from the counter then washed my fork. Some cracklin' bread would taste real good with the pot liquor from the cabbage, but I couldn't make any because the stove was acting funny. Half of the time the dang thing wouldn't cook at all. I looked back up at the clock and saw another five minutes had passed. I like to be on time, and if it got too late, I might as well miss confession altogether. If I did, I was really going to be upset because I really wanted to speak with Father Donahue.

Making my way to the front of the house, I double checked each room on the way. I don't believe in wasting electricity. My pocket book and sweater were sitting in the chair by the door so that I could grab them on my way out when Virginia got there. Taking a seat in the chair, I looked out of the window to see if she was driving up the street. Even I was surprised to see all of the dust collected on the blinds. In my minds eye, I could see Mother shaking her head at me; she couldn't stand sloppy house keeping. Where was that Virginia? What I needed was a car. Mine was beyond repair, and without my rental property, I couldn't afford to get a new one. That is why I was waiting on Virginia in the first place. My disability couldn't come through soon enough. Lord knows I hated being so dependent on other people. Cause when you are, only one of two things is gonna happen—they'll either boss you around, or let you down. At least that's how it's always worked out for me.

Just as I was about to go back in the kitchen and check the clock, Virginia blew her horn. I don't know why she blew that dang horn like she the one been waiting. I swear. I couldn't wait till I got my hands on that money. One of the first things I would do was buy me a car.

She had her grandbaby in the car. I didn't think Sherril liked me. All she ever did was look at me without saying a word. I mentioned it to Rachael; she claimed that the child is shy and didn't talk much to anyone. I know it was foolish for a woman as old as me to be worried about whether or not a little girl liked her, but I usually get along well with little children.

One summer Sherril stayed a week with Virginia. Well, Virginia had some errands to run and asked me to watch the child. I did. Sherril didn't say much then either, but I guess we got along okay. That is until she scared me half to death. I just happened to look out the window, and there she was walking down the street. I liked to have a fit. Sherril was only four and could have easily been hit by a car, snatched or anything. I went tearing up the street to get her. We came back to the house with me fussing all the way.

When she had decided that she'd gotten enough of my mouth, she looked me straight in my eye and said, "I hate you. Nobody loves you. Nobody but God."

I told Virginia, and we both got a good laugh off that. Virginia said, "Well, Bea, if the only person who loves you is God, I guess you are doing okay."

"Hey, Sherril," I said as friendly as you please. "You look so pretty today."

She didn't even turn around when she said thank you. She kept looking out of the window, same as she was before I came out.

"Where y'all been off to today," I asked, trying to be friendly. I didn't feel like fussing with Virginia for being late.

"We had some things to get at the store. I wanted to stop and get some cloth diapers for the smaller children."

"I didn't know that Rachael uses cloth diapers. Matter of fact, I didn't think anyone used cloth diapers anymore."

"Well, she doesn't, but she needs to. She can save a lot of money by using cloth."

"So she decided to use cloth diapers, how much money she trying to save?"

Virginia sighed and kept on driving. I hate it when she sighs like that. It's her way of saying, without saying, that she doesn't like whatever it is you are talking about. The cloth diapers were all her idea. When Virginia gets an idea in her head, it doesn't matter if you want to do it or not. I love my sister, and I'm not trying to squash her. She is a good person, but she's too controlling. How did she know if that girl wanted to use cloth diapers?

Before I knew it, I asked exactly that, only I said it a little nastier than I meant to. "Now how do you know that girl want to use cloth diapers?"

"Huh." She sighed again. "Bea, we have to do a lot of things that we don't like in this life. I've had three babies myself, and all of them used cloth diapers. Surely, she can use them on these two. Rachael has two babies in diapers; she told me that they go through two packs of diapers a week. When I went to purchase some for her, I couldn't believe that they cost ten dollars a pack. That's twenty dollars a week and at least eighty dollars a month. If she uses cloth diapers instead, she can take that same money she was using for pampers and put it into a savings account. In twelve months that will be nine hundred and sixty dollars plus interest."

I was the one that worked in the bank, but that was only as a secretary. Seems like when I see a bunch of numbers on paper, they all get kind of jumbled up in my head. One thing I couldn't deny though, Virginia could save some money. Still, Rachael should be the one to decide, since she would be the one doing all of the work. I didn't say anything though. I was on my way to confession, and having an argument beforehand would just give me one more thing to confess.

"Bea," Virginia said, clearing her throat. "I got a call from Faye. Do you have any idea what she was talking about?"

Of course I knew what she was talking about, so did Virginia. Both of them got on my nerves. Faye's nosey behind was trying to get into my business; she called Virginia to see if she would spill the beans. Folks can be so sneaky. Two can play that game. I decided to play dumb and see where Virginia was going with this. "Ain't no telling. Faye is my friend, but she likes to get herself too involved in people's business for me. Half the time, she don't even know what she's talking about."

"She seemed to think that you were upset over some friend that you have."

Virginia never would have approved of my friendship with Eunique. First of all, she would have thought that he was to low class for a lady like me. Second of all, she would have thought he was too young. Humph! Come to think of it, R. Thomas wouldn't have liked him either. The two of them always were real careful about who they let get close to them. Me, I could just about be friends with anybody. If R. Thomas had been around, he wouldn't have even let him step foot inside the door. Ain't no use in thinking about all of that now, here is where I am. Still, I wasn't ready to tell Virginia about Eunique.

"You know I don't have any real friends, at least not like R. Thomas."

"Bea," Virginia sighed, "R. Thomas was our brother and we both loved him, but it is time for you to move on."

"Well, Virginia, you have your children and your grandchildren, but what have I got?"

"Perhaps I am mistaken, I thought they were also your nieces and nephews."

"It's not the same and you know it," I said in a huff.

Virginia pulled into the church parking lot, parked the car, and turned to look at me. "Listen, Bea, I know that something is going on with you. I am tired of having these conversations. If you are not going to let me help you, I am sending you to someone who will."

"What do you mean sending me?"

"Just calm down. You know that you haven't been feeling well. You are tired and irritable all of the time. I try to get you to exercise and you won't. You are overweight and frankly, that cough of yours is starting to bother me. Dr. Evans says that you have a heart condition."

"Dr. Evans! What are you doing calling my doctor behind my back?"

"I didn't call him. He called me because you won't do like he asks you to. He's been trying to get you to take better care of yourself. You refuse. He wants you to start seeing a counselor. He called me out of desperation."

"Well the two of you can call each other all you want, but

how am I supposed to pay for this counseling? You know I'm not working, and I don't have insurance. "

"You are right, I did know that. Which is exactly why Dr. Evans and I are trying to get your disability started. We also arranged for you to get Medicare. All you have to do is complete the tests to qualify for the disability. Didn't you think that Dr. Evans was going to call when you walked out of his office during one of your tantrums?"

I folded my arms across my chest. This town was full of nothing but spies. I should have known that the women I saw the other day was going to say something to Dr. Evans, she did work for his practice. But that still didn't give them the right to go running off at the mouth to Virginia, even if Dr. Evans was Mother's god son and had been raised with us like a brother.

Virginia changed her tone and started talking to me like I was her five-year-old granddaughter. "Look, I know that you like your privacy, but this is serious. It's time for you to quit acting like a stubborn child."

What could I say? She had me there; it wasn't like I didn't need the money. "Just be here to pick me up in an hour," I grumbled, getting out of the car.

I went inside the confessional and said my prayers. "Receive my confession, O most loving and gracious Lord Jesus Christ, only hope for the salvation of my soul. Grant to me true contrition of soul, so that day and night I may by penance make satisfaction for my many sins. Savior of the world, O good Jesus, Who gave Yourself to the death of the Cross to save sinners, look upon me, most wretched of all sinners; have pity on me, and give me the light to know my sins, true sorrow for them, and a firm purpose of never committing them again. O gracious Virgin Mary, Immaculate Mother of Jesus, I implore you to obtain for me by your powerful intercession these graces from you Divine Son. St. Joseph, pray for me."

After saying my prayer of confessional, I wasn't about to lie to no priest, so I asked him, "Father, what do you do when you can't get over something."

He didn't answer me right away. I could hear him fiddling with a candy wrapper on his side of the partition. " Exactly, what do you mean?" he asked finally.

I was so 'shamed, I had to close my eyes. "I told you about that man, you know Eunique, the one that conned me. Well, I can't seem to get past what he did to me."

"Exactly what are you saying?"

I could hear him fooling with a piece of candy on the other side of the partition. I took a deep breath and began wringing my hands. "I'm saying that I can't make myself forgive him. Seem to me like he needs to pay for what he did to me. It's just not right!"

"Pay for it?" he asked, the scent of his cinnamon candy filling the air. "You haven't gone to the police yet?"

"No," I answered, a tear rolling down my face. "I'm too embarrassed." I could just imagine how fast the news of misfortune would go through town. I wouldn't be able to go anywhere without folks laughing and talking about it.

Father Donahue coughed. "How do you propose he pay for it?"

"I could kill him," I said, punching my fist into my thigh like me at sixty-four, killing a thirty-some-year-old man was the most natural thing in the world.

"Now, Bea," Father Donahue said in his soft quiet way, "think about what you are proposing. How will killing him help you? Will it change what happened? You are a good Catholic woman, and I know that you believe the teachings of our Lord and Savior Jesus Christ. Vengeance is mine sayeth the Lord. You need to purge any thoughts of revenge."

"And let him get away with it?" I asked through clenched teeth.

Father sighed, and the scent of his cinnamon candy filled the air between us. I could almost taste it. "First of all, unless you go to the police, he will get away with it. You misunderstand. Handing it over to God doesn't mean that he will get away with anything. "

That said, Father Donahue closed with a prayer, telling me to fast and pray on it until my next confession.

I did exactly that. I got home from confession at eight and didn't eat a thing until noon the next day. I was starving to death by that next afternoon. All I had was two jugs of pink grapefruit cocktail. I'd spent the whole night praying and meditating so hard, I saw rosaries in my sleep. I was purging.

The next afternoon my answer came clear as a bell. When I went to get the mail, there was a flyer from some finance company. According to the flyer, I could get a loan for at least twenty-five thousand dollars. All I had to do was call the number at the bottom of the flyer.

Forget about what Mr. Eunique Johnson had to say about old people and loans. He was the devil that had gotten me into this mess. I went straight to the telephone. After the man from the finance company took all of my information, he said I qualified for a loan of fifteen thousand dollars. All I needed to do was go to his office to fill out the forms and bring him all of the information he needed. I had to get my proof of residence, last year's income tax papers, and the title to my house to show that I owned it.

I gathered my papers together and looked through my book of prayers. On bended knee, I prayed. "Almighty and ever-faithful Lord, gratefully acknowledging your mercy and humbly admitting my need, I pledge my trust in you."

CHAPTER SIX
RACHAEL

After several weeks of living with Virginia, she and I developed a regular morning routine. At first, I tried to fight it, but finally gave in. The two of us couldn't function together in the kitchen, at least I couldn't. The first couple of days, we spent bumping into each other. We spent the following week trying to stay out of each other's way. That got old, too. Virginia had her way of doing things, and I had mine. To my horror, the ladies liked her way of doing things better.

She took their breakfast orders like a short order cook. I wasn't about to be bothered with all of that. To my way of thinking, as long as what I was serving was not poisonous and relatively tasty, hush and eat it.

Witnessing Virginia running around like a chicken with her head cut off irritated me to no end. She worked as hard as any Waffle House waitress fixing one child French toast, the other child cinnamon toast, making one's eggs sunny side up and the other ones scrambled. Not only that, but the ladies also insisted on eating out of their favorite bowl and cup every morning. Which had to be in their favorite seat, with their favorite place mat, fork, etc... A bowl is a bowl; get over it.

Some mornings after being up with the baby, I was not in the mood. God forbid I sit the wrong lady in the wrong seat. All hell would break loose. Of course Virginia never forgot whose seat was whose. She was perfect.

Adding coal to the fire, whenever I refused to give them what they wanted, they told on me. Now see, from my vantage point, Virginia didn't do enough to discourage that behavior. My daughters were turning into little brats right before my eyes. They were due for some major attitude adjusting. One morning Sherril wouldn't come down when I called her to eat breakfast. When I called she responded, "I am brushing my teeth."

I reminded her that we don't brush our teeth until after we eat.

She looked at me and said, "That's not what Grandma said," as if everything Grandma said had to make more sense than what I said.

I stayed upstairs in the morning, so I wouldn't be tempted to kill anybody. I only went down to get a cup of coffee and feed the baby. At least I still had total control of him.

His diet consisted of nothing but the best. I made sure I only fed Elliot fresh vegetables and fruit, no red meats, pork, or fish. In addition to breast milk, I gave him plenty of water to drink. I would love to have maintained the same for the other two. As babies, I followed the advice of experts when introducing them to solid foods, starting with vegetables and then adding fruits so that they would not develop a preference to sweets. I made sure they drank plenty of water, and when it came to snacks, I gave them plenty of fresh fruits. About the sweetest thing they ate on a regular basis was peanut butter. I had a sweet tooth of my own to deal with, so I didn't buy sweets. I wanted to avoid them.

All of that was before we came to live with Virginia. Since moving in with her, their idea of water was Sam's Choice

Flavored Seltzer. Virginia swore it was real water. I told her that it was really just a clear soda, but that's what she liked. She also liked frozen cakes, Popsicles, red meat, canned foods, sodas, ice cream, and condiments. I cringed every time my kids loaded their plates with ketchup or salad dressing.

Initially, I gave into our new diet. Being from the Midwest, I grew up on red meat. Steak and roast beef were two of my favorite foods. After about two weeks of this, I noticed little bumps erupting on my forehead. I bought a loofa and started scrubbing my face in earnest in the morning and at night before I went to bed. Nothing, the bumps were still there. My next step was to use a strong cleanser for my face. Instead of clearing up the bumps, I developed dry patches on my face. Finally, I decided that the bumps were due to my change in diet. I decided to stop drinking coffee, drink real water, and return to my old diet.

As luck would have it, that week Virginia came home loaded with ground beef. There was a big sale at the grocery store that she couldn't pass up. I told her "I decided not to eat red meat anymore since my face has been breaking out."

She looked at me and kinda smiled. "People have been eating red meat for hundreds of years, and now they are saying it will kill you."

True, I'd heard that argument before. "Maybe, but I'm not taking any chances, cancer runs in my family."

Even though I cooked it, I refused to feed it to the baby or myself. I let Sherril and Vee eat it for two reasons: one, Virginia gave it to them; and two, I didn't feel like arguing with her about it. Besides, as soon as we moved into our own place, I planned to put them back on our old diet.

A few things were bothering me: I was horny, bored and tired of acquiescing to maintain the peace. My friendship with Bea was fine, but I needed to be around people my own age. To take my mind off my problems, I tried to strike up conversations with some of the mothers at Sherril's school, but it was all so one sided.

A lot of kids at Sherril's school came from the military base. I didn't realize that the military installation was so big. The military families that attended the school were a little cliquish. Most of them were the children of officers who chose not to go to the school close to the base. One night the class mother called the house, she was getting everything together for the class Halloween party.

"Hello, I would like to speak with Mrs. Anderson."

"Virginia Anderson, or Rachael Anderson?"

"Rachael."

"This is she. How can I help you?"

"Hello. This is Mrs. Jackson. My son Brian is in your daughters class."

"Oh, hello."

"The parents are planning a class Halloween party, and we need your help."

"No problem."

"Well the party is scheduled to begin at noon. You are required to bring the paper goods. That would be the plates, cups, and napkins. We are expecting you to arrive at 10:30 A.M. for set up. In addition, you will be required to help with games throughout the party and cleanup immediately following."

I was speechless on my end. I didn't know whether or not I was getting ready for the class Halloween party, or battle. I swear, by the time I hung up the phone, I felt like a recruit for the Mother Troop of Classroom A. The next day, I found out that her husband was a captain. I don't know what the deal was, maybe as his wife she had become accustomed to giving people orders.

There was one real friendly lady; she had a little girl named Laura. Turns out Laura and Sherril were becoming fast friends. I was glad that Sherril found a friend, but I couldn't help feeling sorry for Laura. She was one of those kids that you knew from a young age would always march to the beat of a different drummer.

I know that it is superficial, and I felt really bad for even thinking it, but Laura was the goofiest little girl I had ever seen. She looked like a Holly Hobbit reject, with buckteeth, wild hair, and she was pigeon toed. Poor girl, she was only five and already wearing bifocals. What a pair of bifocals they were. They were broken, with a wad of masking tape holding them together at the bridge. The other little kids in the class had a field day teasing Laura. I hated how poorly the other kids treated her.

I was happy to see that Sherril was learning the values I worked so hard to instill in her. Sherril didn't seem to notice anything different about the little girl. I watched them play together on the playground. The two of them carried on like the best of friends. I could see why, Laura had a lot of spunk.

Laura sure didn't get her spunk from her mother. Susan, her mother, was a real introvert. It sounds mean, but Susan was the perfect candidate for a makeover show. I know that my style *du jour* was a pony tail, but Susan's hair was all over the place. Looking at her made me want to go over and fix her up, flatten her hair, adjust her shirt, do something!

Since we were both knew in town and not affiliated with the military, Susan and I were the new kids on the block. So, naturally, we gravitated toward each other. Like me, she had two smaller children. Hers were always whining, crying, pushing, pulling, but never sitting still and being quiet. She always looked like she woke up not more than five minutes before she was scheduled to be somewhere, pulled everyone's clothes out of the laundry basket, grabbed a quick bagel, crackers, or something for them to munch on, and then shoved everyone into the station wagon with the hope of arriving on time.

The worst thing, though, was the way she answered questions. I learned to expect a response from her no less than a good forty five seconds after I finished my question or comment. Maybe it was because she was accustomed to being so preoccupied by her children. She'd lost track of the normal response time of say five seconds. Even when she was not dealing with her child–which was hardly ever–she just stared at you with her mouth hanging open. I wanted to take my hand, gently place it on her chin, and close her mouth.

Aside from our kids, Susan and I had absolutely nothing in common. At least my horny problem would be fixed by the weekend. I was at a loss for what to do about everything else.

At midnight I was lying in bed waiting for Richard, he was supposed to get in around eight. I had all of our bags packed, ready and waiting. My plan was to get in the car and leave the minute he pulled into the driveway. Virginia pretended not to see me put our bags by the door. So what? I was ready to see some tall buildings, my friends, and people who didn't look like Beverly Hillbilly rejects. Every time I heard a car going down the street, I popped my head up to the window to see if it was him.

I flopped down on the bed when I saw it was a red car and not his blue one. I missed my husband. I missed feeling like a woman in every since of the word. Instead, I was feeling like some stressed out milk producing robot.

I lay on the bed, rocking from side to side, singing an offbeat tune in my head.

For Better

For Worse

For Better

For Worse

That's what I'd signed on for, right? Okay, I could deal with it. I had a good man, a risk taker, but he was still a good man. Turning over on the bed, I looked at his basketball picture. What an afro. Ha!

Sleeping in the room he grew up in made me miss him even more. Virginia left the room the same way it was the day he'd left for Morehouse, complete with Brady Bunch bunk beds. I'd learned so many things about him staying in that room. I knew what size Boy Scout uniform he wore. That he had a thing for Knock'em Sock'em Robots, and that he'd lost his virginity at sixteen–he didn't throw away the note that Tina wrote him the day after. Cleaning out one of the drawers I found a sex manual. He bunny eared the foreplay chapter. I blushed just thinking about what a good student he was.

Needless to say, I missed sex, but I missed being his wife even more. I missed him bringing me coffee in bed. I missed my back rubs. I missed my *Deep Space Nine* watching partner. I missed having him in my bed with one crumb snatcher bundled close to him, the other in between us, and the third nursing me.

Now I was the one who had to run beside Sherril flying down the hill on her two-wheeler so she wouldn't fall. I had to do his Yurtle the Turtle imitation and play bounce 'em cowboy. That stuff is hard when you don't have anybody helping you do it.

The kids missed him, too. Sherril had started having nightmares about cats, and Vee walked around with his picture all day long, pointing and telling everybody a thousand times, "Daddy, see, see."

We have definitely been blessed with our better times, and there have been some doozies in terms of worse. We'd made it through the loss of jobs, the deaths of family and friends, credit denials. We'd gone through our share of illnesses, including my being restricted to complete bed rest for four months during my last pregnancy, Richard's broken hand, and the time he had walking pneumonia.

But none of that compared to us living in separate places. For better for worse, I know that you make a vow, but damn I wish somebody could tell you how to deal with the worse. It would be so much easier if I could say I had a cheating, no good, low down dirty so and so. But I didn't.

From the start, Richard had my back. Beginning with the time he typed my term papers one peck at a time because I couldn't type. He was the man who co-signed on my student loans because I was being a brat and wouldn't speak to my parents and then kicked me out of bed when I wouldn't get up for class on time.

When I met him his senior year at Morehouse, he told me that he planned to be a millionaire by thirty. I was impressed.

Here was a man who had an internship with IBM, sold sub-sandwiches out of his Honda Accord at night, and was there promptly at 7:45 to pick me up from class at night. What ever happens to a dream deferred? The last thing I wanted to be was the reason for his deferment, so how could I ask him not to pursue his dream?

I couldn't. That would have been tantamount to asking the man not to breath. I had a man with a plan, a plan that he was willing to work. Okay so it wasn't a conventional plan, but a plan nonetheless.

While I lay there, I considered leaving Virginia's and going to stay with my parents. Unfortunately, there was nothing to do there either, and the weather was worse. My constitution couldn't tolerate a Michigan winter. Besides, there was no point in even thinking about going to stay with my parents. Richard would never agree to let me and the kids go that far. Doing so would be tantamount to divorce.

It was well after one o'clock and Richard still hadn't come. I was worried. I know it's cliché, but what if something had happened to him. He could have at least called. I felt the disappointment in me growing. Three hours ago when the clock struck ten, I figured I would have to put up a fight to get back to Atlanta right away, so I readjusted my plan. My getaway would have to begin in the morning.

Early the next morning, I felt Richard lying beside me. Beats me how I didn't feel him climbing next to me in the twin bed. For a few minutes, I let myself enjoy his presence. I missed the smell of Zest soap combined with his body's scent. I pushed myself into the curve of his body, and inhaled, even the smell of his morning breath was welcoming because it meant that he was there. It is hard having a relationship with someone through the phone. Instinctively, Richard drew me even closer to him and brushed his lips across the back of my neck. I had to remind myself that I was still angry that he was hours late and didn't even bother calling, but that didn't stop my body from tingling.

Virginia was rustling around outside the bedroom door. There was no way that I was going to do anything with her in the house. The twenty-year-old bed we were sleeping on was so rickety it creaked if you blinked. I sucked in my breath and hoped that Elliot, who'd started to stir, would not wake up. It wouldn't have made a difference anyway, because Sherril and Vee came bursting into the room. So much for sex, my kids must have had some sort of radar that went off anytime their father and I were about to get busy.

"Daddy," Sherril screamed, excited. The baby jolted upright and started howling.

I got up to get him, and the other two kids took my place in bed. I sat down on the opposite bed to nurse the baby.

"Where were you, Daddy? I waited and waited," Sherril asked, her nose pressed up against his, despite his morning funk breath. Vee snuggled against him with her thumb in her mouth. Lucky for her she had no consciousness of time, she was happy to see him no matter how late he was.

Richard gave his answer and although I was looking down at Elliot, I could feel him looking at me. His voice was full of apology. "I had to work, baby, and I couldn't leave until I was finished."

"Humph," I said, and rose to get a clean diaper. I stood in

front of the dresser with my back to Richard taking longer than necessary to find a clean undershirt. He could kiss my ass. He had to do more explaining than that.

"What kind of work, Daddy?" Sherril asked. I smiled; the child was up to a good start.

"I had to drive to Chattanooga for a meeting, and the meeting wasn't over until late. But I wanted to see you so much that I came here right after it was over," he said, kissing and tickling her.

I started calculating mileage—in good traffic, Chattanooga is at least a good hour and an half from Atlanta, and it took six hours to get from Atlanta to Albany. That gave Richard a two-hour credit, but it still didn't explain why he hadn't called. Cell phones work in Chattanooga. When I thought about it, I didn't remember him telling me about any important meeting in Chattanooga either. Normally, I wasn't a jealous woman, mainly because Richard hadn't given me reason to be. But, this distance thing wasn't working for me. I'd never been in a long distance relationship. The saying might be that distance makes the heart grow fonder, but in my opinion, it gave too much opportunity for missteps.

Richard took all three kids downstairs to make breakfast. Their laughter and the smell of bacon and coffee drifted upstairs to me in the bedroom. Instead of joining them I burrowed down in my covers. Let him deal with the kids for a while. It was about time I got a break. I love my kids, but even I needed a break from being crawled on, tugged and pulled.

I heard a car pulling out of the driveway and noticed that the house was quiet. A few minutes later, Richard entered the room bearing a plate. Although I wanted to ignore him, the smell of bacon and the steam rising off of an omelet was more than I could resist. Grudgingly, I took the plate.

Richard sat down on the edge of the bed, holding a cup of coffee. He watched me take a few bites in silence then handed me the coffee.

I breathed in the bittersweet scent before taking a sip. *Yum, hazelnut*, I thought as I let the flavor settle in my mouth before swallowing.

Richard watched me take another sip. "How long before you talk to me?" he asked.

Not wanting his eyes to soften my heart, I looked away. "I am talking. I just didn't have anything to say."

"Right. I know you, girl," he said, brushing a piece of stray hair out of the way and letting his hand brush across my face.

I took a deep breath, partly because too many thoughts were rushing through my head, but mainly because I wanted to take in his essence. I missed my husband. Instead of saying so, I whined, "You don't know how hard it is for me here all by myself. I waited for you all night, and you didn't even have the decency to call."

"I did call. I talked to Momma last night. She told me that you were asleep."

In my most humble opinion, that was just a wee bit much. Had I been in Virginia's shoes, I am quite sure that I would have woken me up. But, in an effort not to say anything unkind about the mother of the man I loved, I literally bit my tongue. "She didn't tell me."

He shrugged me off. "She probably didn't want to wake you

up. She told me that you hadn't been getting much sleep because Elliot was up nights."

I bit the inside corner of my mouth. "Well why didn't you tell me about your meeting before?"

Richard settled down on the bed beside me. "I did tell you, remember. I told you about a promoter that wanted to meet with us about a rehearsal space."

I did remember him telling me that. "You didn't say he wanted to meet in Chattanooga."

"What has that got to do with anything?" Richard asked, puzzled.

"Nothing." What was the point of taking the conversation any further? I didn't have anything to accuse him of. I didn't know if I should ask him the details of the club, or ask him to lay down point for point exactly what they'd discussed in the meeting. The fact that my husband and I were living in separate cities didn't mean that he'd turned into a low down, dirty cheat. Besides, it wasn't like we were legally separated because we weren't getting along. My moving into his mother's house was something we'd agreed upon for our mutual benefit.

"So the kids are gone?" I asked, deciding to try and put thoughts of doubts out of my head for the moment.

"Yes," he answered, pulling my gown up over my head and rolling on top of me. "We have to make up for lost time."

I felt my face grow hot. After years of marriage, I still blushed when he talked dirty, even though I loved it. "Yeah, but first we need to brush our teeth."

We returned from the bathroom and went at it like a pair of nymphomaniacs. I'm not one to brag, but for the next hour, I let him manipulate my body like I was a yoga guru. And, I loved every single second of it.

After we finished our lovemaking, Richard and I were lying in bed enjoying each other's company. I thought that I Virginia's car coming up the street. *Damn it,* I thought. I wasn't finished yet. I grabbed my robe off the floor and peeked out of the bedroom window. The car pulled into the driveway of the house next door. I was just about to release the shade when I saw a white Ford Explorer parked in our driveway. "Did you rent a car?" I asked, turning to Richard.

He was pulling on his pajama pants. "No." He headed for the bathroom. "That's Rosalyn's car.

The first time I met Rosalyn, Richards' business partner, I felt something was amiss. As far as I was concerned, he acted too nervous. The man kept talking about how much the two of us had in common; he wouldn't shut up. You can't make people like each other, either they hit it off, or they don't. As a matter of fact, the harder you try to make people like each other, the harder it is for them to get along.

Why was it so important to him that I be her friend anyway? I didn't have to work with her, he did. He didn't act that way about the other people he worked with. Besides, once when she called, after we said good bye, I heard her say something like, "What is wrong with her?" before hanging up the phone.

I could tell her exactly what was wrong with me. She was calling my blankity blank husband, at my blankity blank house, on my blankity blank phone, that's what was wrong with me. I could sound however I wanted to on my telephone. When I told Richard, he accused me of jealousy. Why did he go and say an ignorant thing like that. My not liking it didn't have anything to do with being jealous, at least not at that point. I didn't get jealous until he started defending her! I'd look like a fool taking up for some man that left a message insulting my husband on his answering machine. To me it was a matter of respect plain and simple. At any rate, we ended up arguing. I know that it sounds cliché, but most women would not put up with the shit I dealt with. Really, they wouldn't. I don't mind Richards' female friends, and he has quite a few of them. I even let one of his friends spend the night. She wasn't some ugly woman either. To the contrary, she had a body that wouldn't quit.

I followed him into the bathroom and climbed into the cold shower. "Why are you driving her car?"

"My brakes went out," he said, lathering me up.

I pushed him out of the way, and stood under the water. "You didn't mention that before," I said, turning around to face him.

He stared at me, working his jaw. Richard snatched a towel off of the towel bar. "Let me get this straight," he said, drying himself off like he was trying to rub the skin off of his body. "I've been working non-stop for weeks, trying to save money. I drive half way across the state to get here, and you are tripping," he said, pointing at me.

I stepped out of the shower and grabbed a towel. "I'm tripping? Please. Hell yeah I'm tripping. You drove another woman's car."

"To see you?" he said, throwing his hands in the air.

We stood staring at each other's naked bodies. I decided not to give him the pleasure of seeing mine and jerked the towel around myself. I stormed into my bedroom. Richard was hot on my heels.

"You know that she is gay?"

"No. I know that you told me she is."

"Oh, so I'm a liar now?"

"You tell me?"

"Baby, she is gay. There is nothing going on between us."

I started crying. "Put yourself in my shoes. There you are, hundreds of miles away, lonely, horny…and you are a man. You're probably ten times hornier than me."

"Damn." Richard threw his hands in the air and sat down completely naked, holding his head in his hands. My eyes went straight to the gusto. He caught me looking and snatched a pillow to cover himself. "Have I ever cheated on you?"

"No, but so what, there is a first time for everything. I want you to stop seeing her."

"Baby, I couldn't do that if I wanted to. What am I supposed to do, tell everybody that the deal is off because my wife doesn't want me to work with Rosalyn? Besides, she is gay," he said, emphasizing each word.

I stared him down. "For all I know, she could be bi-sexual."

"Okay. You're right. I'm sorry. I shouldn't have driven her car down here. But I haven't seen my family in a month. My son can sit up and hold his bottle, and I wasn't there to see it. Little Virginia is saying full sentences. I missed Sherril's Halloween party. I wanted to see y'all and she offered. If I was messing around with her, I would at least have enough respect not to rub your face in it."

I breathed deeply. "I don't want you accepting anything from another woman. Women are no different than men. If a man lent me his car, don't you think that he'd expect something in return?"

Richard laid his head on my shoulder. "You're right."

I popped him in the head. "The next time you better rent a car."

Richard and I got dressed and went downstairs to have lunch. I chopped the vegetables for a salad while Richard prepared the ground turkey for hamburgers.

"So what have you been up to?" Richard asked.

I shrugged. "The usual, taking care of the kids, hanging out with Bea?"

Richard stopped to look at me. "Have you done any writing?"

"No," I tried to think of something to change the subject.

"Why not?"

"It's not that easy…"

He put down the bowl and pulled me to him. "It's not that hard either. You've been talking about writing since the day I met you."

We looked at each other. "I know." I sniffed. The freshly sliced onion was bothering my eyes. "I know." I wiped my eyes. The onion that I was cooking was really strong. "It's not that easy." I wiped a tear from my eye and looked up, blinking.

"Open your mouth," Richard commanded. He took a piece of bread and placed it in my open mouth.

"What is this for," I mumbled.

"It'll stop your eyes from stinging." He went over to the cook top and pulled two frying pans from the cabinet underneath. Next, he placed a pat of butter in one of the pans and lit the stove.

He was right. I looked like a loon holding the bread in my mouth, but my eyes stopped stinging. After I finished cutting the onion, I took the bread from my mouth and began slicing red and green bell peppers. "I don't know what to write about." My life wasn't that exciting. I am sure that there were some writers who could make anything exciting. But I didn't think that anyone would be interested in a story about me changing diapers.

Richard took a handful of ground turkey and rolled it into a bowl. He repeated the process and placed both burgers into the frying pan. "You could write about a jealous wife who thinks that her husband is having an affair with a gay woman."

I flung the dishtowel at him. "That is not funny."

Richard ducked. "I'm not trying to be funny. I'm serious. A girl at work is always telling us about these stories she reads from *True Romance*. I know you could write something like that."

"I don't know…" I didn't even read romance, how could I write it.

Richard took the burgers from the pan and put them on a plate. "All you have to lose is time."

He was right about that, and there was one thing for sure, I had plenty of time.

CHAPTER SEVEN
BEA

I'll be dang! Trying to do like the doctor said, I bought seventy dollar shoes so that I could start walking. Dr. Evans told me to start off easy by just walking around my court. I walked all the way around the court and stopped to get the mail when I stepped into an anthill hidden under pine straw.

I ran into the house as fast as I could, stopping every few steps to stamp my feet and try and swipe the ants off. I rushed to the bathroom and got out the Witch Hazel I kept in the medicine cabinet. Sitting on the toilet, I tended the tender ant bites as best I could. The light was dim, and Lord knows my eyesight ain't half what it used to be, but I must have counted at least twenty bites.

It wasn't easy for me to go out and spend that much money on a pair of walking shoes. I did it anyway. Dr. Evans ran all kinds of tests on me. If I never saw the inside of another waiting room, it would be too soon. According to him, I have congestive heart failure, high blood pressure and Lord knows what all, scared the mess out of me when I heard him say congestive heart failure. That's what R. Thomas died of.

I was sitting on the porch rubbing my foot when Rachael came round.

Rachel called out to me from the car. "You want to ride with me to McDonald's?"

I'd used up the Witch Hazel I had by then, and my foot was still stinging. "Yeah, just hold on a minute," I called back. When I stood up, my foot throbbed so I stepped lightly on it.

"Why are you limping?" Rachael asked when I got inside the car.

"I stepped in a bed of ants." I rubbed on my legs.

Rachael looked down at my legs. "They do look a little red. You need to stop rubbing. Did you put anything on them?"

"Witch Hazel," I answered, wincing. I tried not to touch my legs, but I couldn't stop rubbing.

"Stop rubbing," Rachael commanded, looking at me out of the corner of her eye. "Look, I promised Vee that she could play on the playground. I'll drop the two of you off at McDonald's and run over to the drugstore for you. That way you won't have to walk around."

I nodded my head in agreement.

"And stop rubbing, that will only make it worse."

Rachael dropped Vee and I off at McDonalds, and she and the baby drove to the drugstore across the street. While I was waiting for her, I kept on rubbing my legs. The pain was getting worse.

Rachael came back from the drugstore and took a tube of something out of the bag.

"What is that?" I asked.

"Hydrocortisone," she answered, taking the top off the tube.

Whew, my legs were killing me. "I asked you for Witch Hazel," I snapped.

"The pharmacist said that hydrocortisone is good for insect bites. But I knew you would say that so the Witch Hazel is in the bag." Rachael knelt down to put some of that hydrocortisone my foot. "They do look a little irritated," she said, rubbing the cream on my legs. "But it's just a few ant bites. The itching will go away if you stop scratching. I hope this doesn't stop you from walking altogether."

I was hot! Here my legs were throbbing and burning, and she come talking bout me exercising. "I guess you don't know anything being from up north, fire ants bit me. They can be dangerous. I remember seeing on the news how a man died from some red fire ants. He and his neighbor were arguing when the neighbor pushed him into a bed of 'em. Those ants bit the poor man, and he had a heart attack, died before the ambulance even got there. It was big news because the neighbor got put on trial for murder. I can't remember if he went to jail or not. Still, that let me know right there that fire ants can be serious." As it was, my ankles and feet where I got bit were all red and swollen.

That baby screamed his little head off all the way home. I thought that I was going to lose my mind. Between his yelling and my legs, I couldn't get home fast enough. The first thing I did when I got home was fill the tub with warm water so I could soak in the tub with some Epsom salts. Even that didn't help. Something was seriously wrong. My legs were especially burning where I got bit, and they had started to swell all the way up to my knees. I got up out of the tub and put on my robe without even bothering to dry off.

I had to cruise my bedroom furniture like a child just learning how to walk to get to my bed and the phone on the bedside table. By the time I got Dr. Evans on the phone, I was sitting in a puddle of bathwater. After describing my complaints, he told me to head straight to the emergency room. Thank goodness he volunteered to call Virginia for me. I didn't have the patience to deal with her in my state. Only reason I called him in the first place was because Virginia wouldn't take me to the emergency room unless he said to. Rachael wasn't the only one who thought I was trying to get out of exercising. My God, if I didn't want to exercise, all I had to do was not exercise. I didn't have to lie about it. Last time I checked, I was a grown woman.

I heard the horn blow and couldn't believe Virginia got to my house so fast. For once, she was on time. I didn't even have time to take a whore's bath. Decent women took care of themselves before seeing the doctor.

"Hold on, I'm coming. Stop banging on my door like a damn fool!" Shoot! I already explained to her that my feet and legs were hurting.

I should have figured. It wasn't Virginia banging on my door, it was Rachael. No wonder she got to me so fast.

"I'm sorry, but I blew and you didn't come," Rachael said.

I took a step. "Ahhh," I cried and snatched my foot off of the ground. It felt like someone stabbed my leg with a bolt of lightening when my foot touched the ground. I leaned against the door, taking the weight off my foot.

"Oh!" Rachael gasped when she saw my leg. "Oh, Bea, I am so sorry. Oh my God. Your leg is twice the size that it was this afternoon. I'm so, so sorry."

Now she wanted to show concern.

I pointed to the chair on the other side of the room. "Just grab my purse over from that chair."

Rachael ran and grabbed my things from the chair. "Here," she said, putting her arm around my waist. "Lean against me."

The two of us looked a sight, hobbling to the car. When we finally made it, Rachael slowly leaned me on the car and carefully took her arm from around my waist. "Look," she said, opening the car door. "I'm sorry I didn't believe you when you told me that your legs were bothering you."

"Chile, that ain't nothing. Y'all never believe anything I say anyway." I really meant Virginia, but she wasn't there, so I took it out on Rachael instead.

"You're right, I'm so sorry. It's just that Virginia told me that sometimes you get carried away, and she asked me to make sure that I encourage you to exercise. Believe me, if I knew it was this bad, I would have taken you to the hospital right away."

That's for sure, I wasn't feeling well. Sitting in the emergency room all night wasn't going to make me feel better either. I was worrying about how I would pay somebody's hospital bill. Shoot! Now I wished I had listened to Virginia when she was trying to explain to me all of that rigmarole about Medicare and Disability. If I asked her again, I would have to hear her mouth about not listening the first time. I thought about asking Rachael, but the pain in my foot and leg was getting to me, so I decided to wait till later.

The woman at the emergency desk taking my information acted like she thought I was some kind of fool. I figured from the way she was looking at me that not too many people come to the emergency room for ant bites. To plead my case, I told her about the man on the news. "Last year a man died from red ant bites." I might as well have kept my story to myself, she kept on looking at me, popping her gum, like I was the tenth fool she'd seen that day. Seems like I was the only one that knew you could die from red ant bites.

Rachael brought me a nice cold Coca-Cola from the machine and took the hospital forms out of my hands. I was relieved; my legs were paining me too much for me to even think about fillin' out forms.

It took them forever to call me into an exam room. At least the nurse who came in had enough sense to take me seriously. One look at my legs sent her running to find the emergency room doctor. Finally!

I tried not to be embarrassed when the doctor came in. I wished I didn't have to put on the ugliest pair of shoes I owned. The shoestrings were missing, and my toes were sticking through the holes in them. My feet were so swollen, they were the only ones that would fit.

The doctor ran his finger along the swollen part of my legs. "How does this feel?"

"Pardon me." I was so busy thinking about what a mess I looked I didn't hear him. I wondered what he thought about fat people.

"Your leg, how does it feel when I touch it?"

"I can't feel it."

He pressed harder. "How about this?"

"Ouch!"

"Let me have a look at your feet. You did say you stepped into an anthill?"

"Yes." This was exactly why I wanted to wash up before coming to the hospital. What if my feet smelled? I held my breath and said a silent prayer that my feet didn't stink when the nurse took off my shoes

If they did, the doctor didn't seem to notice. He went about examining them like nobodies business. "Are you under a doctor's care?"

"Dr. Evans is my doctor. He has been for almost thirty years." *Oh Lord now what, I hope I'm not going to die.*

"And are you on any medications?"

At least I thought to bring all of my medicines with me. I had put them inside of a plastic bag, which I gave to the doctor.

"I'll be right back," he said, taking the bag.

"I'm not going to die am I?" I asked the nurse taking my blood pressure. She didn't answer. I could tell she was not the listening kind of nurse who cared about her patients. She was the kind of nurse who only cared about the job at hand, I asked again anyway.

Rachael came and stood at the head of the bed, stroking my hair.

Instead of answering my question, the nurse told me that the doctor would be back shortly. She probably thought I was a foolish old woman. Well, let her think whatever she wanted. I ain't got but two legs and two feet, raggedy ones at that. See how people treat you when you don't have any money. If I had on jewelry and furs, she'd have answered my questions right quick.

"Let me ask you something," Rachael said with a concerned look on her face. "What makes you think you are going to die?"

"I saw on the news where this man was fighting with his

friend and got pushed into a mound of fire ants and…"

"You already told me all about that, Bea. Maybe he died because he was allergic, or maybe he died from a heart attack. Who knows, but you're in the hospital, and I'm sure that they're doing everything possible for you. I know it's hard, but stop worrying."

I closed my eyes and tried to relax. "You think I am a silly old lady."

She laughed and waved her hand like it was nothing. "Puhleez! I didn't say anything about you being foolish, but you do tend to get carried away."

Thinking about what she said put me more at ease. I decided to change the subject, get my mind offa things. "What did you do while you were in Atlanta?"

Rachael stared past my head. "Nothing, we didn't go," she said, brushing her bangs up out of her face. "We just stayed in town. Too bad though, it would have been nice to be in a city with beautiful people and tall buildings."

I looked at her standing there rolling her tongue around the inside of her check. Something was bothering her. I wanted to ask her what was wrong, but I can't stand people getting in my business. "Beautiful people! What do you mean beautiful people? You sound so dumb." I laughed. "I been to Atlanta plenty of times, and believe me, all of the people are not beautiful. It's ugly people living there, too."

"That's not what I meant, thank you very much. I know that all of the people in Atlanta are not beautiful. They're more cosmopolitan…"

"Cosmopolitan?"

"Yeah, you know, fashionable, worldly, whatever you want to call it."

I took a good look at Rachael. She was a pretty girl. Nice figure and she sho' didn't look like she had one child let alone three, but she could use some fixin' up. Everything about the poor chile looked tired. Her hair was hanging from her head all limp and scraggly like, and her face was a bit peekish. "It's hard for a young girl like you to be away from her husband. You ain't got no friends, just the company of two crazy old women and three children."

"Amen and praise the Lord!" she said, throwing her head back laughing.

"A girl your age like the company of a man. Believe me I know, I used to have me a boyfriend. We met when I lived in Boston, and we were going to get married, too, but things didn't work out."

Rachael was sitting facing the door. She pointed her eyes in the direction of the door. I turned my head to see who was there. I hoped it wasn't that nurse. I had enough of her for one night. The doctor stepped in.

I swear, he looked like a red haired Doogie Howser. They must be letting younger and younger folks into college. That doctor didn't look any older than twenty-one. He didn't waste any time getting down to business. "I just spoke with Dr. Evans, and he tells me that you have been diagnosed with a heart condition."

Thinking it was something bad. I started to get up from the table.

"Calm down, calm down it is nothing to get upset about." He gently pushed me back on the table. "You did the right thing by coming to the emergency room."

Rachael asked, "What has her heart condition got to do with the ant bites?"

I really started to grow fond of that girl, because this is exactly what I wanted to know.

"Well," he said to the both of us, "because of her heart condition, her blood isn't circulating through her body as fast as it normally would, and this slows down the bodies ability to send white blood cells."

"White blood cells fight off infection?" Rachael asked.

He snapped his fingers. "Exactly. Because they were not able to get to the bitten areas properly, the infection started spreading!" As excited as he was, you would have thought that we were talking to Alex Trebec on Jeopardy.

All right now, he had just said that everything was okay. A spreading infection didn't sound okay to me. And what about those white blood cells? I dropped back on the table and closed my eyes. Did I want to hear the rest of what he had to say?

The doctor laughed and rubbed my arm. That made me angry! What in the world was so funny, my legs falling off? "Am I going to be able to keep my legs?"

"Bea!" Rachael said. "Remember what we said about you getting carried away."

Even with my eyes closed, I could tell she was shaking her head. So I decided not to say anything. Just then, the nurse came back in. I heard something rattling and opened my eyes to see what it was. An I.V. Oh lord! I fell back down. I should have known. I wasn't going to die or lose my legs. I didn't even listen to the doctor go on about fighting the infection. Instead, I was thinking about the I.V.

It's bad enough to get a shot, but in the case of an I.V., it is a shot that doesn't come out. When you get a shot, you can close your eyes, turn your head, grit your teeth, and squeeze something in your hand. Not so with an I.V. It hurts when they put it in, and then just when you get used to the feeling, your hand starts to feel numb. As for using the bathroom, don't even think about it unless you're prepared to work. First off, you have to get the I.V. untangled from the bed frame, chair or whatever else is in the way. Then you have to maneuver it into the bathroom. If all else fails, you have to call the nurse, and that's the worst. As far as nurses are concerned, you using the bathroom is not a priority for them. They tend to get around to it when they're ready, regardless of how bad you have to use the bathroom.

The nurse started to lift my gown. "Will you please turn on your side?"

As I turned, she lifted this giant needle in her other hand.

"That is the I.V. needle!" I said, my voice shaking like a bowl of jelly.

The doctor shook his head, still smiling. "Before we start the I.V., I want to give you a good dose of antibiotics. Relax, that way it won't hurt as much. Trust me, you're in good hands." He motioned toward the nurse.

I watched the doctor walk out of the room, thinking how dumb it was for him to tell me to relax when I was about to be stuck with a giant needle. "Ouch!" I hollered, pulling away from the pain as the nurse gave me the shot.

"I could finish faster if you'd be still," the nurse grumbled.

The witch! She wasn't the one who had to stand the needle. I tried to be still and wondered why in the world this woman decided to be a nurse if she was going to be so nasty about it. I was too tired to whine and fuss anymore, so I let them do what they wanted.

On her first try, the nurse missed my vein. I gritted my teeth and tried to lay still as she poked around my arm, looking for a good vein. Finally, she finished with the I.V. Great! She put the needle in my hand and taped it in place. I was happy to see Nurse Hatchett leave the room, but knowing that my hand would be sore for days cut that happiness short. Rachael started rubbing my shoulder. All of it was too much, and I started crying. It should have been my baby with me rubbing on my shoulder.

After the nurse left the room, Rachael tried consoling me. "Bea, it looks like we are going to be here for a while. Why don't you tell me about your boyfriend?"

I sniffled. "What boyfriend, I done had plenty of boyfriends?"

"Excuse me, Miz Thang," Rachael teased. "The boyfriend you had in Boston."

I chuckled lightly. "I liked Boston, it was a nice city. The only thing wrong with it was the cold weather. Even the weather was nice when you had someone to cuddle with. Virginia's husband Richard, Sr. had family in Boston. I stayed with them when I first moved there. Back then they still had ballrooms where you could dance and listen to live music. We would go to this one place in particular, Roseland. Girl, the big time acts used to play at Roseland. One time I even went to hear Louis Armstrong sing my favorite song, you too young to know about 'Hello Dolly.'"

Rachael squinched up her face. "I'm not too young to know

'Hello Dolly,' but I thought Carol Channing sang it."

How sad, I thought, shaking my head. Young folks these days sure don't know their history. Carol Channing may have sung the song, but Louis Armstrong made it popular. "Anyway, we used to go there every weekend, and every time we went, I'd see this real good-looking man staring at me from across the room. Oooh! He was tall and well built with a café au lait complexion. At first, I tried to pretend like I didn't notice him staring at me. Then I got to wondering why he never said anything. He saw me week after week, and never said anything. One day I got all my nerves together and walked straight up to him and said, 'Look, do you want to buy me a drink, or are you going to keep on staring at me forever?'" I laughed just thinking about how young and sassy I was.

"You can't tell now, but I used to be a fine woman. I never been small, but I had a real nice figure and long pretty hair. There were more than a few men who didn't mind my dark complexion. At first he stared at me like I was a crazy woman, but then he started laughing and said, 'Well, my name is Claude, and I guess you got me.' Claude went ahead and bought me a drink. The time flew by while we spent the rest of the night getting to know each other."

"So it was love at first sight?" Rachael asked with a half smile on her face.

Conjuring up an image of Claude in my mind, I tried to decide if it was love at first sight. "I thought he was fine and all, but looking back on it, it was his spirit that I fell in love with. Something about talking to Claude put me at ease. He seemed to understand me. It didn't take long for us to start spending all of our free time together. Six months went by, and he asked me to marry him. Of course, I wanted to, but I didn't know how he would feel about the fact that I had a child. I told him anyway. I didn't know where my son was, but I still wanted him back in my life, husband or no husband. Claude loved me, he was real understanding about the whole situation. If he could have, he would have killed the father of my child. He couldn't understand why I never told my parents about what happened."

"I agree with Claude, I don't see how you kept it secret," Rachael said, shifting around in her chair.

I started twisting the bed sheets around in my hands. Who was I going to tell? The one person who I could talk to about it was my daddy. And, even he never bothered asking me about the father of my chile. In a way, that kind of bothered me more than the rape itself. "One way or the other, Claude insisted that the man should pay for what he'd done to me. I figured the man still lived in Macon. I asked around and got his phone number. It wasn't hard for Claude to convince me to call the man and demand some money from him. I ain't ashamed to tell I did it! I don't care what people think about me either. I guess getting money out of him was little enough for what he did to me."

Rachael stopped fidgeting with her purse and looked at me with narrowed eyes. "You mean you actually called him?"

My face grew hot, but I pushed the shame away. After all I'd gone through, what I did was nothing. Lifting my chin, I took ownership of what I did for revenge. "I sure did. I politely called him up and said, 'Hello Vincent, this is Bea Walker from Albany. I'm sure you remember what went on between you and me when you were doing some work out at my daddy's house. Well I have me a son by you and we need us some help. You might as well be the one to give it to us. Don't bother trying to deny me either, or I'll be glad to tell your wife all about it.'"

Rachael's eyes went all around the room like she didn't know what to say. Finally all she managed a "Wow."

I looked right through Rachael. "I know it was evil of me, but I felt good!"

"I just can't believe that you did that. I mean, I can see why, but still."

I felt Rachael's eyes staring at me, but I kept my eyes on my hands, winding my fingers through the sheets. The tears that I was holding back started burning my throat.

The doctor knocked on the door, and opened it slightly.

"Come on in," Rachael said, waving him inside. She got up, and moved to the foot of my bed.

He came in the room and looked and my leg. "So, how is my favorite patient feeling?" he asked, wrapping both hands around my leg and pressing lightly from my foot to my knee.

"I'm not in as much pain as I was when I came in, but it still feels a little uncomfortable."

"Just give it a little longer. The medicine we gave you is working. See how you let me touch your leg? Before you wouldn't let me do that. The swelling has stopped and the pain is easing. I spoke to Dr. Evans again and we both agreed that we would feel better if you stayed over night. We want to keep and eye on you."

"Huh," I sighed.

Rachael touched my good foot. "Bea, it's okay. We just want you to get better."

"Listen to your daughter," the doctor said. "We're just going to keep the antibiotics going and the pain medicine we gave you will help you sleep."

Rachael massaged my good foot. "I'll stay with you until you fall asleep."

The doctor winked. "See, you are in good hands. Dr. Evans will come by and see you tomorrow. By then, we should have a better idea about when you can get out of here. In the meantime, I want you to relax."

The doctor said his goodbyes and left the room. Rachael returned to her seat at the side of my bed and took my hand in hers. I wondered what Rachael thought about what I just said. I couldn't tell from the look on her face. She was easy to talk to, for all that I had told her, she never made me feel bad about what I had done. She was so calm about darn near everything. "You think I should be ashamed, huh?" I asked.

Rachael inhaled. "It sounds like you are ashamed. It's like I told you before. You won't let go of the guilt. You haven't forgiven yourself for what happened. So, when you did do something about it, you did it in a way that made you feel even worse about yourself. It's not about what I think about you. It's about what you think about you."

I was thinking about what Rachael said before I drifted off to sleep. I was ashamed of what was done to me. If I hadn't been so fast, Vincent never would have had the opportunity to put his hands on me. And, what happened with Eunique felt like being raped all over again. I invited him in my home, thinking that he cared about me, and he played me for a fool. I was stupid. Nothing like that ever happened to Virginia, and I knew why. She was smart, pretty, and successful. She had accomplished everything I hadn't, which led me to believe that Mother was right all along, maybe I was just a failure.

CHAPTER EIGHT
RACHAEL

When I finally left Bea at the hospital, I was exhausted. I hoped what I said to her got through. She deserved to feel better

I stopped to hang the car keys on a peg near the door in the mudroom before entering the kitchen. "Thank you for watching the kids. How did they do?" I asked Virginia who was washing dishes in the kitchen.

"Oh they were fine."

I smelled chicken. Until then, I didn't realize how hungry I was. "I'm sorry I didn't call you from the hospital," I said, opening the refrigerator, and looking inside. "But I didn't want to leave Bea. You know how dramatic she can be."

"That's Bea," Virginia agreed. She tapped me on the shoulder. I turned away from the refrigerator and she offered me a plate of food.

"Thank you," I said, accepting the plate and sitting down at the kitchen counter. It was baked chicken, cabbage, and carrots. I tasted it. "This is good. It taste like honey mustard. Anyway…" I said taking another bite, "her leg was in pretty bad shape. They gave her an I.V. to start her on antibiotics. They're keeping her overnight."

"Did they say how long she has to stay?"

"No. Dr. Evans has to see her in the morning. I feel horrible. I should have realized how bad it was when she first showed it to me. I just thought she was exaggerating." I shrugged my shoulders.

"Well, we all know the story of the little boy who cried wolf. I can see how you thought she was exaggerating."

Virginia finished washing the dishes and grabbed her purse off of the counter. She stopped in the mudroom to grab a sweater and turned to me before leaving. "I have a key to Bea's house. I'm going to swing by there and take her a few things for the hospital."

I felt a pang of guilt when she left. Virginia was always looking out for Bea. I debated whether or not I should tell her about the con man. On the one hand, I didn't want to lose Bea's trust, but on the other hand, Virginia could help her get out of this mess. From my own experience, I understood Bea's need for secrecy. It really wasn't about keeping secrets as much as it was about how she saw herself. In the end, I decided to keep her confidence. But, I was going to have to get on the ball in regard to Legal Aide.

The following day, Virginia took the day off from work, and the two of us took turns visiting Bea at the hospital.

I entered Bea's room and an elderly white man stood with the assistance of a cane to offer his hand. "Hello. I'm Father Donahue."

"I am Rachael, Bea's nephew Richard's wife." I said, shaking his hand. He had a firm grip.

"You look good," I said to Bea, who was sitting up in bed in a blue flannel nightgown and matching sleeping cap. I was pleased to see that she felt well enough to receive visitors besides Virginia and me. I know from experience that there is nothing worse than a bunch of people visiting you at the hospital, and you looking all stank and raggedy. I took a sit on the heating unit by the window.

"Father Donahue has been my priest for years." Bea smiled.

Father Donahue threw his head back and laughed. "Don't say it like that, Bea. You're making me sound old."

I laughed. I could see why she liked him so much. Knowing what high esteem Bea held him in, I appreciated his coming to see her. "Bea speaks very highly of you."

"Thank you for helping with one of my most faithful parishioners." His eyes twinkled. "Yes, we have quite a history together. Would you care for a piece of candy?"

I smelled cinnamon candy. "No thank you. I'm not going to stay long. Virginia is watching the kids for me, and she wants to be here when Dr. Evans comes. I just wanted to make sure that Bea is okay."

"I was saying to her that I hope she was feeling better in time for mass on Sunday."

"Oh no, Father, I doubt that I could make it in my condition even if I do get out of the hospital." Bea sighed and lay back on her pillows.

Father Donahue turned to me. "Maybe your niece can help."

"Oh that shouldn't be a problem." I felt so guilty about how I treated Bea the other day, taking her to mass was nothing.

She sat up immediately, happy as a clam.

Virginia wasn't expecting me at home for another hour. Without the kids, it was the prime opportunity to find out what I could about Legal Aide. On my way to the car, I stopped at the information desk.

"Hey," I greeted the woman sitting behind the desk. This woman's make up was immaculate, and so was her hair. Although she had on a hospital volunteer uniform, you could tell that she was a snazzy dresser.

"Hey, honey." She smiled. "How can I help you?" she asked in a voice that sounded like Minnie Mouse.

I had to look down at my purse so that she couldn't see my facial expression. I wasn't expecting such a girlish voice from such a mature woman. "Could you tell me how to get to the nearest library?"

"Oh, honey, I wouldn't have the slightest clue. I haven't been to the library in years. But hold on, let me see if I can find out for you."

She picked up the phone and hit speed dial. "Betty," she said into the receiver, "I have a lady here who is asking for directions to the library. Uh huh, okay…I'll see you in a minute." she hung up the phone. "Betty will be here to help you in a minute"

"Thank you." I smiled sweetly. One thing I liked about living in the south was that you could still find plenty of people who didn't mind going the extra mile.

Betty, was a senior volunteer with light blue hair. "Hey, darlin," she said to me before reaching the info desk. "Are you the lady that's looking for the library?"

"Yes ma'am." I nodded

"Oh, honey, my grandchildren love to read."

"That's wonderful," I said enthusiastically.

"It's a wonder that they do. I couldn't get there daddy to pick up a book to save his life. Thank goodness for their mama."

"Well," I replied, "you know what they say… a woman's …."

"…man's work is never done," she said in unison with me.

"So, where is the closest library? " I took a pen out of my purse.

"Let me see, you need to head west on Pine, then a right on North Jefferson and take a left onto 3rd Avenue. Honey, it's not even a mile away. You probably passed it on your way here. Isn't that always the way it happens?"

I listened closely while writing the directions on an old receipt.

"Yes, ma'am, it sure is. Now, let me read this back to you."

"You go right ahead."

"I go west on Pine, right on Jefferson and left on third."

"That's it."

"Thank you so much." I backed away. I didn't want her to get her second wind. I only had an hour before I had to get back home.

The directions were right on the money. She was right, I had passed the building on my way to the hospital. I walked inside the library and took a deep breath. I loved the smell of books. When I was molested as a child, reading became my refuge. The library was kind of like a home away from home for me. It was the place where I had my first kiss with Scott Alexander. I smiled at the memory. I went straight to the librarian desk to sign up for a computer.

Thank goodness there wasn't a waiting line. I only had forty-five minutes left before I needed to get home. I went straight to the computer and got on the net. I typed Legal Aide into the search engine. In just seconds, the search engine returned ten pages worth of results. I needed to refine my search. I typed in

Legal Aide, Albany Georgia. Bingo! I didn't have enough time to read off all of the information, so I printed it out. Copies were only 15¢. I printed off all of the information that I thought I needed.

I felt so much better on the ride home. I'd taken the first step. Now, all I needed to do was convince Bea to go to Legal Aide.

"We come bearing gifts!" I called to Bea who was in her room recuperating after her hospital stay.

Bea was sitting up in bed watching her stories. Her face lit up when the kids and I entered.

"Hey, I'm so glad y'all came by. I never thought I would say it, but I'm sick of watching TV."

Vee grabbed the shopping bag I was holding and plopped it down next to Bea and started rummaging inside.

Bea was none responsive.

"Go ahead, Sherril," I said, pushing her forward. "Give Aunt Bea your gift."

Sherril handed her a homemade get-well card. "Vee messed it up," she explained before letting go.

Bea took the card and opened it. "It's so pretty. Dear Aunt Bea, get better. Love Sherril," she read aloud

Vee had managed to open up the bag, and she was taking out the food I'd packed, spilling it all over the bed. I went to grab it.

"Let me do it. I wanna to do it," she said, hopping up and down.

"I'm sorry, but she likes to help," I apologized

Vee grabbed a sandwich wrapped in paper towel and held it to Bea's lips. "Open wide," she said, trying to imitate me feeding the baby.

Bea took a bite of the tuna sandwich and I watched a glob of tuna thick with relish spill from the side. Her face screwed up and she puckered her lips.

I grabbed a glass of ice water off of the nightstand and gave it to her. "She made it herself," I explained. "Sherril, take Vee outside with Daddy."

"Richard is here?" Bea asked.

"Yeah, he took time off from work so that he could come down for Halloween. He's outside raking up the pine straw." I took a pillow, placed it across Bea's lap, and laid a napkin on top of the pillow. I handed Bea the lunch that I'd prepared. Hopefully, it was better than Vee's.

I started straightening up the room as best as I could without going through her things. I collected the newspaper that was strewn all over the bed and folded it together and picked up a few dirty clothes and placed them in the hamper next to the bathroom door and stacked newspapers and magazines into neat piles. I took the small trashcan beside the nightstand and emptied it in the kitchen trash.

"Sit down!" Bea commanded when she finished eating the fried chicken, rice and salad. "You making me nervous."

I sat down at the foot of the bed. "So how are you feeling?" I asked.

"Not too good."

I should have figured, I thought. I don't believe she'd ever answered that question with the simple word fine. But at least this time she had been in the hospital. "Is your leg bothering you?"

"No."

"So what is it?"

She handed me some papers.

I opened them up. They were hospital bills. "Ohhh," I said when I read the total. "But I thought that Virginia was helping you get Medicare."

"She is, but it hasn't started yet."

"Well, have you talked to the financial counselor at the hospital?"

"For what," she snapped.

"You're a senior citizen living alone on a fixed income. How practical would it be for them to think that you could pay them off right away?"

"Those people want their money. They don't care about how old and broke I am. If only I hadn't been conned out of my money."

"Bea, you won't know unless you try. Speaking of which…" I got up to get the papers from Legal Aide out of my bag. "I got some information for legal aid."

"For what?" she asked, eyeing me suspiciously.

I took her plate and replaced it with the papers. "For you, you need to try and get your property back."

Bea shoved the papers off of her lap. "Why should I believe that anything else would work when I couldn't even walk to the mailbox safely?"

I grabbed the side of my head in frustration. "That was just a coincidence and you know it."

"Well, excuse me, Miss High and Mighty. I guess you don't know anything about money problems, what with you living with your mother-in-law."

Ain't that nothing, here I was trying to help her out, and all she could do was give me a one, two, sucker punch in the stomach. It was on. "Stop talking about it if all you're going to do is complain. I can't believe that you could be so selfish."

"How am I being selfish," Bea asked, raising her voice. I'd never seen her so riled up, but I didn't care.

"Because, your parents worked hard to leave you something behind and now that you've lost it, you don't even have the tenacity to try and get it back. Have you stopped to think about what kind of position I am in by not telling Virginia, not to mention my own husband. And then, when I do try and help you, you pitch a fit like a little kid. Well, I've tried to be your friend, but if you can't help yourself, I am telling the family. It's all this secrecy that got you in this mess in the first place. You could have easily put your property into the family corporation. Instead, you decided that you didn't want them in your business. Well here's a news flash—none of us even think about your business. We are all working hard trying to live our own lives."

I stopped ranting when I heard Richard and the kids outside the window. Richard walked up to the window and knocked. Bea and I turned towards the window and looked as Richard waved. Bea returned a tired wave.

Richard and the kids started making faces and dancing around like nuts. "Go on boy before my neighbors see you acting a fool," Bea laughed.

Richard blew her a big kiss before returning to his work on

the yard. I felt kinda bad that I'd been so harsh, but she needed to hear it. She couldn't have been more shocked if I had gotten up and slapped her in the face. Bea picked up the papers with tears in her eyes and my heart softened. "Most problems don't fix themselves, you got to do something about them."

"So you say, but as soon as I get ahead, Satan snatches me back."

I rolled my eyes. "Satan is not the problem here. It's you being stubborn. Why are you concentrating on everything that is going wrong? Look at the positive things in your life"

"Positive, what positive? I ain't got no positive things in my life."

"Yes you do. You and I are friends right?"

Bea nodded her head.

"Well that's one positive right there, a new friendship. How about Virginia? How many people can claim a sister who would have gone out of their way for them the way she has done for you? You need to go ahead and talk to her and your nephew about that man who took your property. I can't be the only one telling you that."

She studied my face for a minute. "If your advice is so good, why don't you follow it? You come in here looking like death warmed over. All that pretty hair pulled back in that raggedy ponytail, no make up, and why you wear them big baggy clothes? You got a nice figure, wouldn't hurt to show it off a little."

It was my turn to be shocked. What could I say, she was telling the truth. There are few things worse than someone pointing out your hypocrisies. I didn't even feel like brushing my teeth in the morning. Didn't have enough energy, just walked around all day running my tongue along the back of my teeth, thinking about how much I hated the yucky feeling in my mouth.

I touched my ponytail. "You aren't the only person with problems."

"So, what is wrong with you?"

"Don't try and change the subject. I am serious. When Richard and Virginia find out about you losing the property and they will eventually I don't want to be put in the position where I have to lie to them. You need to promise me that you are going to call Legal Aide."

"I promise," Bea said quietly.

I got up to leave and gave her a huge hug. "I have to leave now, we're taking the kids to Boo at the Zoo. I need to get the kids home to get them into their costumes."

I tried to focus on the kids as I got them dressed in their costumes, but my thoughts kept going back to Bea. I really hoped that she would take the time to go through the information I'd given her. My mind stayed on Bea as we drove to Boo at the Zoo, the Halloween celebration at Chehaw Nature Park. The kids looked so adorable. Sherril was dressed as an Indian, Elliot was a pumpkin, and Vee was dressed as a pink M&M. We had only gotten two feet from the car when Frankenstein walked by. One look at his green face and Vee went ballistic.

"Ahh!" she screamed at the top of her lungs.

Richard picked her up. "It's okay, it's okay. He's not real."

"I scared. I scared! " she continued screaming.

Before we could get her calmed down, three Draculas and a kid in a mask walked by.

Richard and I looked at each other. We didn't have to say a word. We all climbed back into the car and headed for home. We took the kids to the neighbors for a little candy and called it a night.

I got up early Sunday morning to go to church with Bea. I started going through my clothes hanging in the closet. All I'd worn for the past few months was my mommy uniform that consisted of t-shirts, jeans, and hiking boots or gym shoes. I put on a new dress, but changed my mind when I went to put on shoes. For starters, my stockings looked like they'd been in a catfight. I don't know what I was thinking putting them in a drawer in the first place, they belonged in the trash. When I finally found a pair of knee-highs minus runs, my shoes were too tight. High heels are funny that way, the more often you wear them, the more comfortable they are. But go a week or two without wearing them, and your foot feels like a sausage in the casing, stuffed. Finally, I decided on a pair of black and white hounds-tooth dress slacks, a white sweater and a pair of patent leather flats. I wasn't up to doing anything fancy by way of my *coiffure,* so pony tail it was. Only I made it neater than usual by slathering on baby lotion—I didn't have any brown hair gel. Looking at my image in the bathroom mirror, I decided that was as good as it was going to get.

When I went downstairs, Sherril and Virginia were sitting together sharing a morning cup of coffee. Sherril was trying to read the Sunday funnies and kept stopping every few minutes to ask for help reading a word. "What's this word, Grandma?"

"Fan-tas-tic," Virginia said, making sure to pronounce each syllable.

Vee was sitting in Richard's lap, helping him feed the baby who was seated in his infant seat on the counter in front of them.

I grabbed a bagel out of the refrigerator, thanked Virginia and was out the door.

It was early November and the morning temperature was already sixty-five degrees. Even so, the smell of fall was in the air. I didn't really fell like it when I initially agreed to go, but now that I was on the way, it felt good going to church. Bea was coming out of the house when I pulled into her driveway.

"What are you doing eating?" Bea asked when she got in the car.

I looked at Bea before pulling out of the driveway. "What do you mean? It's eight in the morning. This is my breakfast. I don't want my stomach growling during the service."

"You aren't supposed to eat an hour before mass. You can't make the sacrament now."

"What?" I asked, stopping at the stop sign on the corner.

"I keep forgetting, you're not Catholic."

"The sacrament is what y'all call communion? Oh. Is there anything else that I should know?"

"Yes, you need to wear this."

I turned to see Bea waving a lace doily like the one she wore on her head. Wow, I thought, all of the three major religions asked woman to cover their heads at one point or the other. It's a good thing I decided to wear my hair in a ponytail.

The inside of the sanctuary was beautiful. It was like stepping on the set of a gothic movie. The woodwork was rich and ornate, the perfect compliment to the red carpet and cream walls. The walls on either side were decorated with ornate pictures that showed fourteen events leading from Jesus arrest to the crucifixion. The sunlight shined through the leaded glass of the windows, creating a bejeweled dance of light throughout the chapel. You couldn't help but feel the presence of God.

Unlike the churches I'd grown up in, the service was reserved. I put the doily on my head and followed Bea's lead. Three men in robes entered the chapel followed by another priest and Father Donahue. The congregation stood and watched as they approached the walked down the center isle. The three men in plain robes sat in the front row. The priest knelt before the alter and kissed it. Father Donahue led the congregation in prayer, telling us to be especially mindful that we were in the year of the Eucharist. I had no idea what that meant. When I finished praying and began looking at the people around me, the church contained a mishmash of people; old your, black, white and some nationalities that I didn't recognize.

After prayer, we took a seat, and the choir began to sing. For such a small group, they sure did make a powerful noise. There were only six people in the choir total. I saw two women wearing head coverings and two men. I couldn't see the other members because they were standing behind a large statue of an angel whose golden wingspan his them. After a responsive reading, something in Latin and another choir selection, Father Donahue was dressed ornately. His robe was a beautiful green satin with elaborate gold embroidery. He stood in front of his parishioners with a calm demeanor and spoke in a voice so mild, you had to really pay attention in order to hear. The message centered on heaven and faith.

Calmly, the priest spoke, "Is your life earthbound or heaven bound? The Sadducees had one big problem—they could not conceive of heaven beyond what they could see with their naked eyes! Aren't we often like them? We don't recognize spiritual realities because we try to make heaven into an earthly image… Do you live now in the joy and hope of the life of the age to come?"

I gave some serious thought to what he was saying. Was I guilty of this? I certainly was. I knew for a fact that my outside situation was determining what went on in the inside instead of vice versus.

I listened as Father Donahue continued. "The way that Catholics understand sacrifice, two elements are involved. The first centers on an outward sign, which should exist for the support of the second element which is in the interior disposition. Without the belief or faith on the inside, what you do on the outside doesn't matter. Note Isaiah 29:13: 'This people honors me with their lips, but their heart is far from me.' So I ask you today to be mindful. Are your actions empty?"

You see that was the hard part for me. I wanted to have faith, I just didn't know how. I looked at the people sitting round me. Did any of them possess the secret to having faith? Maybe the key to having faith was the desire to have it. Maybe, God took over from there.

My thoughts were interrupted when the choir started their Gregorian chanting. It was beautiful and reminded me of the Disney movie *The Hunchback of Notre Dame*. I know that it was just a cartoon, but that was the most passionate cartoon I'd ever seen. Well, beside *The Lion King*. Anyway, I loved the idea of sanctuary in the Hunchback movie. I was also struck by the notion that God existed for everyone, including the lowest of the low like Esmerelda the Gypsy. It was the classic battle of good versus evil. I was thinking these thoughts and before I knew it, the service was over.

CHAPTER NINE
RACHAEL

I watched with curiosity as Bea prepared the turkey. Laughing at me, she said, "I know this looks crazy, but I promise you, there is nothing better than drunk turkey." She stuck a clove of garlic and several sprigs of rosemary into a beer can. Next she put the beer can in a roasting pan, centered the bird's cavity over the beer, and sat the turkey in an upright position over the beer. Bea basted the turkey with her own special blend of seasoning, wrapped the wings in foil and placed the roasting pan inside a brown paper bag.

The smells of Thanksgiving dinner permeated the kitchen. I was glad Bea had come over to help with the cooking. Holidays are the only time when it's okay for more than one woman to work in the kitchen at a time. The macaroni and cheese was cooling on the stove, and it looked picture perfect. The candied yams were done, and the turkey was in the oven. Forget Butterball, Bea was cooking a wild turkey. I'd never had wild turkey before. When Bea took it out of the butcher's wrapping, it looked a little bony. Bea swore that if you cooked it right, you'd never go back to the store bought kind.

Bea placed the bird in the oven then turned to me giggling. "Stop looking at me so crazy. This is how Mother used to make it."

"Well, I have to taste it first. I've never seen anyone bake a

Turkey with beer and a paper bag. It won't catch on fire in the oven?"

"Not as long as the bag doesn't touch the sides. What do you think people did before they invented cooking bags?"

I hunched my shoulders. I didn't have a clue. "What is the beer for?"

"Keeps it moist."

"So did you fill out the forms for Legal Aide?" I asked. I'd given her more than enough time to fill the paper work out, but she kept putting it off with lame excuses.

Before she could answer, Richard came in. Instead of lending us a hand, he fixed a plate. The holidays are one time when it must be good to be a man. Except for at my mother's house, they get to sit back, relax, and put their feet up while the women work like slaves. Besides watching the game, all he could do was talk about Rosalyn. I was in the kitchen with Bea cooking Thanksgiving dinner. Virginia was out with Sherril and Vee, delivering food baskets for the church.

Richard sat smack dab in the middle of the counter I was working from. "Baby," he said in between smacks, "you should see her house. It's built on a lake, and it is so peaceful out there."

I'll bet, I though, shoving my knife in the center of the onion I was dicing. I slammed the knife down on the counter, went over to the sink, snatched a piece of paper towel from the roll, and jerked on the water.

Bea looked at me, shook her head, and walked over to the counter where Richard was sitting. "Move, boy," she said, shoving him out of the way and looking into the cabinet under the counter. "We got work to do."

Richard stared at me while Bea fiddled inside the cabinet. "Mumph, this is good," he mumbled, offering me a bite of his macaroni and cheese.

I smelled the macaroni and cheese. Mmm, it had just the right amount of nutmeg, but I wasn't making up with him that easily. "No, I tasted enough." In fact, I had nibbled on just about everything that Bea and I cooked. Every good cook knows that you have to taste what you prepare, and Bea was a good cook. No wonder she was so big. Her greens were to die for. They contained just the right amount of tart. Bea swore that her secret ingredient was the tablespoon of sugar. As if the greens weren't good enough, her candied yams were even better. She added a dash of lemon zest to them to give them that special something.

"Anyway, she got that house for a steal."

"Oh really," I commented with raised eyebrow. He was so into the food on his plate that he didn't catch it.

He took a long swallow of iced tea. "Yeah, but I can't stay inside long because she has cats. Fifteen minutes is all I can take before my eyes start watering and I break out in welts.

"Hurray for kitty cats," I said, and shoved the stuffing in the oven. Jealousy is a bitch, it feels like a virus of the worst kind sitting in the pit of your stomach, the heat slowly reaching out to the rest of your body until it finally makes you go crazy, saying and doing things you normally wouldn't. I didn't want to be one of those jealous women that go around nagging and accusing, but then how do you quell your intuition?

"What's your problem?" Richard asked.

"Oh you know what my problem is," I said over my shoulder as I left the room. We didn't need to have this discussion in front of Bea.

Richard followed me up the stairs to my room. "What was that all about?"

I looked at him sitting at the foot of the bed steadily munching away, which pissed me off even more. The least he could have done was put down his plate. "Stop smacking," I ordered with contempt.

He hesitated before putting his plate on the dresser. "Well?"

"I don't know how you got to be so close to this Rosalyn, but you talk about her all of the time. Rosalyn, Rosalyn, Rosalyn. Oh her house, oh her boat, oh her lake," I said, doing my best imitation of him. "What the hell are you doing at her house and boat?"

"Baby, we had this argument, remember? She's the last person you need to be worried about."

"Oh, I need to be worried about some one else?"

"Come on, Rachael, you know that's not what I meant. I didn't drive all the way down here with no sleep and no food to argue. I wanted to have a nice Thanksgiving dinner with my family."

"Right."

"What, you think I like being away from my family?"

"Well, you damn sure don't seem to mind."

"Girl. Every night I sleep on a couch in a room full of cigarette smoke and sweaty ass—excuse my French—niggas. You and the kids are in a nice, warm, clean house."

"But it's not my house."

Richard dropped his head. "Come on, baby," he said lifting, his head to look at me. "We both agreed to this."

That was true. "But I didn't know that it would be this hard. What am I supposed to do while you're living out your dreams?"

"Are you for real?" he asked, looking at me like I'd said the moon was made of cheese. "You have all of the time in the world to figure that out. Instead, you've been moping around since you got here. It's like I'm married to a whole other person."

"I hate it here."

"Baby, you haven't even given it a chance. I know it's not Atlanta, but come on. How am I supposed to be able to do what I need to do if I am worried about you all of the time?"

"Well, if you are so worried about me, I sure as hell can't tell. All you do is talk about what you want and that damn Rosalyn."

"That's not fair," he said, shaking his head. "Everything I do I do for us. If I get this contract for the studio, we all benefit."

"What contract?" I asked, eyeing him suspiciously.

"Rosalyn thinks I should go to Midem."

"What is Midem?"

"It's this huge music conference in France. Anyway, she wants me to meet some people over there who are looking to get something started in the states. It's a long shot, but it might be what we need to get the studio over this hump."

Oh God, I knew that this whole studio biz was something that I agreed to, but at the time I didn't realize that it would be to the exclusion of me. "When do you go?" I asked, on the verge of tears. France? When he said France, a million thoughts went off in my head. Foremost of which was that I should be going. I don't know that I wanted my man overseas with another woman. "So is Rosalyn going?"

"No, baby," he answered, massaging my thigh. "I'm going

with Byron. But we can't keep doing this. I agreed that I was wrong to drive her car, but I have to work with a lot of very attractive women in this business. Hell, in any business. I can't do what I need to do for my family if I have to worry about whether or not my wife trusts me during a business meeting. It is business. Do we have friendly conversations? Yes of course we do, just like any other business associates, but it is not like we are going out for romantic dinners. If I was interested in her, do you think I would talk to you about it?"

I admit, I thought about what he said and he raised some good points. But, I still didn't like this whole Rosalyn business. I shifted my leg so his hand fell off of me. "You never said anything about it before." I was the one who always wanted to go to France. When we first met, I was trying to raise my GPA so that I would qualify for an exchange program in France. The only thing that stopped me from getting it was getting pregnant with Sherril. I was going to college full time and working two part time jobs. Of course I didn't go. When I found out that I was pregnant with Sherril, all my plans got put on hold. Getting pregnant got me all messed up. I didn't even finish college. And now my husband was going to go to France without me. No doubt about it, I was jealous. What does a wife do when she is jealous of her husband, I wondered?

I like to think of myself as this intelligent, interesting person who had it going on. I used to act, I dabbled in radio, I worked on political campaigns, and I even did a few stints as a model. But for the last few years, the only thing going on with me was nursery rhymes, diapers, and breast milk. Not that I don't love my family, because I do, but I spent so much time supporting them, I lost track of me. If someone were to come up to me and ask me what my goals were, I wouldn't have known what to tell them. It was easy for me to advise Bea to take care of herself, but I turned chicken liver when it came to taking care of me. The worst part was, I didn't know what I was afraid of. Every time I thought about sitting down to write, I let something else pull me away. Even worse, afterwards, I felt guilty about it. What was wrong with me?

Richard and I had our share of arguments where I called him selfish, and it always came down to his asking me what it was that I wanted. Unfortunately, the honest truth was that I didn't know. Not only did I not know but, I had no clue how to find out. Our arguments would end with him pledging to give me more me time. In the end my me time consisted of driving around looking for something to do or trying to catch up with friends who had real lives. Finally, if all else failed, I would make up an excuse to hang out with Richard and the kids.

Richard took my face in his hands, turned it toward him, and lifted my head. I tried to turn away, but he wouldn't let me, so we sat there looking into each other's eyes. My eyes are not good liars. They prefer the truth. Only I wasn't ready to tell him the truth. Doing so would be an admission of my weakness.

Instead, I jerked my head out of his hands and asked a few mundane questions about his trip. The more questions I asked, the more excited he became.

"I got my passport this week. Do you want to see it?"

"Sure." I swallowed.

When he handed me the picture, I felt myself turning into a green monster. Again, I swallowed.

"When we went to get our passports, you know Byron had to act like he was used to going over seas." Byron was his wanna be a big shot partner. He was always pretending to know things. It is amazing to me how black people will take a white man's word as authority just because he is white. A couple of times, Richard had to call him on it. Still he remained with him because a white business partner brings certain advantages.

Thanks to our conversation, Thanksgiving dinner was awkward. Virginia had the kids gather leaves and pinecones outside. They washed the pinecones and leaves then used them to create a centerpiece for the table. I came downstairs just in time to help the kids tie strings of raffia around dinner napkins and placed bay leaves and sprigs of rosemary in the center of each napkin. I had to give it to Virginia, between the fresh herbs and dried leaves, the room smelled divine. As shitty as I felt, even I had to smile as I watched Vee carry the water goblets to the table, walking so carefully, you would have thought they were made of diamonds. We placed our creation in the center of each plate. By the time we dressed the table with Virginia's good silver ware, China and water goblets, it looked like a spread right out of *Martha Stewart's Living*. In short, the table sparkled.

Richard tried to be sweet and held my hand underneath the table. I was so depressed, I couldn't even taste my food. On the one hand, I knew that he was right. I should have been using my stay in Albany as time to focus on me. On the other hand, how was I supposed to do that? I didn't really know anyone, and for the most part, I felt like a duck out of water.

When he was ready to leave for Atlanta, Richard called me out to the car. "I was going to give this to you for Christmas, but

I think you could use it now," he said, handing me a package.

I looked at the package. I could tell by the way it was wrapped in the Sunday funnies with about a roll of scotch tape that the kids had helped him wrap it. My heart constricted. I reached for the package and opened it up.

"Oh my God!" I screamed. "You got me a laptop."

"Yeah." Richard grinned like a teenager wooing his first girlfriend. "Now you don't have any excuse not to write."

My heart was racing a mile a minute. In Atlanta, we'd taken the computer for the house and put it in the studio. Richard needed it more there. Even when I did want to use it, I had to go over there. Now that I had one of my own, the possibilities were endless. "Thank you, baby!" I said with tears in my eyes.

"Oh, wait, there's something else."

Richard handed me another package. This one was wrapped much like the first but it was the size and shape of a jewelry box. I looked at Richard shocked that he was being so generous. "Oh, baby, we are supposed to being saving. You didn't have to do all this."

"Just take it," he urged, smiling.

I took the package and opened it slowly. "You are so stupid." I laughed when I got it open. It was a Snickers.

"Don't you like it?" Richard asked innocently, pulling me into his embrace. "I thought it was your favorite."

After kissing him, I lay my head on his shoulder. I had a good man. It might not be the easiest thing in the world, but I was going to have to learn how to trust him.

After he left, Richard emailed me about four or fives times a day, urging me to get to work. After putting the baby down for his nap and setting Vee up to watch *Dora the Explorer*, I was sitting at the coffee table trying to write. It was a cold night in Georgia, I typed. No, I decided that sounded too much like the song "Rainy Night in Georgia" and deleted it. I stopped to think for a moment and typed another sentence. The night was cold. No, I decided, not enough imagery. Three sentences later left me feeling like Billy Crystal in *Throw Momma from the Train*. How could I be a writer if I couldn't even write one sentence?

The phone rang, interrupting my work. I wanted to finish at least a paragraph and ignored it. By the tenth ring, I knew it had to be my mother. She was the only person I knew who would let the phone ring that many times.

"Hey, Mom."

"Hi, look are you still coming home for Christmas, cause Nicole and her family are coming. So if all of you guys are coming, I need to figure out where everyone is going to stay."

The instant I heard her voice I began to feel better. She still had that affect on me. I absolutely adored my mother; she was my best friend. She was the first person I called when I lost my virginity. I cannot imagine what it would be like to have a relationship with her like the one Bea had with her mother.

"Yes Mom, we're coming."

"Are you sure?"

"Yes."

I was so looking forward to going home for Christmas. If I had to walk to get there, I was going.

"Well do the kids need anything?"

"No, not really."

"They don't need underwear or anything?"

Underwear, why would they need underwear? A red flag popped into my head. "Mom, why do you keep asking me about underwear? If you want to buy some, buy it. What's the big deal?"

She got quiet for a second. "Well how is Virginia? I like her, she is so nice."

Click! The light of revelation came on. "When did you talk to Virginia?"

"What difference does that make?"

"None, I was just curious, so when did you talk to her?"

"She called me the other day."

The light in my head started flashing the Proceed With Caution signal.

"She called you, why in the world did she call you?"

"Girl, I don't know, but she did. Why are you upset about that?"

Why was I upset! I had plenty of reasons to be upset. I was upset because my husband was going to France. I was upset because while he was there I would still be in South Bumble Town. I was upset because I missed my friends. I was upset because even when my husband did come and visit, I was too depressed to have sex with him even though I was horny. And worst of all, I was upset because I used to be good looking, but I'd turned into this pasty person that I barely recognized in the mirror. But I couldn't say all of those things to my mother. As cool as my mother was, and as close as the two of us were, I couldn't tell her that I was ugly, horny and lonely. Instead, I told her that I was not feeling well.

"You aren't pregnant are you?"

Perfect. Why did my life's entire crisis revolve around the belief that I was pregnant? By this time I was too disgusted to deal with her any further I merely responded, "I dunno," and hung up the phone without giving her a chance to piss me off even more. Briefly, I felt better; misery does love its company.

Riding my high, I went downstairs to speak with Virginia. She and Sherril were setting the table. How do you tell your mother-in-law, who is allowing you to live in her house rent free and teaching your daughter how to set a proper table, off for calling your mother? As soon as I entered the room and saw how they had the red tablecloth with place mats and silver ware in the proper place on top of folded napkins I lost my nerve. My God, they were putting out water glasses. What could I say, stop calling my mother and telling on me? I felt so foolish.

She saw me fidgeting around in the doorway and asked, "Is something wrong?"

"Um, well, yeah, I just got through talking to my mother." I took a deep breath. "My mother seems to think that my children are going without the necessities of life. Somehow she has concluded that they are without socks and panties."

There I said it. I may have sounded a like a smart aleck, but whatever.

Virginia fixed me with her stare, making me feel uncomfortable. As if reading my mind, she spoke. "I did mention some things that she might get for the children."

Hmm, she just mentioned some things; this put me in a quandary. Did I just make a fool of myself? Maybe, maybe not, at any rate, it was time for me to lay my cards on the table.

"I wish you wouldn't tell her things like that. My mother was really worried by what you said." Okay, I exaggerated a little. "The next time you think the kids need something, I would prefer it if you talk to me."

I left the room; I'd been hateful enough for one night. Christmas couldn't come fast enough.

CHAPTER TEN
BEA

I don't even know why in the world Rachael agreed to come to mass with me again. During the service, all she did was sit and look at the ears of the man sitting in front of her. If that ain't the most ridiculous thing I ever heard of. After the service, she comes out talking about some man with hair growing out of his ears. What kind of thing is that to be paying attention to in church? She didn't say anything about the sermon; she probably didn't even listen to it at all. Still, it was nice of her to come with me.

After the service, I asked if we could stop by the carhop, I like carhops. When I was young, colored folks weren't allowed to go. It always seemed like it would be so much fun to go to the carhop with your boyfriend and sit in the car eating, talking, listening to your favorite songs on the radio, and stealing kisses when you thought the people in the next car weren't looking. What a shame that colored and whites couldn't drink coca-colas in the same parking lot, but those were the times.

I love root beer floats. I thought having one might put Rachael in a better mood. Feel good food is what got me so fat. I couldn't even enjoy the taste my of root beer float with her sitting beside me in a huff, the creamy smooth flavor was lost. Trying to lighten the mood, I changed to my favorite station. For the longest, there wasn't too much on the radio that I could listen to. Then I found the oldies station. Even though most of the songs weren't from my time, now and then they played a couple of tunes that I could get along with. I started snapping my fingers to the beat.

Looking at Rachael crouched up on the door pouting, I nudged her and asked, "What is going on with you? You don't have much to say today."

"What ever happened with you and Legal Aide?"

"I made an appointment to go into the office." I couldn't believe how easy it was for me to lie like that. Those papers were sitting in a stack underneath my bed.

She hunched her shoulders. She didn't feel like talking to me, but so what. Didn't matter anyway, I already knew what was wrong with her. It had to be that damn nephew of mine. First, he came to see his family in some woman's truck. Then he spent the Thanksgiving holiday talking about this woman's possessions. I think the young folks calling them SUV's or something. It wasn't even his truck; it belonged to some woman he claimed he was working with.

Now ain't that just like a man. I swear, somewhere on this God's green earth, men take a class that teaches them how to be the fools that they are. There must be, how else could they all act so foolish? Here he was, hundreds of miles away from his family, and when he come to see them, all he could do was talk about this woman he working with. The more he talked about her, the madder Rachael got. I don't know why Richard didn't notice her slamming cabinet doors and banging pots and pans. I thought she was going to break a frying pan across his head. If it was me, I would have. Instead, she snatched the baby out of his arms and took him upstairs for his bath. I should have slapped the fool for her. I thought I taught him better than that with his Harry Belafonte looking self.

"Are you upset about this lady that Richard is working with?" I asked, knowing the answer ahead of time.

"Why do you ask me that?" Rachael's eyes searched mine like somehow I knew something she didn't.

Poor thing, just that one question and she looked nearly fit to be tied, she might as well have said yeah. "Chile, I ain't no fool. I was a married woman once. Don't no decent lady want another woman sniffing around her husband. Why you so ashamed about it? Richard is your husband, you supposed to be jealous."

She tried to pass it off with the wave of her hand. "Says you. Anyway, I never said I was jealous. I'm just sick of being here."

"So you pouting because you not jealous? Do I have stupid stamped across my forehead? You can call it what you want to, but I know the truth even if you don't." Like a duck on a June bug, I put it right out front where she could see it.

Rachael slumped back against her chair. I watched as her body caved in. Pushing her float aside, she confessed, "They may not be having sex, but there's other means of infidelity. The two of them are far too friendly for my taste."

I pushed her float back in front of her. "I know what you mean," I said, putting the straw to her lips.

Rachael took a long sip from her float, leaned her head back against the seat, and shut her eyes tight. I didn't say anything; sometimes folks just want to be left to their own thoughts. Just as I finished the last of my root beer float, a song came on the radio that took me way back. Snapping my fingers, I started to hum along to the music. "Sitting at the dock of the bay." I turned to look at Rachael. She wasn't having it. "Did I ever tell you about when I lived in New Mexico?"

She shook her head no.

"Well, you know my husband, Larry. He was a staff sergeant in the army. Right after we got married, he was stationed in New Mexico. If not for having to live with him, I would have liked it there right fine. You wouldn't know it 'cause we are still friends today, but he was a horrible husband."

"How so?" Rachael asked, her eyes still closed.

"The bottle, that's how," I said with disgust. "Never marry a hard drinking man, course I probably don't have to tell you that, you at least have that much sense. When I met him, I was on the rebound. Claude was the love of my life! But I had to leave him."

Rachael opened her eyes and you would have thought that she just lost her favorite friend in the world. "What happened to Claude?"

My chest grew heavy just thinking about it. "R. Thomas had done left Columbia University by that time. He didn't go back after that Jewish girl went and got married, I thought that it was for the better. Wasn't no sense in Mother staying in that big ole house by herself, and I wasn't about to go back. Virginia had her job, and she'd met Richard, Sr. In her letters, Mother would drop hints about R. Thomas acting peculiar, but we didn't think too much about it. It got to a point, though, where Mother couldn't control him anymore. He started doing things that caused attention like going to whites only places and acting like it was the most normal thing in the world for him to be there. Luckily, there were white people who had enough respect for Mother that they just brought him home, like the priest at the Catholic church downtown, but it was just a matter of time before he got himself in trouble that Mother wouldn't be able to get him out of."

Rachael finished her float and placed it on the tray hooked to the window. "So what did you do?"

I pressed my float against my chest and let the cold of the glass calm my nerves. "Since I was the one closest to R. Thomas, Mother asked me to come home to help her. Of course I did. What else could we do? You know there's no way we could have put him in the hospital, in those days, coloreds weren't allowed. Jail is where they sent you. She took him to the doctor, but they wanted to give him shock treatments. You wouldn't believe the things they do to sick people."

"That must have been so hard for you," Rachael said, turning to look at me. "How did you deal with that?"

I turned away from her. I didn't need anybodies sympathy. It was just that simple. I may not have done many good things in my life, but at least that was one of them. "I loved my brother. R. Thomas might have been hard to fool with at times, but I loved him. People didn't understand nothing back then about the mind. It took years before they found out you could take drugs to help R. Thomas's kind of sickness. He hated that lithium, said it made him feel the world through a cloud, whatever that means. I came on home like Mother asked, thinking that as soon as R. Thomas got over his heartbreak he would be okay again. Well, that never did happen."

I looked down into my empty glass. If I had a penny for every time I wished things would have turned out different, I'd be as rich as Madame CJ Walker. "Claude didn't come with me, his job and family were in Boston. I promised to come back, but one year turned into two. He tried to wait on me; I guess two years is too long for most men. He ended up getting this woman pregnant. He did what any decent man would do and married her. Sounds silly to you probably, but abortions were illegal. I told you what it was like for an unmarried woman to have a baby. That's why I understood when he told me he had to get married. Might not have liked it, but I understood."

Rachael sighed. "Well that's crappy. I don't think I would have been as understanding as you."

"Right about that time, Larry was always asking me out. He wanted me something awful. Spending time with him took my mind off Claude. I wasn't a bit surprised when he asked me to marry him. I knew all along that was what he wanted. Mother, on the other hand, had a fit."

"Why?"

It's not funny now, but I had to laugh when I thought about how stupid I was. "She begged me not to marry him. 'Bea, believe me, he is not of your station. What do you have in common? Look at his family, they are some of the biggest rogues in this, town and, believe me the apples don't fall far from the tree.'"

I sighed. "To tell the truth, I partly married Larry out of spite to Mother. That and the fact that I wanted to have me a comfortable life. Colored folks didn't have as many opportunities as we do now. Here was a man with a career, petitioning me to marry him. I jumped at the chance to leave town for good."

Rachael shrunk down in her seat. "I don't think I even want to know what happened next."

"No sooner than he got me away from my family, I realized

that Mother was right. That man drank from the time he came home, to the time he fell asleep. The more he drank, the meaner he got. I didn't know what to do. For the most part, I had a sheltered life. When was I ever around any drunks? You couldn't have paid me to believe that a man could marry a woman one month and be beating on her the next."

"He beat you?" Rachael said with a look of shock on her face. "I would have knocked him upside the head and left him the very first time that he hit me."

"Yeah, well it's easy to be the Monday morning quarterback. Anyway, it didn't take long for me to get sick of all of that. One night Mr. Larry came home full of sweet talk. Girl, he came up with more than a few excuses, he was under a lot of pressure dealing with Charlie all day. The people under his command couldn't half be counted on. He just went on and on. I took that as a sign that he wanted to change. I promised to forgive him for everything so that we could start from a clean slate."

"Please tell me you didn't fall for that," Rachael begged. "Once a dog, always a dog."

"Tell me about it. The very same night he did all of that apologizing, he took me out to eat. Only, he invited someone else to go with us."

"What do you mean, someone? This was supposed to be a makeup date, why would he take someone else?"

"No, no let me finish," I said, holding up my hand. "It wasn't just someone, it was another woman."

"Ooh," Rachael said just like a little girl. "He didn't."

I closed my eyes and slowly nodded my head. "I'll never forget that woman; her name was Delane Ross. Sounds like it belongs to a movie star, but honey, she was pure street trash! Don't nothing stop a whorish woman. Not even the idea of fooling around with her husband's best friend."

Rachael leaned toward me. "I have got to hear the rest of this."

I watched in the rear view mirror as Delane painted her lips ruby red. She gave me a wink when she looked up and caught me staring.

I gave her my best fake smile. That is, I smiled just enough to let her know that I was only being friendly. She winked back at me.

Skanch, I thought to myself.

"So, Larry," she cooed. "Are you going to save a space on your dance card for me?"

Larry laughed. "Eh, heh, heh, heh."

I cut my eyes at him and looked back at her. "He doesn't dance," I snapped.

We pulled up to the Coyote. The Coyote was really popular with the colored men on base. It reminded me of one of the Honky Tonks in Albany, not that I'd been in one before. It was nothing but an old barn with a corrugated tin roof. The only difference was, there was no *Whites Only* sign posted. It was one of the few places near the base where colored people could go for entertainment. Colored folk were allowed in, but we had to stay on one side of the place along with the Mexicans. Only white folks were allowed to go past the jukebox.

Larry parked the car, got out, and came around to open the door for me. I stood beside the car as he opened the door for Delane.

Watching her get out of the car was like watching a burlesque show. She made a complete production of it. First she stuck out one leg, and then she leaned forward, placing both hands on the seat like she was preparing to take a dive. Her bosoms nearly popped out of her dress. Finally she stepped on out of the car and ran her hands down the length of her red dress.

"I'm not too wrinkled am I?" she asked, giggling. Her voice was a combination of Betty Boop and Marilyn Monroe. Nobody talked that way for real.

"No," I answered. Larry couldn't speak for drooling. I snatched his hand and dragged him inside. As tight as that dress was, there was no way it could hold a wrinkle. In comparison, the linen summer dress that I wore looked plain.

As soon as we were seated at a table inside, Delane opened up her compact, checked her face, and applied more rouge.

My goodness, I thought, I wonder what she looks like underneath all of that makeup. Elvis Presley was playing on the jukebox.

I looked around. It wasn't crowded yet, but the people were steadily coming in. Several couples sat at the tables around us, enjoying themselves. Larry waved at a few of the people he knew from the base. Delane did too. She seemed to be acquainted with several of the men. They kept coming waving to her.

One of them came over to our table. "How's your husband doing?" he asked, staring down at her chest.

"He's fine." She waved her handkerchief over her chest filling the air with the smell of her cheap perfume.

I looked at his eyes following that handkerchief back and forth like a pendulum.

"Where is that waitress?" Larry asked abruptly.

"I'll be seeing y'all later. Take care now." He nodded, kissed Delane's hand and walked back to his table.

I looked around for the waitress. I didn't see one on our side of the room, they were all assisting the white customers. "I think we have to order at the bar," I said, directing my eyes across the room to where the white customers were being served. "I'll have a steak, baked potato, salad and a coke."

"That sounds divine," Delane purred. "I think I'll have the same, but make mine a whiskey sour."

Larry went to the bar to place our orders.

Delane started moving to the beat of the salsa music coming from the jukebox. "Don't you just love all the horns and the drums?" she asked me. "It makes me want to go wild." She shook her head up, down and to the side. Her hair swung about her head, and when she stopped, it looked kind of funny.

I tried not to laugh. "Um," I said, touching my hair, "I think you need to straighten your wig."

"Oh," she said, losing that sex kitten voice. She straightened her wig and looked to me for approval.

It was still on crooked, but I nodded my approval anyway.

Larry came back with our orders. He handed me my plate and Delane hers. "Thank you," Delane said, fluttering her eyelids. The sex kitten had returned.

Larry headed back to the bar for his food and our drink orders.

"Let me help," Delane said and sashayed to the bar with him.

All of the men in the place turned to watch her hips move from side to side. The woman at the table next to us elbowed her date in the side. He had to shake his head before he continue with their conversation.

All during dinner, Delane went on and on with oh Larry this, and oh Larry that.

"Oh, Larry, I don't know how you do it. The pressure you must be under. I mean, you are responsible for feeding all the men on base."

Larry blushed. "Well…" he stammered, "I just try my best."

"So what is that you are eating? I'm too chicken to try any of that Mexican food. I hear it's spicy," she said.

"Tamales," he answered. "You should try them."

Delane reached over with her fork and took a piece of his tamale.

I felt my face flush, and I literally saw red. I got up from the table without excusing myself. Come on now, girl, I said to myself, don't make a fool of yourself. The last thing you want to do is to start acting colored.

I went to the bathroom and splashed cold water on my face. Just be cool, I said to my image in the mirror.

Instead of going back to the table, I walked over to the juke-box. A white man was studying the songs on the jukebox. This man seemed like the type that got around, a regular Marlboro man.

"Excuse me, sir," I said, tapping him on the shoulder.

"Yeah," he answered, turning to look at me.

"You see that couple right there?" I pointed at Larry and Delane. He turned to see Delane reach her fork into Larry's plate again. "That's my husband. What do you think of the two of them?"

The Marlboro man laughed. "Looks like your boy has him a little something on the side."

That is exactly what I was thinking. I walked back to the table. "I'm ready to go," I said to Larry.

"Okay, just let us finish our food," he answered.

I looked down, and his plate was empty.

"Now," I demanded loudly.

Several people at the tables close to us turned to see what was going on. I turned and stormed out of the Coyote.

Larry and Delane came out a few minutes behind me.

Delane climbed into the backseat. "The food got to your stomach?" she asked me.

"No," I said, looking her eye to eye. "It's something else."

"Woman what you talking 'bout?" Larry asked, laughing nervously.

My foot was tapping away at the car floor, but I didn't say a word. I don't know who they thought they were fooling with. Maybe Delane's husband didn't mind if his wife gave it up to half the base, but I wasn't about to stand for it. The further we drove, the madder I got. I looked At Delane in the rear view mirror. She was putting on more lipstick. God I couldn't stand her.

I don't know what came over me. I reached into the glove compartment and pulled out Larry's gun. "Get out," I commanded, gritting my teeth.

Delane screamed. "Ahhh! You gone crazy! Larry, do sumpin wit dis witch."

You see there, you can take the cat out of the alley, but you can't take the alley out of the cat.

Larry was swerving all over the deserted road. "Have you lost your mind!" he roared.

My heart felt like it was about to jump out of my chest. But, I didn't lose my cool. I don't know how I held that gun steady. "I said get out, and don't you stop neither."

Larry slowed the car down, "Bea…"

"I said keep going." I shot the gun off into the roof of the car.

Delane screamed, opened the door, and jumped out into the night. I looked back in the mirror and saw her rolling around on the ground. Serves her ass right, I thought

Rachael screamed, "I can't believe you made her jump out of the car without stopping."

I laughed so hard I almost messed myself. The waitress turned around to see what in the world was so funny.

"Umm are you okay?' the waitress asked like laughter was the same as the cooties.

Neither one of us could stop laughing. Finally, Rachael managed to let her know we were okay by way of paying the bill.

The waitress left. Rachael turned to me. "So you left her out in the middle of the night?'

"Of course I did. Delane didn't care about me, why should I care about her. By then, I was feeling good. I turned to Larry and told him not to even think about helping that witch."

"He didn't ask you to go back?"

"No. But, he cussed me out under his breath all the way home. The more he cursed the more scared I got. Normally when he beat me, he would take me out to the country somewhere and do it. The military didn't go for domestic violence. Even though he would be drunk, he had enough sense to know he didn't want to fool with the MPs."

"So you called them right?"

"Who, the MPs?" I asked, turning to her. "No I didn't call them. Then again, I was going to be a sitting duck. He had to be planning something. You can't pull a gun on someone and expect them to let things go. Plain and simple, I had to leave. Larry stopped the car in front of the house long enough for me to get out, and took off down the street. When he got back, he would be drunk and ready to go at it. Well, not this time. This time I wouldn't be there when he got back."

"You should have left him before that."

"I got inside the house, went straight to the phone, and called a cab. While I was waiting for the cab, I threw my clothes into a suitcase with one hand, and held the gun in the other. My heart was racing the whole time. I asked the cab driver to take me to the bus station with no clue as to where I was going. I bought my ticket under a false name like they do on Perry Mason. That man was crazy, it would be just like him to come after me."

"So where did you go?"

"The bus I took was headed to Mexico. I got off as soon as I got to a place that I felt was far enough away. I found a motel that had these little one-room deals you could rent month to month. You call them efficiencies, and that's what I got. You know, some people live in motels almost their whole lives. I rented it for only one month since I didn't have a clue what my plans were. I let Mother know where I was. Wasn't no sense of making my family worry. She sent me some money right away. She was so happy I left Larry, she probably did the two step."

"I'm sure she was," Rachael said, yawning as she turned on the car.

I got all of my trash together and handed it to her so that she could put it in the garbage can outside her door. "I'm telling you all this for a reason; you need to know that women don't need to take a lot of mess. I could have left that man long before I did. To this day, I don't know of any woman who can stop her man from cheating, a man will do what he wants to do. But, you can stop the damn woman from messing with you, and if you make it hard on her, after a while she'll get the good sense to leave you alone."

CHAPTER ELEVEN
RACHAEL

I didn't even mind the sixteen-hour drive to Michigan for Christmas. That was the most time I'd spent with just my husband and kids since the day before forever. The farther we got north, the higher my spirits lifted. When we hit the Tennessee/Kentucky border, I thought I would burst. "Look you guys," I said, pointing out of the window. "Snow."

Richard started singing off key, and I rushed to find a radio station that was broadcasting all carols all the time. I hit pay dirt when the second station I turned to was in the middle of "Santa Baby." In my pitiful imitation of Eartha Kitt, I started dancing in my seat and singing, "Santa baby, da, da,da,da,… So hurry down the chimney tonight."

Richard groaned. "Girl, how you going to mess up Eartha Kitt? If you're going to sing it, at least know the words."

Sherril didn't have a clue what he was talking about, but she was so happy to have all of us together and in good spirits that she began laughing deliriously.

When the Temptations started singing "Rudolph the Red Nose Reindeer," everyone started singing. I know it sounds crazy, but even the baby started humming along. Okay well, he wasn't in tune with the rest of us, but he was trying to sing to the best of his abilities. Vee was in the habit of talking to him like I did. She bent over him and said, "You like that don't you, boy.

Rudolph the red nose reindeer had a very shiny nose." Her singing cracked him up.

We were tired, but full of holiday cheer, when we finally reached my parents house. One thing about my mom, she loved Christmas. Everything at her house screams Christmas. She placed citrus fruits stuffed with cloves throughout the house to give it that oh so special holiday smell. Whereas normally, her house was Oriental Chic, with ebony and mahogany furniture. For Christmas, she lost all sense of co-ordination. As long as something was red, green, gold, or sparkly, she would find a place for it. She placed hand towels embroidered with ginger bread men across the backs of her white club chairs. All along the half wall of the kitchen was her display of a Christmas village. Inside of her china cabinet, she placed red glass Christmas ornaments. The *pièce de résistance* was the tree.

Every year, Mom dedicated her tree to someone in the family. If a person graduated, got married, or there was a new addition to the family; that year her tree was decorated especially for them. This year marked my son's and my sister's son's first Christmas. Mom decorated her tree in baby blue in celebration of both Elliot and Cameron's first Christmas. The tree was huge. Even though I though it looked perfect, Mom wasn't finished decorating. Five minutes after we walked in the door, she dragged me with her to the nearest twenty-four hour superstore. My parents' house was full of food, singing, laughing, playing, and even a few arguments.

Despite the fact that I was tired out of this world, I couldn't help but share Mom's excitement. "What did you get the kids for Christmas?" she asked while dropping an Easy Bake oven into the shopping cart.

"I got two baby dolls, and a couple of Barbies."

"What did you get for Elliot?" she said, picking up three Barbies without looking and throwing them into the cart.

Looking down into the cart, I realized that she had three of the same Barbies. "Mom, these are all the same dolls."

"Well get some more," she said without looking as she threw in a Barbie car, and Barbie beauty salon. She kept throwing toys in the cart, and I took them out just as fast. She was determined to spoil them rotten.

This went on for the next thirty minutes before we finally made our way over to the children's apparel. In addition to the toys, Mom also picked out Christmas pajamas for all of the kids so that we could take pictures of them all dolled up opening their presents.

After picking out outfits for the kids, Mom stood still, appraising me up and down. "You look horrible."

"Gee thanks," I said, touching my hair self-consciously.

"Well, would you rather I let you take a bad picture?"

"I look that bad?" I looked down at my jeans.

Mom pushed the cart toward the women's clothing department. "Like shit. What is going on with all those patches on your jeans. Look around you, it is Christmas. Pep it up. You look tired and worn out. What are they doing to you down there?"

"Nothing," I explained. "I have three small kids to take care of."

Mom stopped pushing the cart to turn and look at me. "Virginia and her sister don't help you? I don't like that. I'm surprised. I would have expected Virginia to…"

"No, Mom, that's not it. She does help, they both do. It's just that Virginia has her way of doing things, and I have mine. Besides, her sister has her own set of problems."

"You can't let her problems become your problems."

"But she is my friend."

"What's that supposed to mean? You need to take care of your best friend first."

"My best friend?" I asked, confused. I didn't know what she was talking about. "Serrita lives in Atlanta."

"Nah fool. I'm not talking about Serrita. I am talking about you. Your best friend is you. You can't help anybody if you don't take care of yourself. Come on now. I raised you smarter than this." Mom pulled a red sweater from the rack and held it against me. "See there, you don't even have the sweater on, and already you look better." She continued rummaging through the clothes rack. "How are you and Richard doing?"

I shrugged. I tried not to go running to my mother with my marital problems. I'd learned early on in my marriage that it was best to keep our problems between us. In the beginning when we were married an I'd go to Mom, she would hold on to her anger toward Richard long after I'd gotten over it. Or, she would make snide comments when he came around. All in all, it just added fuel to the fire.

She stopped rummaging through the racks and took a long look at me. "Well, it must be hard being so far away from one another. You need to do things to spice it up a little. He's involved in a business where he has to deal with a lot of temptation."

"So what do I do?"

"For starters, you need to stop acting like he sent you away to prison. It's not like he's off to war and you don't know when he is coming back. You are staying with his mother to save for a house, get over it."

"What are you talking about? I haven't said anything?" I felt like I was on trial or something.

"Honey, please. You don't have to say anything. It shows in your demeanor. If I can pick up on it, don't you think he can?"

I thought about her question. Of course he could pick up on it. That's why he walked on eggshells around me. "You are right," I agreed reluctantly.

We picked out your basic red sweater and black skirt. Before heading to the beauty section where I purchased some make up. Mom wouldn't let it go at that though. "So, what is going on with you?" she asked.

"What do you mean?" I asked.

"I mean, have you made any friends, are you doing any volunteer work, what?"

"Well, Richard's Aunt Bea is my friend and I help out at the school."

"Uh, uh. You need to do something for yourself. Find a hobby, girls your age like to work out. Do that. Or maybe you could do some volunteer work for something that doesn't have anything to do with the kids."

"Richard did buy me a computer so that I could start writing."

"Have you been writing?" she asked, pushing the cart toward the check out lines.

I took over pushing the heavy basket. "Not yet." I said apologetically.

"Why?"

"I don't know. I guess I don't have anything to write about."

"Then write about that," she offered like it was the easiest thing in the world.

The next morning, my sister and her family got in from California. By that afternoon my parents' home was a hustling bustling mess, and I was fully enjoying it. Damn, it was good to be back at home where you could do or say whatever you wanted because the people around you were family. They might talk about you like a dog and get on your nerves a little bit, but the love was unconditional.

I realized one of the things that I missed the most about home was the noise. At any given moment, there were sounds of people going through cabinets, laughing, talking, fighting, listening to the radio, and just being together. The noise of life filled my parents' house.

Mom didn't waste anytime assigning everyone a job. My sister Nicole was put in charge of running errands, my cousin Melanee was responsible for the macaroni and cheese. My little sister Dionne was awarded care of all of the kids and had all but the babies putting away shoes, dusting and as busy as Santa's elves. The men were all assigned the task of cleaning Dad's den, which took them twice as long as it should have because Dad kept stealing them off to do God knows what. As for me, I was put in charge of the stuffing. Of course this didn't stop Mom from tasting it from time to time. Sticking a spoon in the bowl, she declared like a technician, "It needs more butter," and promptly dumped in a stick of butter and a can of both cream of chicken and cream of mushroom.

Richard walked pass just as she finished pouring in the cream of mushroom. "What is that supposed to be, heart attack food?"

"Taste it," Mom commanded and handed him a dab of stuffing on the end of her mixing spoon.

Richard reached and took a pinch of stuffing off of the tip of the spoon. He pretended to be afraid to taste, but the look on his face once the stuffing hit his taste buds told the true story. His face portrayed a look of pure ecstasy. He grabbed a spoon off of the counter and went after the bowl of stuffing.

Mom playfully hit him upside the head and handed him a mop and bucket. "In my house you have to work before you can eat."

We all laughed as he stole a spoonful of the dressing before making his getaway.

Unfortunately, we were not spending New Year's in Michigan. We decided to head back to Georgia on the 30th of December so that we could beat some of the New Year's traffic. The moment I took a seat in the packed car, I felt a weight pressing on me, which grew worse the closer we got to Georgia. We left at night so that the kids could sleep most of the way. We'd only been driving for an hour when Richard took my hand. "We need to talk."

"About what?" I asked sleepily. The combination of warm air coming from the air vent and the hum of the motor was putting me to sleep.

"Our plan," he answered.

I woke up instantly. "What about it?

"I thought that it would be easier to save. But I didn't realize exactly how many bills we had until I added them all up togethr."

"We'll just keep paying one thing at a time."

"Yeah, but at the rate we're going, we'll only have a small amount set aside for a down payment. I wanted to save at least $10,000 for a down payment."

"We're still on the right track. We have over five thousand dollars saved up."

"Yeah, but you have to look at how much of that is owed out. We owe $2,000.00 in credit card bills alone. We don't have to pay everything off. Some of the bills, like your hospital bills, we can just pay down. We need to at least start thinking about where we want to buy."

"I know," I agreed. "But with you working and traveling all the time. It's hard for me to get up to Atlanta. I'm not trying to ride Greyhound with three kids, but I could do some research online. At least that way we can narrow our search."

"Have you been using the computer?"

"Yes," I said, shrinking down in my seat.

Richard glanced at me. "You haven't been writing," he sighed.

"I've been looking into it."

"What is there to look into?"

"I dunno: style, technique, the submission process."

"None of that means anything if you don't write."

Whatever. I didn't want the first thing I wrote to be something stupid. What if I didn't have talent. Then what. Would I have to change my dreams?

"You have paralysis of analysis."

"Huh?" I said.

"Stop analyzing everything and just do it."

"Are you ready for your trip?" I asked in an attempt to take the spotlight off myself.

"Mm hmm."

"So what is Midem, again, and what do you plan to do there?"

"It's a big music conference in Cannes. Basically, I'm going to network. There is a group that records at the studio. Rosalyn and I have them signed to a production deal and we're trying to get a deal. We thought that it might be easier to break them overseas before trying to get a deal in the states."

"So what is the name of the group?"

"N-O-T-E."

I nodded. "Note, what does it stand for?"

Richard smiled. "Not of this Earth. We thought that the name was catchy."

"It is."

"I have a package for them in the side door. Take a look."

I looked in the compartment on the side of my door. Sure enough there was a package of NOTE. It was the picture if two black men and a white woman. One of the guys was tall and baldheaded with a long tail at the nape of his neck. The other was short with a short afro. The woman was dark haired and petite. She had natural good looks.

I put the CD in the player. They sounded pretty good. I could see why they went with the name Not of this Earth. There music didn't fit any particular genre. It was kind of a cross between Seal and Soul II Soul. I listened to the music until I finally drifted off to sleep.

The trip from my parents to Virginia's was over fifteen hours, and I did my share by driving—six hours of it. Under the best of circumstances, the drive takes a lot out of you. The last few miles all I could think about was climbing into bed. When we finally reached Virginia's, the kids were excited to see her. They couldn't wait to show her everything they got for Christmas. Their excitement grew even more when she gave them the gifts she bought. Instead of going straight to sleep, I watched them open their gifts and play with the toys. By the time they finished with the presents, I didn't feel like I could keep my eyes open any longer.

Go figure that's when Virginia called me into the kitchen where she was busy cooking. "You know you really do make a good salad," she said. "Would you mind making one for me?"

It takes a special kind of fool to believe that they can do anything in another woman's kitchen without being "directed."

"You see," she said, placing the lettuce in a colander, "you have to make sure to rinse it thoroughly."

I can't begin to imagine what my facial expression was. I stared at her in disbelief as she rinsed the salad before handing me the spray so that I could take a turn. She walked over to the cabinet where she kept the salad bowl and pulled it out. "The salad tongs are in the silver ware drawer."

"Yes I know. I cleaned out the drawer, remember." Did I mention that she only had one pair of salad tongs?

"Now, you can set the table," she directed like I was a little kid.

"Sherril, come help Grandma." That little piddly stuff like setting the table and putting ice in glasses, Sherril could do. I started at her age; that's how I learned. Besides, I was exhausted by the drive.

I couldn't believe it when Virginia walked up to me and told me to fix Richard a plate. She must've thought I didn't hear her right because I didn't act right away, so she repeated herself.

She began explaining, "He's tired, he has been on the road all day and needs to relax and watch the game."

Why she wanna go there? "And?" I asked, the indignation flowing.

She was kind enough to fix the plate herself. Though I stopped smoking years ago, I wanted a cigarette. Since I didn't have one, I sat right down beside him on the couch, took that plate, and started eating it. It was better than Christmas dinner.

Virginia stood at the kitchen counter looking across the pass way into the family room and continued pleading her case. "I'm sure that he is really hungry."

"He knows where the kitchen is," I replied, kicking him in the leg. This was the first time he'd bothered to take notice of me since we'd walked into the house, and he started watching another one of his all-important football games. He looked at me totally confused. Whatever, I continued smacking away while I finished the food on my plate. Kicking him made the food taste that much better. I looked at him and rolled my eyes. Finally, he got his raggedy behind up off the couch and into the kitchen to get his own plate. I had half a mind to belch aloud when I finished eating, but decided that belching would have been going too far.

Richard had been in France for five days, and I still hadn't heard from him. I couldn't believe that my husband had the nerve to cross the ocean. I'd tried to show interest in his trip, and what did it get me? Not even a funky little phone call. I felt miserable. I got up that morning to use the phone and saw an international number on the caller I.D. It had to be Richard. Who else would have called from overseas. I got so mad that the walls of the house were closing in on me. I needed someplace to go, something to do, anything, but sitting around feeling tired and funky. Bea called and said she bought a car and needed to go and get some things from the auto parts store, I was more than happy to go with her.

Bea was as happy as I was upset. Sitting back in her car, I leaned against the seat and turned on the radio. I tuned in to the local R& B station and turned it up. Apparently, my groove was too much for Bea; she snapped the radio. "I'm an ole woman. I can't be driving around listening to that loud mess. How can you think with that noise?"

"Who said I wanted to think?"

"Chile, you might as well stop pouting about that man. He'll be back soon enough. Not like he gonna be gone forever."

I rolled my eyes and snorted.

"If that is what you're upset about, you might as well get over it."

The second time I rolled my eyes, she laughed.

"Roll your eyes if you want to, but you look a mess. When the last time you combed your hair or put on something besides them raggedy jeans."

"Whatever," I said, taking in a deep breath and pulling at the rip in my jeans. What difference did it make what I wore? The only people who saw me were my kids and two old ladies. And besides, I did comb my hair. I just didn't curl it. Again, what was the point? I wasn't going anywhere.

"How do you like my new car?" Bea asked.

I looked around. "My dad used to have a car like this one. A Caprice Classic. Ours was a tan color, almost yellow." Bea's was blue, but I think it used to be green. Whoever did the paint job did a pretty good job on the outside, you couldn't even tell it had been repainted. But on the inside, it looked like they were in a rush. All along the top of the door, the original green was visible, as if the person doing the painting couldn't be bothered with making sure the blue paint carried all the way to the top. Not wanting to hurt Bea's feelings I commented on how clean it was.

"I know it's not much," she said self-consciously. "But I like it."

"You haven't told me about your holiday." Since she was trying to cheer me up, the least I could do was try and be positive. Bea deserved to be in a good mood driving around in her new car, even if I felt miserable.

"It was fine, dinner with Virginia, nothing fancy. I love Christmas. When I was a little girl, we used to have big fun at Christmas time. I remember the time Daddy got this white man dressed as Santa Claus to come over to the house to bring us our gifts. I thought he was the real thing. I went running up the stairs trying not to yell because I was supposed to be in the bed. I threw open R. Thomas's door and dragged him to the top of the stairs. Look, I said, it's him, it's him, it's Santa Claus! I had to hold R. Thomas back from falling down the stairs he was so excited. We could hear Mother talking to the man. She told him to follow her to the back yard. We went running to the back room, which overlooked the backyard. We got up on the sofa and peeked out so that we could see what Santa Claus was doing. All we got to see was a truck with something in the back covered by a tarp, when we saw Mother coming in the back door, we rushed back to our room. Chile, that morning when we woke up, you will never guess what was in that backyard."

"What?"

"A merry-go-round, we had our very own merry go round! Oh we were some blessed children sure enough."

"Hmm," I smiled. I'd had some pretty good Christmases myself: seesaws, tea sets, ice skates, dolls, but it had never been in my thought processes to expect a merry go round. "Yeah you were, how old were you then?" It was nice to hear a happy memory for a change.

"Oh I was a big ole girl, too big to be believing in any Santa Claus. I had to be at least ten or eleven. That morning me and R. Thomas was running around telling every one how Santa had brought us a merry go round, bragging to Virginia that we even saw him. She wasn't paying us no mind though. She looked at me and said, 'Bea. That man was not Santa Claus. He was just a man that Father hired to come and put up your merry go round.'

"Mother told her to mind her manners! 'Virginia you may not believe in Santa Claus, but don't spoil it for the younger ones.' That was the first and only time I can ever remember Mother taking my side over Virginia's."

"I can't imagine Virginia ever being anything but perfect," I said, despite myself.

Bea coughed. "Virginia never was a real playful child like R. Thomas and me. Most times, she didn't even play with the dolls that she got for Christmas. Instead, she kept them locked up in a trunk in her closet. She wouldn't even let me play with them. She said she was saving them for her children."

"Huh," I mumbled. "Why does that not surprise me?"

Bea laughed. "I heard that. I know that Virginia can be a little bossy sometimes, always has been, but she means well. A lot of what she says makes good sense."

"She still gets on my nerves," I snarled. "Richard has been gone for a week, and I still haven't talked to him. When he finally called last night, Virginia didn't even give me the phone. Ugh! Now why wouldn't she let me talk to my own husband?" Just thinking about it made my scalp itch.

"What?" Bea asked, clearly confused. "She didn't put you on the phone?"

"Can you believe it?" I asked with indignation. "She kept right on talking to him like his wife wasn't in the house. She didn't come and tell me they were finished talking either, instead she hung up. Now why would she do that?"

Bea looked out of the corner of her eye. "Is that all that is bothering you?"

"No!" I hit my hand on the dashboard. "I bet he didn't even ask to talk to me!"

"The boy is coming home eventually. Just cuss him out when he gets here. That can't be all that's bothering you."

"Okay fine," I said, pointing my finger at an imaginary Richard. "He comes back today, and then before you know it, the weekend will be over, and he'll be right back in Atlanta. And I'll be stuck here," I said, pointing my finger back at myself.

"You talking like a crazy person. I wish I were young enough to be as innocent as you! You can't see the grass for the meadow. You got everything. You got your husband, your health, your kids, and you got a nice place to stay. Don't you know how much I would give to be in your place?"

If that wasn't the pot calling the kettle black. I liked her nerve. Bea did nothing but complain. Talking to her only frustrated me more. I didn't care that there was some truth to what she said. Staying in someone else's home is not an easy thing to do. Little things get magnified into bigger things, and eventually, you get to a place where you get tired of walking on eggshells. I started praying to God to help me hit the lottery so I could move back to Atlanta. I was slowly but surely going nuts.

After leaving the auto parts store, Bea came over to Virginia's, and we watched Oprah together. Lo and behold, the show was about lottery winners. One of the women on the show in particular caught my interest. She was a single mother, blonde, and very attractive. She had just broken up with her baby's father and needed a place to live. One night, on a fluke, she bought a lottery ticket.

Damned if the lady didn't win one of the biggest lotteries ever. It turned her whole life around. She worked as a secretary for a law firm so they helped her make a plan for her money. She was able to get a house for herself and cars for her and some of her family members. Bea and I listened to her talk about how winning the lottery hadn't changed the type of person she was on the inside. Too bad that couldn't be me. That night I bought my very first lottery ticket. From that point on, I couldn't get the thought of winning out of my mind.

Bea backed me up all the way. I was going to pray for the lottery, and she was going to pray over her hospital bill–even though I urged her to go to the financial aide counselor at the hospital. In addition, we both agreed to pray for each other. Once, she claimed she won the lottery by praying to her Patron Saint. She swore that the same prayer would guarantee my winning and gave me a prayer card. With it, I was supposed to say it and ask her Patron Saint for the lottery number. I figured it couldn't hurt. What was God going to do, strike me down? I took the prayer card.

I waited until everyone was in bed and took out the card. I kneeled down in front of a night-light. Bea told me to use a candle, but I didn't have any. I hoped the Saint wouldn't mind a night-light; basically, it was the same symbolism. I tried meditating on the card by reading it repeatedly, but the more I looked at the card, the more I didn't like it. It was hard to meditate on anything while staring at a picture of a pale Christ on the cross with blood dripping from the nails in his hands and feet and a blood soaked crown of thorns on his head.

I could get with asking for forgiveness. At the same time, everything about that prayer pointed to the fact that I was wicked and undeserving of God's blessing. Praying, "Oh God, I am so wicked, please let me win the lottery," just wasn't flowing.

Finally, I decided to use my own prayer and pray straight to God. Seems to me that if you have something to say, you may as well say it yourself. Why use an intermediary? I thought about what I'd learned as a kid in church. My Baptist teaching ran deep. Even as I prayed I could hear Rev. Floyd's voice admonishing me that I needed to pray in the name of Jesus, otherwise, God wouldn't hear me. So, I ended my prayer for the winning lottery number in the name of Jesus. Instead of feeling good about it, I felt stupid and ashamed.

All night I tossed and turned, wondering whether or not God would decide to listen to my prayer. For the past couple of months I had been pretty hateful. I probably wasn't deserving of a blessing, especially one as big as winning the lottery.

As soon as Virginia left the house the next morning, the phone rang. It was Bea. It had become our morning ritual to call each other at ten, as soon as the first talk show came on. Then we would sit on the phone for at least the next three hours talking about how pitiful the people on the different shows were.

"Did you pray like I told you to?"

"I tried."

"What do you mean you tried?"

"I dunno, I guess I didn't like your prayer."

"Dumb face, it's a prayer. You don't have to like it. All you have to do is say it."

"What good is saying it if you don't believe it. You might as well be saying Mary, Mary, quite contrary."

"You should know better than to use the Virgin Mother's name in vain. That is blasphemy, and blasphemy is an unforgivable sin."

"I'm not using her name in vain. I'm using it to make a point. And the point is, I don't believe in the prayer," I answered nonchalantly.

"Why do you have to make things so hard? Your patron Saint has the faith for you."

"Uh, huh. Well that seems lazy, why can't I have my own faith." I regretted telling her what I really felt.

"Look, fool!" she shouted through the phone. "You can have it, but you don't! That is why you need a saint to go to God on your behalf."

I thought about that for a minute, but it still didn't make any sense to me. "Yeah, well I'll go to God on my own behalf, unless the saint plans to go to heaven for me."

"I ain't got time to be talking to no stupid people," Bea yelled and hung up the phone.

She was like that. One day she would be nice as you please, and the next she'd be calling you names and hanging up in your face. I laughed. By the time her stories went off, she would be ringing my phone again.

This whole faith thing was bothering me. Faith is supposed to be the substance of things hoped for and the belief in things unseen. Well, I had plenty of hope and just as much trouble with belief. It's not that I didn't want to believe, but I had doubt.

There is this song that I sang at church as a little girl .The refrain was 'Peace be still.' Christ made a reference when he was out on the water. I guess it could be taken one of two ways; maybe Christ was talking to the disciple as the fears and doubts were starting to rise up in him, or maybe he was referring to the waves in the water. Either way, he calmed the spirits so that God could do his work. I wanted to have faith like that.

CHAPTER TWELVE
BEA

Miss know it all Rachael got on my last nerve talking about how a sin is a sin and what not. God knows where my heart is; besides, I make confession. At least most times I do. I was trying to do the best I could, that is more than I can say for most folks. Anyway, I noticed a long time ago that the people who do the most complaining about your religion, are the ones who have no religion at all. Rachael ain't no exception. Tried to help her out by giving her a prayer, all she could do was complain. I don't know what all she was complaining about in the first place. She had a husband, beautiful children and a place to stay damn near free. If anybody should have been complaining, it's me. I was the one with barely a pot to piss in.

Between my health and my money, I was going crazy. Even with the fifteen thousand loan I took out, I was broke. Between buying a car and hospital bills, that money was mostly gone. To add to it all, my stove broke. I had my friend Melissa bring me her hotplate so that I could cook. I'm a big woman and I like to eat. It takes too long to try and cook a whole meal on one hot plate. I kept trying not to worry about it, but the more I did, the madder I got at that Eunique.

I still had thoughts about killing that man. My thoughts of revenge were starting to scare me. I felt so violated. In my dreams, I was a girl again, and this time it was Eunique violating me.

Only this time I did something about it. Instead of laying there trying to pretend it wasn't happening, I took a brick and started smashing him in the head with it. His head turned to jelly as I smashed it over and over.

You know how you wake up from a dream still half asleep and acting out? That's how I woke up—still half asleep, wiping the blood from his head on my gown.

I'm not crazy, but all day long, my palms itched. I took to wiping my hands clean on anything that was at hand, my dress, the sheets a hand towel. I'd be there wiping away till I looked down and realized what I was doing. I decided to ask for help in my next confession before I went completely off the deep end. There had to be some kind of prayer Father Donahue knew to get me through this.

Looking at me rubbing my hands on my skirt, Father Donahue rubbed his hand across his forehead, took a deep breath, and asked, "Are you really that bound and determined to go to hell?"

"No, of course not," I answered, sitting on my hands so I would stop trying to clean what wasn't there. "I know we been over this. I promise you, I been praying, meditating, and all of that, but I feel like I been ra…well you know, all over again. The devil himself has planted these thoughts in my head, and I am telling you right here, Father, I just can't seem to shake them!"

Father Donahue sat there quietly, rubbing his hand in circles around his face. "So what you are telling me is that you choose to follow the devil as opposed to our Savior?"

I tried to jump up, but my body gave out, and I fell back in the chair. "That's hardly what I meant! You know me better than that."

He nodded his head in agreement. "You're right, I do know you better. Simply think about what it is that you are saying."

I pressed my lips together. This was too hard. "But I get so upset. You don't understand what it's like." Trying to get him to understand what I was saying, I moved to the edge of my seat. "I feel like I have to do something before I go crazy."

"Bea," he said my name in that same voice that my daddy used when he was serious about something, "I'm merely pointing out the obvious. When you concentrate on God, everything else falls into place. Have you given any thought to go to the authorities? Jesus instructs us on the necessity of following the law of the land."

I sat in my chair, twisting my hands in my lap, feeling like I was having a hot flash. I know that wasn't it 'cause those days were long gone, but I was definitely in the hot seat. Father Donahue had a quite peaceful voice, but his eyes on me reached my heart, making me feel like I was explaining myself to St. Peter himself. The thought of going to the police and explaining how I'd been conned was more than I could handle. I couldn't bear the thought of telling another soul how stupid I was. The shame of describing just how much I trusted Eunique, and how easy it was for him to convince me to turn over my property was too much. It may have been the right thing to do, but the right thing ain't always the easy thing. It sounds silly, but I felt like the wrong answer could send me straight to the depths of hell. I've always tried to be a good Catholic, so I agreed to pray with Father for forgiveness and strength.

After we finished our prayer, I got me some holy water to take home. Having it comforts me. I like the idea that the water starts out as just ordinary water coming out of a faucet, the priest prays over it and poof, the same water gains dominion. Virginia and her children think that I'm superstitious, but what do they know?

Her children were some crazy little fools. Ever since they were young, they loved to play practical jokes on me. One time her youngest, Lynette, snuck into my house and turned on my radio. When I heard it, I thought I forgot to turn the radio off. I went into the living room to turn it off. Before I could get settled into my bed to finish watching my stories, I heard the radio again. Maybe I had turned it down instead of turning it off. I went back into the living room to turn it off for good. This time, I even double-checked to make sure that it was off. I wasn't even half way down the hallway to my bedroom when I heard music coming from the front again. This time it was loud. I hurried to the bedroom, got my holy water, and ran back into the living room to sprinkle it around. I was saying more prayers then I knew I remembered. When I heard laughter, I started throwing water all over the room. I figured I needed to give those bad spirits something to consider. Lynette started laughing so hard she fell out from behind my sofa. I was so relieved that all I could do was laugh right along with her.

Superstitious or not, when I got home, I put my holy water on the nightstand. I like to keep it close by in case I ever need it. I climbed into my bed to watch a little television. Even with all of the channels on cable, there was nothing on worth watching. Finally, I got tired of flicking channels and turned off the television. I could have spent some time cleaning up my house, but I wasn't in the mood. My house was such a mess. There were clothes still in the dryer from way back when and the linoleum on the kitchen floor was little more than patchwork. Eunique was supposed to fix that floor after I signed my property to him.

Most of the time, I didn't even venture out into the rest of the house, not that it was that big anyway. Two bathrooms a kitchen, living room, and two bedrooms were all I needed. For the most part, I stayed in my bedroom. As such, it was the biggest mess.

I had papers everywhere. I started going through the papers so I could throw some of that mess out. I picked up one envelope, saw it was a bill and put it with a pile of bills stacked on my nightstand. The second piece of paper was another bill. It joined the pile. The third fourth and fifth papers were all bills. I got so disgusted, I climbed back into my bed. Ever since the loss of income from my properties, my finances were in a mess. It was hard to keep up with everything, my utilities, my credit cards, and my life insurance, before I took out the fifteen thousand dollar loan on the house. Now that the loan money was almost gone, things were damn near hopeless.

Bed didn't provide me no relief either. The middle of my mattress sagged, so I had to make sure I stayed on the edge. Wasn't no use even thinking about buying a new bed. The bed I was layin' in used to belong to Mother. It was a king sized bed made of walnut. The posts were carved in the shape of swans, and the headboard had a swan carved in the center. Mother bought it right after Daddy died, claimed she didn't have the heart to sleep in the bed she and Daddy shared all those years. When she had it, the bed was decked out in the finest of everything: 100% cotton sheets, and a silk duvet. Thank God I had the sense to hang on to the sheets, even though they had become thin as a pair of sugar sack panties.

The doorbell rang. I struggled to raise up off of that sagging mattress. I found myself rushing to the door, hoping that it was Eunique. Maybe I was wrong, maybe he had a death in the family and was so broken up that he needed some time to himself for a while. The truth of it was, I missed our friendship. Walking to the door, I realized what sad shape my house was in. I used to look forward to getting the house ready for him to come over. Almost like getting ready for a date, 'cept we weren't boyfriend and girlfriend. I would spend all day cleaning and cooking. And then, if I was in between hair appointments, I'd take and grease my hair and roll it in strips of torn paper bags. If you ask me, paper bag curls come out pretty way better than sponge rollers, and they easier to sleep on.

Before opening the door, I raked my fingers through my hair. I didn't even want to think about how long it been since I'd had anything done to it. Glancing at my reflection in the mirror over the sofa, I decided that I looked like something the cat dragged in. My gray roots had grown so much it was a shame. My head looked awful, like someone took the tips of my hair and dipped them in black ink.

To my surprise, standing on the other side of the door was Red.

"Ain't you going to ask me in?"

"Oh," I said, trying to collect myself. "I been kinda under the weather." I coughed. "So please, excuse the mess." When I realized that Eunique had conned me, I lost the desire to do near bout everything. That ain't the half of it; my house was falling down on my head bit by bit. I had a busted water heater, a broke down stove, and a disabled washing machine. At least I my refrigerator was still working.

"Girl, you look like you been wrestling the devil." He didn't bother waiting for me to invite him in. He came on inside and took a seat. I knew he intended to stay whether I wanted him to or not.

I pressed at the wrinkles in my housedress. "Yeah, well, my washing machine is on the blink." The only clean clothes I had were my drawers. That was only because I washed them out by hand. Which ain't a bad thing. When my daddy was a boy, all he had was two pair of underwear made from flour sacks. Washing them out by hand wasn't nothing to him. He didn't intend for me to have to do it though.

"I came round to see about you because ain't nobody seen you around lately," Red said, looking around and shaking his head.

"Well I haven't been feeling like going out much."

"Uh huh." He sat back on my sofa. "The two of us have been friends for more years than I can count. You know that I love you like you my own family."

"Yeah," I said, my eyes boring holes in him, waiting for the shoe to drop.

"Your daddy never intended you to live like this."

He got that right. I closed the door and took a seat in the chair opposite the sofa. It was one of the last pieces of furniture that Eunique had helped me move from the house. "I know. That's the killing thing. Eunique didn't just take from me. He took from my daddy, my mother—hell—he took from my whole entire family. Some folks ain't got no conscious."

"So what you gonna do about it," Red asked, clasping his hands together in his lap.

How did I know? Shrugging, I asked him, "Do you remember when I first got all my houses?"

"Yeah," Red answered, looking me straight in the face.

"Well, I used to have a devil of a time with the people that rented them. I never wanted to be no slumlord. I tried to be kind to the people. People take your kindness for granted."

"Not always, Bea."

"One house I owned didn't have indoor plumbing, so I had it installed. A normal person might want hot running water and the convenience of not having to use slop jars or go outside. Them folks didn't have the sense God gave a flea. If I hadn't seen it myself, I wouldn't have believed it. They destroyed my bathtub. Fools disconnected the plumbing and used the bathtub as a coal bin. Those people were too country for their own good. I never was able to get that bathtub cleaned out. Had to trash it and get a new one."

Red laughed. "I remember. They were as country as the day is long."

"Sometimes it felt like I was pouring money down a hole. As soon as I would fix one thing, they would break something else. I'm not talking about ordinary wear and tear either. R. Thomas swore that people didn't give a damn about how much we tried to keep those houses nice, even if they were the ones living in them. He said that they just thought that we had money to burn. Maybe he was right."

"When R. Thomas wasn't sick, he made right good sense."

The thought of R. Thomas making sense made me smile.

"Yeah, that's why I hired John Bend to manage the houses for me. He was already managing R. Thomas's properties. That didn't help much either. For one thing, we were always butting heads. The main problem was that I wouldn't let him evict people when they got behind on their rent. I didn't want to be in no way responsible for women and children getting put out on the street. Every time that John told me that he was going to evict a family, I would go and try to talk to the people. I didn't want to have to explain to God in Heaven why I put a family out on the street. In the end, they would stay in the house an extra month and still not pay any rent. Some of them would just move without telling us. I didn't get mad though. Who wants to see their stuff out on the street?"

"You always have been a softie."

"Well, a lot of good it's done me. You remember Mrs. Howard? She had two of the raggediest children I ever saw. They always looked hungry, like the children you see on the world hunger commercials. They always had that begging look in there eyes. I'm sure their mama had a story, but I don't know what it was. As usual, I stopped by their house because they were always late on the rent. While we were talking, she let it out that they didn't have any food. I went right out and bought them some groceries. They wasn't no piddling groceries either. I bought the good stuff. That night Mrs. Howard and her children had a steak dinner."

"I don't know, Bea." Red sat forward and rested his elbows on his knees. "Seem to me like you were always doing something for somebody."

"When I went back and talked to John about Mrs. Howard,

he hit the roof. 'Mrs. Roberts, I know that you're trying to help, but these people are taking you for a ride. Every time you talk to them behind my back, you undermine my authority.'"

"He had a point there, Bea."

"So you say. He made me mad when he started talking about me undermining his authority. I told him I thought that those were my houses and that you were working for me! He threw his hands into the air and walked over to his desk. A few days later, I got his resignation letter. That's not the thing that got me. The thing that floored me was what I found out from R. Thomas. R. Thomas told me that Mrs. Howard didn't have it as bad as she made out. She wasn't rich by any means, but she wasn't dirt poor either. She worked and just about every dollar that she made she gave to Father Divine. Supposedly, that is why Mr. Howard left her. He couldn't see himself giving money to a fancy preacher. I can understand that, any woman who would starve her own is a mess and then some. Plenty of people tried to buy themselves a miracle from Father Divine. You always knew when he was coming to town, because every time he did, folks was late paying their bills."

"So what's the point of this story, Bea?"

Looking through the slats of my dusty blinds, past my overgrown yard, and onto the empty street, I answered him, "I don't know. For the longest time, R. Thomas and me would sit around dogging poor Mrs. Howard out. True to her nature, Virginia would say, 'Everybody has to have hope.'"

I turned away from the window and faced Red. "I needed me some of that hope."

"Well, old friend, the best I can tell you is talk to that attorney nephew of yours."

I couldn't bear to look Red in the face. "I can't."

"Bea, look at me," he demanded, gently taking my chin in his hands, catching the tears rolling down my face. "Could it get any worse?"

"Attorneys cost money, every time you so much as talk to one they send you a bill."

"This is your nephew we are talking about."

"I can't ask him to work for free. He has a family to support."

Red got up and walked over to the phone that was sitting atop the marble phone stand that was Mother's favorite. Holding out the telephone he threatened. "Either you call him, or I will."

"It's too late to call at this hour." I folded my arms across my chest.

I grabbed my mouth and cringed as I watched Red dial the number. "Hello, Edward, this is Red. No, no, I'm doing fine, it's your auntie. She has a situation that she needs your help with."

A situation, huh. Red had some nerve. Before he could say another word, I got up and snatched the phone from his hand. "Edward?"

"Aunt Bea," he said, his voice full of sleep.

"I'm sorry to call so late," I returned staring daggers at Red. "But Red insisted."

"No, no it's okay," he said waking up. "What's going on? I'm sure you wouldn't call if it wasn't important."

In resignation, I returned to my seat across from the sofa while still holding the phone to my ear. I didn't know that my heart could beat so fast. A part of me shut down as I heard myself telling him the pitiful tale of my friendship with Eunique. Red sat across from me on the sofa and held his hand on my knee as I talked.

After listening patiently, Edward spoke, "Does Momma know?"

"No."

"Aunt Bea, you need to tell her."

"You know how your mother is."

"Never mind that, you don't need to go through this by yourself."

"Last time I checked, I was grown."

"All right, Aunt Bea. It's too late to argue about that now. I have to handle a few things at the office tomorrow, but I can come by in the afternoon, and we will go and have the necessary papers filed."

"I'll be ready at twelve." A knots formed in my stomach.

"Don't worry, Aunt Bea. We can get through this."

"Thank you, baby." I hung up the phone and turned to Red. "You satisfied?"

"I sure am," he said, getting up and making his way to the door. Before walking out, he turned to me and said, "By the way, you're welcome."

CHAPTER THIRTEEN
RACHAEL

I was dying to see Richard when he returned from his trip. He didn't get in until Monday afternoon, so Virginia was at work and Sherril was at school. I was upstairs putting Vee and Elliot to take their naps when I heard him come in. He came running up the steps looking for us. I turned to him. "Shhh," I said, holding my finger to my lips. Vee insisted on taking a nap with Elliot. I had to stay in the room and rub her back until the two of them fell asleep. Otherwise, Vee would keep Elliot awake. Tip toeing past stuffed animals and other toys, I made my way out of the room and quietly shut the door.

My sister-in-law once told me that for the most part, when she gets angry with someone, she wants that person to leave her the hell alone. Not her husband. When she was mad at him, she wanted him right there front and center. That is exactly how it is when you are married, you might be mad at him, but you don't want his butt going anywhere. Uh uh, you want him to stay home, or at least come home and feel your wrath.

I went downstairs and found Richard in the den reading a copy of *Sports Illustrated*. "I 'm sick of you and you mother treating me like I don't count around here," I said through clenched teeth.

Richard sighed before putting down the magazine. "What are you talking about?"

I stood in front of him with my arms folded, tapping my foot on the ground. "You and your mother. This is the second time that you have called and she didn't give me the phone."

"Okay, first of all, you need to sit down and stop acting like you gonna whoop somebody's ass. And second of all, you were asleep, what was I supposed to do."

I covered my face with my hands before inhaling and taking a step back. I felt the coffee table against the back of my legs and took a seat. "So what if I was asleep, you should have insisted that she wake me up. I am your wife! She didn't even bother to tell me that you called. The only way I know is that I saw the number on caller ID. Besides, you were gone for a whole week before you even did that. I can't believe you. You would go ballistic if I went out of the country and didn't call you first thing when I hit the ground. But then again, I wouldn't do that."

"Are you finished," he demanded, working his jaw like he couldn't wait to get a few things off of his chest.

"No! I'm not finished," I said, mimicking him. "You should have told her to wake me up."

"You know what?" he asked rhetorically. "I am sick of this. It's like you're trying to find a reason to be mad at me?"

"Are you crazy? First you're driving other women's cars, then you go over seas and don't call,"

"I did call," he yelled.

"Well, it doesn't count if you don't talk to me and you don't leave me a message saying that you called."

"She said you were asleep, you can't blame me for that."

I pointed at him. "You should have had her wake me up plain and simple. I am your wife. This is the second time y'all have done this shit. I understand that she's your mother, but you're a grown damn man. You should have insisted on talking to me, not her. Remember when we went through all that shit with my mom and you told me I needed to decided who I wanted to be married to? Well, the same holds true here. Period."

We were at a stand still. Back in the early years of our marriage when I'd gone running to Mom over every little thing, Richard had finally gotten tired of the intrusion that I'd invited in. He told me that I had to make a choice, and I did. The funny thing is, once I stopped telling Mom all of our business, the two of them were able to get along much better. They were finally able to build a relationship. I was hoping that the same would hold true in this situation with Virginia. Of course Richard didn't go to her to tell on me, but he hadn't set up clear boundaries either. Without him to back me up, my doing so would be tantamount to kicking at an impenetrable wall.

Finally, Richard spoke. "Fine, I don't like feeling like I am in the middle of you two, but fine."

"What do you mean you don't like being put in the middle? Of course you are in the middle. If not for you, Virginia and I would never have to deal with each other period. I'm not asking you to do anything for me that I haven't done for you."

"So what I am supposed to say to her?" Richard asked pitifully.

"The truth. What is so hard about telling her that you chose me as the woman that you want to spend the rest of your life with and that I come first?"

The night Richard left proved that Virginia didn't bother to listen to anything I had to say. She as much as said so herself when we were talking about the kids.

I was trying to get Elliot to go to sleep on his own. He was six months old. As far as I'm concerned, it was time for him to sleep through the night. Unfortunately, with me sharing his room, it was hard for him to do. As soon as I entered the room, he'd smell my milk and want me to pick him up. Of course I did.

I started putting him down to sleep without nursing him first. He hated it; he just cried and cried. I expected him to cry the first few nights, but eventually he'd learn that I wasn't going to pick him up and he'd start going to sleep on his own. I taught my girls to go to sleep the same way.

Virginia couldn't stand to hear him cry. Almost as soon as I'd leave the room, she'd go in to pick him up. At first, I casually mentioned to her that I was trying to get Elliot to put himself to sleep. I took him from her and put him back in the bed. Naturally, he started to cry when I left the room. Virginia went right back in and got him again. Amazing, Virginia acted like I never said anything to her. The next night the same thing happened, only this time she took him downstairs and started singing and rocking him to sleep. At the rate we were going, he would never learn how to sleep through the night.

At first I wasn't going to say anything, but the more she rocked and sang, the tighter my neck got. Finally, I got up the nerve to ask her if we could talk.

Sitting down beside her on the couch, I came out with it. "I try to put Elliot down before everyone goes to bed so that his crying won't be so disruptive. But does his crying bother you?"

"Yes, it does bother me." She didn't even bother to turn away from the television and look at me.

"Well, I'm trying to get him to go to sleep on his own."

"Lynn tried to get her children to do the same thing, but when my children were babies, I couldn't stand to hear them cry like that."

Hmm, now what could I say? We were living in her house. "How about I close the door so that you can't hear him?"

"That is a suggestion. Is there anything else that you would like to talk about?"

"No, not really." Her asking me the question emptied my head of all the concerns that I had.

"Well I would like to suggest to you that you get Sherril's things for school out at night."

I should have seen it coming; Virginia made it a point to drop casual hints about getting Sherril ready for school from the time that we'd moved in months ago. The first night I went ahead and did it. Eventually I grew tired of her "suggesting." Silly as it was, I was beginning to feel like a kid in junior high.

The first morning Sherril went to school, I had all of her clothes laid out, all she had to do was put them on. While she was getting dressed, Virginia was downstairs fixing Sherril's breakfast and lunch. The last thing that I wanted to be was the number two lady, in the number one lady's kitchen. In which case, I stayed upstairs and busied myself with the kids.

That night after I fed the kids and got them bathed and in bed, I went downstairs to join Virginia watching television. When a commercial came on she turned to look at me and asked, "So did you have a chance to get Sherril's things together for school tomorrow?"

Yeah, I'd had the chance to do it. This was her way of telling me to do it. Why, was she implying that I was lazy? Already in my mind, I had come up with at least three good reasons why it didn't matter if I got Sherril's clothes out at night. If Virginia was going to make her breakfast and lunch in the morning, she didn't need me in the kitchen helping her. I might as well spend that time upstairs getting her ready for school.

I got up the next morning and stayed upstairs to help Sherril get dressed, just as I'd done the day before. Later that night as Virginia and I were passing each other on the stairs, she asked me about Sherril's school clothes again. "Do you need me to help you iron them, are they clean?"

Now why would I send my child to school in dirty clothes? Instead of saying no, which would have led us somewhere I didn't want to go, I said over my shoulder continuing to walk down the stairs, "I'll take care of everything in the morning."

Now here we were, all these months later, and she was telling me she wanted me to get my daughter off to school. I could see if she got to school late or something. What it came down to was the difference between Virginia's way and my way. As I sat on the couch thinking all of this over, she let out a long sigh. I felt a nerve on the back of my neck pop. At that point, I had to ask, "I guess it is important to you that I lay Sherril's clothes out at night?"

"Well yes, I like organization, and I've found that it makes everything move smoothly."

"Well I don't mind getting her ready in the morning, so far it has not been a problem."

Choosing her words very carefully, she responded, "I have found that sometimes when you are trying to help someone, they may not be open to your suggestions. At my age, I do not care. If I think that I am right, I move in that direction."

I felt like I was caught between a rock and a hard place. I appreciated what Virginia was doing for us, and I also respected who she was as a person. But, that didn't mean that I wanted to let her push me around. I didn't want to do anything to jeopardize my relationship with Virginia, my relationship with Richard, or Virginia and Richard's relationship. Yet, I realized that something was going to have to give.

Later on that week as I was giving Elliot his morning bath. I was surprised to see little red bumps on his face. I hoped that he hadn't developed an allergic reaction from something that Virginia might have given him off of her plate. I had asked her not to feed him table food. She thought refusing him table food was ridiculous. As I continued to bathe him, I noticed the bumps on the other parts of his body. They were everywhere. Then it hit me. Chicken pox! Oh, Lord, why me?

I dealt with chicken pox just the other year when the ladies had them. It was awful. The bumps broke out on their eyes, in their nose, their hair, and their vagina. They were miserable. Hell, they made me miserable. What next? I took a long sigh and continued bathing him, trying to see through my tears. Crying was something that I was doing more and more.

That explained why he was so irritable the other day when

Virginia, the kids, and I were running errands. He cried for the better of that ride. Virginia had kept asking me to take him out of his car seat. I refused to. By the time that we got home, the two of us spent the rest of the night avoiding each other.

I know I'd done the right thing, but looking at his outbreak, I felt guilty. The whole time that my baby was crying in the car, he must have been sick. When I felt his head in the car, it seemed hot, but I thought it was because of all the crying. That must have been the incubation period. Hopefully, his chicken pox wouldn't be as bad as the girls.

After giving him his bath, I took him downstairs to fix his breakfast. He was so irritable I had a hard time doing anything because I couldn't put him down. Elliot refused to eat his cereal, even though he was rarely nursing. Finally, I began pacing back and forth across the kitchen floor trying to sooth Elliot. Exasperated, I decided to call Pedia Nurse, even though I knew what to do. I dialed the 800 number on the back of my insurance card. After being transferred three times, I got put on hold, so much for prompt service. With the baby still crying, I hung up and called Richard. I was mad that I would have to handle the chicken pox by myself.

"Hello."

"Elliot has the chicken pox."

"Damn, I bet he's miserable."

"He's pretty uncomfortable."

Richard let out a long breath. I could feel him trying to think of what to say. I was being ridiculous. There was nothing for him to say. He was more than a hundred miles away, and I already knew what to do for chicken pox. My pity ran deep.

"What's he doing now?"

"I finally got him to sleep.'

"Good. Look, I'm sorry that you have to do this by yourself. Maybe I'll come a day early."

Bingo! That was what I wanted to hear.

Two days later, my beautiful baby was butt ugly. His face was covered with pox. They were in his hair and just about every place else you can imagine. He was feeling just as bad as he looked. He wanted me to hold him all of the time, but that still wasn't enough. He couldn't decide whether he wanted to nurse or not. First, he would, then he'd stop. When I took him away from my breast, he'd start howling. By the time Richard came, I was an even bigger mess than usual. The most I'd managed to do for myself before he got there was to take a bath and brush my teeth. That's as much as I was gonna do, forget the rest. I didn't clean my room, and I didn't make the girls clean theirs either. The good thing is that Virginia must have figured I was feeling crappy and left me alone.

On Sunday, she asked Richard to take a ride with her. I was in the mudroom putting a load in the washing machine when Richard and Virginia got back.

"So where did you two go?" I asked casually.

"Out to eat," Richard said, hanging his jacket on a hook near the door. "Mama wanted to talk to me about our finances. She's worried that we're not saving enough money."

He had to be friggin kidding me. "What do you mean she wanted to talk to you about our finances?" I asked Richard in a hushed tone. It irked me that I was not included in this.

What did she know about how much we were or were not saving? She didn't have access to our bank account.

"She doesn't think that the twenty-five dollars a week we agreed to save when we moved in here is enough for us to by a house."

"Duh," I said dropping the lid and hitting myself in the head with the palm of my hand. "So what did you tell her?" I inhaled a large breath.

"I told her that she couldn't draw conclusions without speaking to us and that I wasn't going to talk to her about our finances without you present."

"Whew," I breathed, relieved.

Richard pulled me to him, and placed his forehead against mine. "I'm sorry, baby. You were right. I should have said something to Momma before."

I accepted his apology with a hug. We'd done enough arguing the last time he was here. I didn't want every visit that Richard had to result in another thing that I had to point out where he'd done something wrong. I didn't bother telling him that I didn't want to go into the state of our finances with her at all. So far we were right on track with our savings plan.

Between the physical and mental fatigue of taking care of a sick baby and two children under six, I was half past frazzled. But the thing that bothered me the most was the situation with Virginia. Since Richard had done what I asked, I didn't want to mention it to him over and over. One thing I'd learned from my years of marriage was that men couldn't stand it when women don't let things go. I'd read *Men are from Mars Women are From Venus* enough times to know that by telling her that he wouldn't talk without me, Richard considered the situation a done deal. On the other hand, I was still processing it. Two married people ought to be able to handle their finances on their own. If a third party was going to have input, that person ought to be a professional, not one of the partners mother; no matter how you paint it, one partner was going to end up the third man out. On the other hand, what do you owe someone who goes out of his or her way to help you out? I don't know, my privacy seemed like a big price, too big. But was it? The real funky part was that she had talked to him without me. What to do, what to do?

Wanting to get another opinion or at the very least a little sympathy, I called my mother.

"Hello." From the sound of Mom's voice, I could tell that she was in one of her pissy moods.

"Mom," I said

"What," she snapped.

"Guess what happened now?" I asked.

"Huh," her sigh had that irritated thing to it. "Girl, I ain't got time for guessing games. Just tell me."

When I thought about why I was calling her, I felt really childish. "I don't have anything to tell you really, it's just that ..."

"That figures," she snapped. "If you don't have anything to tell me, quit wasting your money and my time!"

"Mom, I am miserable."

"Here we go with that again."

Ignoring her, I went on, "But I am."

"Okay, you're miserable. So what you gone do, keep calling me about it? What you want me to do? You got a nice place to stay, food, and people who care about you. You say you want to be a writer, so write. Come calling me the day after my birthday, whining about how miserable you are. Girl, please, folks got real problems. Not that made up mess you talking about!"

I missed her birthday! So, that's what was bothering her. Instead of apologizing, I continued in defense of myself. "I am not making up stuff. I am lonely! And Virginia always has something to say. The other day she snuck Sherril into the bathroom and pressed her hair. My poor baby looked like a grease monkey with all of the gunk she put in her hair. Then, Virginia had the nerve to say that I send her to school looking unkempt."

"Lonely is not a problem. If you're lonely, go to church, plenty of people to be your friend there. As far as the child's hair, I told you the same thing at Christmas. Who'd you go crying to then? Nobody, you just put some Liv in my baby's hair like you should have been doing all along."

I simply ignored her last remark. "How am I going to get to church without a car?" Never mind the fact that Virginia didn't mind letting me borrow her car when ever I needed it. I was throwing a major pitty party, and my mom was ruining it.

"Humph, you think not having a car stops people from going to church. If you're as lonely as you say you are, walk. They got churches on almost every corner, especially in black neighborhoods. I bet you haven't even cracked open the cover of that book I gave you for Christmas. Anyway, I don't have time for this. You're not the only one who forgot about my birthday, your dad is up north hunting and hasn't called or anything. And your sister is calling me complaining about mess dumber than yours. She's living out there in California punching people in elevators. I swear, everybody has gone crazy!"

I was speechless. What in the world was the girl doing punching people in elevators? Whatever the reason, hearing something as silly as that was enough to bring me to my senses. Mom was right, I was too old to be calling her crying like a college freshman. This was real life, and I was a grown woman living it. Truth is, I hadn't done much of anything to make my stay at Virginia's in any way pleasant. All I'd done was feel sorry for myself for being there in the first place. "Mom, I'm sorry I forgot your birthday."

"Right. Save your apology for Mother's Day. You'll probably forget that, too." That said, she hung up on her end.

I got off the phone and went through my room trying to find something to give her for her birthday. All that I could find was an unopened bottle of Cacherel. I didn't bother with it because I didn't like the fragrance. Oh well, beggars couldn't be choosers. I found a box and put that in then I spotted some bath salts that the kids gave me. I hadn't opened that either and decided to add it to the box. Acting on adrenaline I pulled out the calendar and looked for all of the upcoming holidays and went all around the house putting in things for each holiday up till Mother's day. For her birthday, she got the perfume; and the bath salts for Valentines Day. I added a penny for Lincoln's birthday; Iyanla Vanzant's book for Martin Luther King's birthday and this and that for the other holidays until finally no more would fit in the box. I had to borrow Virginia's car to get the package to the post office and mail it off. So began the first day of the rest of my life.

Virginia waited for Richard to leave for Atlanta before approaching me. The two of us were cleaning out the refrigerator. Virginia was pulling the spoiled foods out of the fridge and pouring the contents in the trash, and I cleaned the empty containers. "I saw your household budget laying on your laptop the other day and ..."

"Excuse me?" My ears burned, and I started scrubbing the dried spaghetti out of the casserole dish furiously. I know I'd left the information up on the screen, but it never occurred to me that she would read it. It was no different than her leaving her mail on the counter. I respected her enough to respect her privacy. I merely pushed it to the side and went on about my business.

"You really should put more money toward a savings account if you want to purchase a home," she said interrupting my thoughts.

I looked at Virginia's backside holding the refrigerator door open. I tried to choose my words carefully. "Virginia, what you read was private."

"I have more experience in ..."

"Wait a minute," I held up my hand. In the past, I'd

approached Virginia as a child. I could see now how that had been a mistake. If I was going to behave like a child, I couldn't blame her for treating me like one. I needed to talk to her woman to woman, not like a little girl begging for her approval. "I know that you are concerned about us, and I respect that. But you have to respect that our marriage only has room for two people."

Virginia withdrew her head from the refrigerator. She looked like she'd just been slapped. "If that is how you feel. I invited you into my home and…"

"And that doesn't give you the right to disrespect me and disregard my feelings." I took a deep breath and lowered my tone. "We appreciate your help, we really do. But we are grown. You can't treat the two of us like we're some of your students at the school." I looked down and saw that I was scrubbing a clean dish and grabbed another one. Ugh, the leftover bits of moldy fish smelled horrible. I attacked the dish with vigor.

Virginia continued her work, deep in thought. The two of us were treading carefully. "You know that at one time or another all of my children have needed my financial assistance. One of the things that I regret most about how they were raised is that their father and I didn't teach them about money. But you are right. The two of you are grown. I didn't mean to intrude. Sometimes, I just get carried away with trying to help. I've always been the one that people depended on, and it's hard to give that up."

"Thank you for telling me that. I've been thinking that maybe it had something to do with the way you felt about me."

"Oh no, baby, no," Virginia said, reaching out to pat my hand. "I love the way that you support my son."

Virginia and I hugged. I was relieved that I'd finally gotten somewhere in my relationship with Virginia. I thought about Bea while hugging Virginia. Sooner or later she was going to need to know what was going on with her. I just hoped that I could convince Bea to tell her, before I had to.

CHAPTER FOURTEEN
BEA

Within a week of the time that I told Edward about Eunique's con, he had charges filed and a deposition scheduled. The only thing we disagreed on was my telling Virginia. When Edward came to pick me up for my deposition, he wanted to bring Virginia along. I made him promise not to tell her. He only knew because Red had, for the most part, forced me to tell him. Red was suffering from a case of diarrhea of the mouth, but for whatever reason, he didn't tell Virginia. He probably figured that Edward was the next best thing.

Edward, Rachael, and Red kept urging me to tell her, but I refused. I threatened not to take Eunique to court or anything if Red or Rachael told her. Besides, Edward couldn't tell her because he was my attorney. That was enough to make him squash that madness. It was bad enough having him know how foolish I'd been, wasn't no need in dragging Virginia into my mess, too.

Once Edward took charge, I just knew that he was going to be able to get me my properties back. Even for a black attorney, he had won some big cases in town. It was going to be hard though. When he asked me if I had proof of the deal Eunique and I made, I had to tell him no. I tried to get him to see that Eunique and I were friends. At the time, I didn't even think about asking him to sign any papers.

Edward was able to get statements from some of the people

who bought the furniture that Eunique and I were selling. Course he had to promise to help get them out of some other legal troubles. I came to find out that Eunique didn't deal with nothing but riff raff.

Eunique came sauntering into Edward's office with his white attorney like he was the major attraction at a talent show, grinning for the entire world to see. He had the nerve to come over to where I was sitting and offer me his hand.

"Mrs. Richards, I'm glad to see that you are doing well."

The cat got my tongue, but in my head, I was calling him all kinds of filth and trash. I drew my hand from him and turned around in my chair to face Edward.

Eunique's attorney, Mr. Fletcher, was class all the way. I bet Eunique used my money to hire that fancy lawyer. I could see from the look on the lawyer's face that he was surprised to see Edward sitting beside me.

"Ed, fancy meeting you here." He shook Edward's hand, and the two of them exchanged a little small talk.

While they were talking, Eunique kept shooting me the evil eye. I suppose he thought that I was afraid of him or something, fool!

Mr. Fletcher started the show off by pulling out a manila folder from his briefcase. That thing had to be about an inch thick. Eunique sat there smiling like he had thrown out his trump card. I wondered what was in that thing.

Not be outdone, Edward pulled out our evidence. It didn't look nearly as big as the file that Eunique had, but I tried to keep in mind that I had the truth on my side.

"Okay are we ready?" Mr. Fletcher asked, smile disappearing

like he was ready to get down to some serious business.

The woman doing the transcribing, for whom I had to pay, nodded yes.

Mr. Fletcher continued, "Well then your client," he nodded his head in my direction, "contends that Mr. Johnson received her property under false pretenses?"

Smiling, Edward took my hands in his and looked that Mr. Fletcher straight in his eyes. "That is exactly what my aunt," he paused on the word aunt, "contends."

Mr. Fletcher raised his eyes in surprise and looked first at Eunique and then at me.

For the first time that day, I started feeling like things would go my way. Eunique, on the other hand, looked like he had just seen a ghost.

Recovering from his shock, Mr. Fletcher opened up his folder and pulled out the papers that I signed when I turned my property over to Eunique.

I got to give it to my nephew, he couldn't deny that those were my signatures, but he surprised even me when he pulled out his own set of papers. He pushed the papers across the table to Mr. Fletcher. "I did a little checking of my own. It seems that your client has a trail of fraud charges. One ended in a prosecution." I liked to faint in my chair when I heard him say that.

Mr. Fletcher grabbed the papers and started reading. His face turned beet red. He turned to stare at Eunique. Eunique sniffed and hit his nose with his thumb. He started yawning and stretching like a dog in the sun instead of a man sitting accused.

"Why don't we step outside and see if we can work something out?" Mr. Fletcher had on his million dollar smile again.

Edward followed him out of the office, leaving me alone with Eunique and the transcriber. Soon as the door swung closed, that bug eyed demon turned to me and laughed.

Even though I was shaking on the inside, I got up like the Queen of Sheba and walked out of that office. I wasn't even going to dignify him with my presence. I made a beeline for the bathroom and splashed cold water on my face. I didn't want to go back in the room with Eunique, so I stayed in the waiting room talking to the receptionist. When I saw Edward and Mr. Fletcher headed back toward the office, I took a deep breath and stood up. "I think it's time for me to go back in."

"Don't be nervous, everybody knows that your nephew is one of the best attorneys in town, and cute too." She winked.

I nodded.

Back inside the office, we all took our seats and Edward took my hand and turned to me. "Aunt Bea, Mr. Fletcher and I have worked out an agreement. In light of all the evidence, we feel it is in everyone's best interest if Eunique returns the three most valuable houses."

"What!" I couldn't have been hearing him right. I wanted all my houses back, not just three.

Edward held my hands even tighter. "Now before you get worked up, listen to me. He has documentation showing what you owe him in terms of materials and work performed, and …"

Eunique took that opportunity to open his mouth. "She oughta be glad…"

Oughta be glad! Fool! He should have kept that yap trap of his closed tight. I took my pocket book and tried to knock him in the mouth with it.

Edward tried to restrain me.

Mr. Fletcher jumped up and grabbed Eunique, pulling him out of the door. A few minutes later, Mr. Fletcher entered the room alone. "I'll have those papers drawn up and sent to your office to sign by the end of the day." He walked over to Edward shook his hand Edwards hand and turned to me. "It was a pleasure meeting you." He held out his hand.

I couldn't help but roll my eyes. The pleasure certainly wasn't mine.

Taking me home, Edward was full of talk. "Aunt Bea, I know how upset you are, but you have to understand. Eunique had all the evidence he needed to keep all six of your houses. Even though we had our character witnesses, he had the legal documentation showing the work he did to bring the houses back up to code and the receipts for the material. He even paid the back taxes on some of the houses. It may not seem fair, but the judge would have to consider that as real evidence, and he would instruct a jury to do the same. As it was, Mr. Fletcher was doing you a favor because you're my aunt. Even so, he has an obligation to protect his client."

I didn't want to hear none of that. I know it was only three houses, but to me that meant that he was justified, he shouldn't have had anything. A man ain't a man if he don't keep his word. The tears streamed down my face.

Edward jabbed me with his elbow. "I didn't know you had a left hook" he said with a weak smile.

Wasn't nothin' funny. I remember the last time I tried to knock somebody out was back when I lived in Boston. I had found a nice job at the hospital in the cafeteria. Edward's daddy got me the job. His sister Rose was the supervisor. I was responsible for all of the special meals for people with diet restrictions. It was a good job, it paid well, and it wasn't too difficult. Don't you know, I didn't have that job for but two months and along came trouble?

Trouble came in the form of Eunice Brown. We started off as friends, but fell out when I found out how two faced she was. Everything I said to that girl got twisted and retold. I overheard her in the bathroom one day telling another girl how I felt I was better than everybody else. And that I talked about all the people in that cafeteria like dogs!

I couldn't believe it!

Standing up in the mirror combing her hair she claimed, "Her brother R. Thomas is even worse than her, think he too good for a colored woman. He got him a white girlfriend."

I threw that door open quicker than you could think. I called that girl a low down lying heifer and this cow had the nerve to throw her hand towel in my face.

I was on that girl like white on rice. Our supervisor had security come and escort the two of us from the building.

CHAPTER FIFTEEN
RACHAEL

I started my new life by going to the gym. Turns out it was a really cool place. Someone had decided to turn an old church into a fitness center. It was a great idea—the architecture lent tons of character to the place. The nursery was no joke. It was decorated in primary colors, the floor was covered in a foam interlocking number/alphabet puzzle, and there was a ball pit—a real one, not the kind that you get from Kmart. There were playpens as well as a television and VCR. Obviously, a lot of thought had gone into the nursery.

The best thing about it was the free membership that I received by filling out a card in the grocery store.

I almost felt embarrassed about my level of excitement as I packed my bags for the gym. How pitiful, you would have thought that I was going to the gym to find a man, but I had loftier goals. I was in search of companionship of the female persuasion. Nothing kinky, I just wanted to find a friend, someone else who was married with small kids. We could work out together and take the kids to the playground together. I needed a friend to do stay at home mom type stuff with. If I got lucky, maybe she would have good taste and we'd cruise the mall, not that I had any money but still.

After checking the kids into the nursery, I went to the front desk to see what was what. From the list of activities, I picked power walking. I overheard some other moms in the nursery say that it was a lot of fun. Besides, I'd just had a baby a few months ago, no need to knock myself out on the first day.

The five other women in the class were all outfitted in the latest Nike gear. As we power walked past the first storefront, I looked at my image in the window. My outfit wasn't too bad—a black one-piece number outlined in black lace. It was a little chilly out, so I wore an orange neon windbreaker on top of my chic outfit.

The first block I was doing good keeping up with the other ladies, listening to their conversation, trying to contribute from time to time. That was a wasted effort. Most of their conversations revolved around what their husbands did for a living, and apparently, they all practiced law. So that pretty much left me out of the conversation. From their conversation, I learned that there was an upcoming charity event, and all of these ladies were on a quick weight loss plan. By the time we got to the middle of the third block, I had given up trying to talk. I was out of breath just trying to keep up, but they were all chattering on and on without one drop of sweat. No biggy, maybe having a baby had taken a larger toll than I thought.

By the fourth block, I was ready to fall out. Yes from power walking. Whew, that power walking was some serious stuff. My knees hurt, my thighs were burning, and I was even starting to feel something in my hips. I grew increasingly hotter from the physical exertion and took my jacket off. Just then, I passed an empty storefront, and happened to glance at my reflection. I looked like a pumpkin on heroin. What was I thinking? My little workout hairdo was all sweated out; the bangs were plastered to my forehead.

Meanwhile, I noticed the fabulous five, all talking a little less and drinking a little more. Other than that, they seemed to fine. Me, I was dying of thirst, but hadn't thought to bring any water. I thought that this walk was going to be a breeze. Thank God we had to stop at the corner and wait for the light change I needed to take that rest. That is when the Fab Five decided to walk another five blocks. Five blocks! Forget it, I wasn't about to try and go another five blocks. My poor out of shape body couldn't stand it.

Besides, there was a car with two men sitting at the corner waiting for the light change. They seemed to be turned on by my sweat. "Hey, baby," the one on the passenger side with the mouth full of gold yelled out of the window.

Not wanting to seem the least bit interested, I pretended to read a flyer that was posted on a near by telephone pole. Lord knows I didn't want to give them the idea that I was in any way interested in them. "Girl, you sho is fine," Young Goldie said, cocking his head to the side as he flashed me a 75-watt player smile. Wow, he was exactly what I was looking for, a man with a mouth full of gold. Yuk, can you say disgusting?

I didn't know this man and hopefully would never see him again in my life, but I still felt embarrassed. There I was, dying on the corner, with five white women who barely had boo to say to me since we left the gym, and I was embarrassed by two ghet-to fabulous brothas trying to get their game on.

I turned to read the side of the building. The owner of this particular building had advertised little known facts about the city. I love history and little unknown facts. Hearing burning rubber, I looked up only to find my compadres had crossed the street leaving me behind—not that they noticed—and the two men left me in their wake with a string of cuss words to keep me company. It was definitely time to make it back to the fitness center.

I don't know how they did it, but the Nike Noids beat me back. By the time I got inside the gym, they were all pulling mats onto the floor, getting ready to do a cool down. I was too pooped and funky to cool down. The only thing I wanted to pull was my towel out of the locker so that I could take a long hot shower. The shower was an experience in and of itself. There was even a towel lady. I spent more time small talking to her in those few minutes in front of the mirror, than I had the whole time I was with the power walkers. I was trying to make sense out of the mess on my head. "Honey, ain't nothing wrong with that hair that a comb and brush wouldn't take care of."

I laughed. "Please, the more I sweat, the bigger my hair gets."

"Honey, just put all that pretty hair in a ponytail and call it a day."

"I would, but I don't have a rubber band," I said gathering all of my hair together and pulling it to the back of my head.

"That's what I'm here for." She handed me a hair band.

"Thank you. My name is Rachael," I said, accepting the band. "What is your name?"

"Miss Moffet. You don't sound like you from around these parts."

"No m'am I'm not. I from Michigan, but I'm staying her with my mother-in-law."

"What's your peoples name?"

"Anderson. My mother-in-law is Virginia Anderson."

Miss Moffet smiled from ear to ear. "Oh, now. Girl, you like family. Mmm hmm. I know Virginia. She the salt of the earth, poor thing. I member how she near bout drove herself in the ground trying to take care of her sick husband and that family of hers. I was working at the hospital then. Oh yeah, they good people. Those children came to see bout they daddy everyday. He was a good man, as good a man as you likely to find this side of heaven."

"Ahh, thank you. That's so kind of you. I am going to have to tell her I ran into you."

"Yes, well I better get back to work." She picked up a dirty towel. "I just been running my mouth. But I wouldn't feel right if I didn't invite you to revival this week."

She and I continued chatting away about nothing. When the ladies from my class came in, they started making requests like the two of us weren't even talking. She shot me the look and filled their request without missing a beat. Before I left, Miss Moffet gave me a paper with the directions to her church. "Service starts at seven," she said, squeezing my hand.

I needed a place that was not so highbrow.

Fitness center aside, I was still on a quest to get a life. Being the good daughter that I am, I decided to take my mother's advice and find a church home. Granted, I had this little thing about organized religion, but number one; I don't know everything. And number two; I am open to the fact that I could stand some enlightenment. Besides, I was lonely and church was a great place for a person that's new in town to make friends. The problem was finding the right church home for me. The Catholic

Church that Bea attended was nice, but it didn't feel like home. I decided to take Miss Moffet up on her invitation.

The moment I stepped across the church threshold, I felt a comforting familiarity. The Mothers of the church, sitting in their customary seats in the front pews, reminded me of my grandmother and her sisters. As did the smell inside the sanctuary, which consisted of a combination of various perfumes and colognes heightened by the heat of all of the bodies inside. For a Wednesday night, the church was packed. Wow, I didn't want to think about how crowded it got on Sunday. As I made my way into the sanctuary, one of the ushers stopped me.

"Hey, sister. How are you this fine evening?"

"Fine." I smiled.

"Are you visiting?"

How impressive, this usher was really on her toes. With so many people in attendance, how did she know that I was visiting? "Do I look that out of place?"

"Oh no sister. Not at all, we are glad to have you. But, the church is fasting this week, so everyone is wearing a red ribbon." She pointed to a ribbon pinned to her chest. "I notice you didn't have one."

Before I could ask about the fast, the choir started singing. So I took a seat near the door. The choir was jumping. I didn't even know the words, but I was swaying from side to side in unison with the woman sitting beside me. The singing was good, and the congregation seemed to have a true fellowship. Every time they stood up, they were hugging and patting each other on the back. At first, I was put off. I always feel awkward stepping into the personal space of strangers, but I came to church looking to make a connection. The woman sitting beside me reached out and pulled me toward her. "Bless you, sister, bless you. It will be alright".

How did she know? I thought as I took in the scent of Giorgio and Afro Sheen. I forced myself to relax and met her gaze. "Thank you," I said, letting out my breath. She pulled back and looked me full in the face. I felt uncomfortable under her gaze. I took a deep relaxing breath, and forced myself to meet her gaze.

She continued holding my hand, squeezing it for good measure. I felt a surge of energy move through my body and proceeded to sit down in my seat. What was that?

The sermon for night dealt with addiction. I was hanging pretty tight with the message too, but then the minister started talking about people seeking different therapies. "Now you know what I'm talking about," he admonished, his fist raised high in the air. "Folks trying out all of these therapies, when all they need is the word."

"Well," one of the deacons shouted in support.

"Y'all run and spend all y'all's money on a psychologist, when what you need is a Godologist."

"Tell 'em now," someone shouted.

By this time, the man was sweating. "Now see," he said, coming from behind the pulpit and to the very first pew, "the devil is a liar."

One of the deacons jumped from his seat. "Amen, amen,

come on now. That's what I'm talking bout."

"Naw, naw," the preacher said, holding his head down. "Y'all doan here me now. Cuz Gawd, don't need no psychology."

"Well."

"Mmm, mmm. Naw see, all that Gawd needs is Jesus."

The organ player struck a chord.

The preacher bounced up and down on his heels. "I said what you need is Jesus," he shouted. The organist played another chord. A woman in back of me began shouting. I turned in time to see her blue bell sleeve, fluttering in the air as she collapsed in her seat. Two nurses came down and immediately began fanning the woman who was screaming "Thank you Jesus," while rocking back and forth.

The preacher strolled back to his position at the pulpit and declared, "The doors of the church are open." Taking their cue, the choir rose and began to sing.

"In the name of Jesus, in the name of Jesus. We have the victory," I sang, stepping from side to side in unison with the choir. You would have thought that I was wearing a burgundy robe. I looked around at the congregation clapping to the sound of the gospel, this definitely wasn't the church for me. What is it about a person that makes them think that psychology is separate from Jesus? The pastor who performed our wedding ceremony was also a licensed therapist. Inner peace is inner peace. Call it 12 Step. Call it Alcoholics Anonymous. Call it saved. In the end, it is all the same.

I wish I could say that I was impressed by the sermon, but that was not the case. God forgive me. I know that I was sitting in church—the one place where a person's appearance really houldn't matter. But who was I kidding. If nobody in the church :ared about appearances, we wouldn't go through so much trou-)le to look good for church. This preacher looked so out of place .o me because most preachers that I was accustomed to were so well coifed. I think that I could have gotten over the way he ooked if his message had been stronger. His message wasn't strong enough to take me past how he looked. He had on a shiny)urgundy suit. Not only was it burgundy, it was shiny too. Shiny ind loud do not go together. When he came down the aisle, I :ould see that his suit wasn't store bought shiny. No, his shine looked like it came from ironing over dirt or too much starch. Whatever the cause, it looked bad, and the fact that the sanctu- ary was hot and he was dripping sweat didn't help. He reminded me too much of a jackleg preacher as he whooped and hollered about the evils of modern day psychology.

According to Jackleg, people had started giving a fancy name to sin, such as alcoholism and drug addiction. Any Saint could tell them that it was just the devil doing his work. When was the last time that anybody could buy cancer on the shelf at the gro- cery store? When I heard that last little bit, I wanted to yell out. "Everyday! Haven't you heard of cigarettes, you twit?"

Instead, I sat in my seat, quietly thinking things over. Maybe there was some truth to what he was saying. There was no deny- ing that alcoholism and drug addiction were sins. I'd be a fool to think otherwise. I have trouble believing the whole devil thing. The idea that there is this ghost person or spirit out to trick and deceive me is kinda.... I don't know. But I do know that I don't really believe it. What if the true devil is fear? That was the thing that was blocking my writing. I mean that would make a lot more sense. For me every time I don't do the right thing, it is because of fear. That is exactly why I couldn't write. I was afraid of failure. When I really thought about it, the fear of what people would think about me or say about me and in the end it didn't really matter anyway. They are going to think and say what they wanted no matter what you do.

On the way home, I decided that if Jesus could be born, die, and live again by the time he was thirty three, the least I could do was cast fear—the devil—aside and pick up a copy of *True Romance* and see about submitting a story.

CHAPTER SIXTEEN
BEA

Today is the day that I'm going to get my new stove. My friend Melissa let me use her Sears credit card so that I could get it. I tried talking to Rachael about it when I went over to Virginia's that afternoon. I was in the den watching Oprah and Rachael was half watching while she was working on that dang computer of hers. All Rachael wanted to do was fuss. She kept on and on about how was I going to pay somebody back for a stove when I was always complaining about paying off the bills that I already had. She'd been saying for the longest that I needed to call Consumer Credit Counselors. And wouldn't you know, that's exactly what Oprah was talking about. Just to shut Rachael up, I went ahead and called them.

Once I got a live person on the phone, I decided I'd do best by getting right to the point. "So exactly what is it that y'all do?"

"We help work out your financial problems."

"Uh, huh." Well that wasn't telling me nothing. "And how do you do that? Do you help to secure a loan?"

"No, ma'am, we don't. We look at your income, and then we gather all the information on your monthly expenses."

"Mm, hmm," I said to the voice on the other end.

"Next, we factor in what you owe to creditors. From there we try to work out a monthly budget for you to adhere to. We also ask that you get rid of all of your credit cards, and we make payment arrangements with your creditors."

"That sounds to me like Chapter 13."

"No, ma'am. It's not Chapter 13. Would you like to schedule an interview, and we can explain it further then?"

"No, but thank you all the same." I hung up the phone.

"Well?" Rachael asked while bouncing the baby on her knee.

"I don't care what that woman says. Sounds to me like all they offering is Chapter 13."

"Why do you say that?"

Oprah, had gone off so I turned off the television. "Because, Chapter 13 I know about. I filed that back when my husband and me called ourselves getting back together."

Rachael stopped bouncing the baby and looked at me. "I can't believe you went back to him after pulling on gun on him?"

Elliot reached out for me. Every since he cut out all that crying he was a real cutie. "When I left Larry the first time, I started seeing someone else. It burns my heart to think about it. I know I was shameful."

"Were you in love with this other person?"

"No, it was pure lust. It was just nice to be with someone who didn't have so many problems. But you know I couldn't take communion, not when I was sinning so shamefully anyway. I had to make myself right with God, so I went back to Larry. He promised me the world if I agreed to come back to him. He promised to stop drinking, cussing, fighting and acting a fool in general. He never did promise to stop cheating on me though, that would have meant confessing that he did it in the first place. I felt like I needed to give my marriage another chance."

"So how did y'all end up filing for bankruptcy?" I continued bouncing the baby. "His friend convinced him to file bankrupt-cy. He spent most of the money he made drinking and woman-izing. His know it all friend told him that all that debt would go away if he filed. Larry, fool that he was, listened to the advice of his friend and fellow drunk. He didn't bother to find out any-thing on his own. As soon as he filed, we couldn't use any more credit, new or old, and he had to pay off the bad credit that he had. All Chapter 13 did was take him before a judge who made him sign an agreement to pay a set amount each month. Too bad they couldn't make him sign an agreement to stop buying alco-hol."

"That's the funny thing about alcoholics, they drink."

"Smart ass. He didn't keep his word, but I will say he gave a month's worth of half ass effort. That fool spent all kinds of money that we didn't have trying to prove to me what a good man he was. When he did start back to drinking, he started off saying that he was trying to relax after working all day and then going to his part time job. By the time Larry started getting flat out drunk every night, he blamed it on me and my greedy, self-ish, spoiled, and Lord knows what all, that he had to work so hard. Claimed that all I did was sit around the house sucking up his money. I don't know what all else he expected me to do. He didn't trust me enough to let me go out and work. I guess he thought that I was going to leave him again."

Rachael got up to check on Vee who was messing with some-thing behind the chair. "You must have loved him at some point to put up with all of that."

"Not like a wife should. The man's own mama told me that he wasn't any good, and Ma Belle ain't never lied. I found out why he was such a low-down, dirty dog. She claimed that he was just like his daddy. Humph, women don't understand how important it is to study a man's family before they spend two seconds even thinking about getting married, let alone calling themself somebody's boyfriend. I learned that lesson the hard way."

"Ugh!" Rachael exclaimed, screwing up her face and picking up her daughter. "This girl refuses to use the bathroom. Hand me one of those diapers, in that pile," she said, pointing to a stack of diapers on the end of the couch.

I struggled to hand her the diaper while still holding onto the baby.

"Cover your nose," she said, taking the diaper off of Vee. "So how did you end up leaving him the second time?"

The smell coming from that little girl's diaper was sinful. I had to turn my head. "What have you been feeding that chile?"

Rachael laughed. "Virginia's red meat. You see what it does to a person."

I rolled my eyes. I never will understand how folks come to believe that meat that we been eating for hundreds of years was going to all of a sudden start making our guts fall out. "A little red meat ain't never hurt nobody. Anyway, after talking to Ma Belle, I figured my husband wasn't about to change. That gave me the courage I needed to leave his black ass for the second time! She called me one day while he was on duty to see how I was doing. He had called her the night before, with his drunken foolishness, asking her to teach me how to fix a pitcher of iced tea."

Rachael had everything she needed to change the baby in a basket on the bookshelf. Once she cleaned the baby up with wipes, she powdered her down and put a clean diaper on her. She took the soiled diaper and walked to the bathroom off the den where she kept a diaper pail full of water and bleach. She stuck her head out of the bathroom door. "Tea?"

"Yes, tea. How the hell is somebody going to tell you how to make ice tea over the phone long distance?"

Rachael came back into the room and pulled a box of Lego's out from under the coffee table. I watched as she sat on the floor playing with Vee. "You're a better woman than me. I don't think that I could take it. What did his mother say?"

"Oh, honey, Ma Belle and me talked for a long time when she called that day. She told me all about how she convinced him to try and change. But he never got over the fact that I left him the first time. Of course, the alcohol didn't help. Anyway, I was planning to leave him again, but I found out I was pregnant. That pregnancy was so important to me...so important!"

Rachael stopped playing and turned to look at me.

"Finally, I was gonna have me a baby."

"But..." Rachael said and I could see by the look on her face that she was starting to put two and two together. "What happened to the baby?"

"I stared down at the baby I was holding in my arms. He wiped at his eyes, trying to fight off sleep. I rocked him back and forth against my bosom. I can't think of anything that will put a baby to sleep faster that a nice warm bosom. I kept on rocking her son in my lap.

As usual, Larry staggered home late last night drunk as Cootie Brown goin on about some money he'd lost so we couldn't be getting the baby furniture he'd promised me.

"It's okay," I'd said in an attempt to calm him down. "Mother wanted to buy..."

Like a wild man he'd pounced on me pinning me to the bed by my wrist and pressing his knees in my side. "Don't say shit to me about your momma. She think I can't do for you? The two of y'all always thinking yawls better than somebody."

His breath smelled like he flossed with chitlins. I turned my head, and he tightened his grip on my wrist and pressed his knees harder.

"The baby," I whispered.

"Oh shit," he muttered.

Like a fool, I thought that he was sorry, and then he started to vomit on himself, the bed, and me.

"Get yo lazy black ass up and clean this shit up."

I nearly became sick myself, cleaning up his filth. I exhausted myself, pulling the sheets out from under him while he lay passed out. I took off my gown and dropped it in the tub with the soiled sheet and began scrubbing them on the washboard we kept by the tub. The back and forth motion it took to scrub calmed my nerves. I finally finished and hung the sheets over the tub, before cleaning myself.

The next morning, I got up and started cooking the food that I needed for Larry's card game later on. I cried out with pain, my arm was sore in the spot where Larry grabbed me last night. I put down the pan, heavy with barbecued ribs, counted to five, and picked it back up, holding my breath until I placed it in the oven.

I didn't know how long I could go on like this. I looked over to the counter. The potato salad was finished, I'd completed baking the cakes, and the tomato cucumber salad was marinating in the sink. Good. I could take a moment to get off of my feet before Larry woke up.

I sat down on the couch and felt something poking me in the behind. Shifting my weight, I looked underneath me. It was Larry's empty bottle of whisky. Disgusted, I tossed it to the side. I got up and started cleaning the house as quietly as I could. Larry sober was a completely different person than Larry drunk. The sober Larry was sweet and tender, would do anything for me and would never raise a hand against me. The drunk Larry was a low-down, dirty son of a bitch. Drunk, Larry didn't give a damn about me one bit. I'd married Dr. Jekyl and Mr. Hyde. I lived on tender hooks, holding my breath until I knew which one I would be dealing with for the day. Lately, Mr. Hyde was the only one showing up.

I went back and forth like a child on a see-saw, thinking about whether or not I should leave him again. Larry must have sensed it. He wouldn't let me out of his sight. He arranged my entire day, setting up visits with the wives of his friends or telling them that I didn't mind keeping their children. I put up with it because of the sin I'd done when I left him the last time. I'd promised God that I would be a good wife, so Larry's abuse was something that I would just have to deal with.

I took the sheets from the bathroom, put them in a laundry basket of dirty clothes and went outside to join my neighbor Elizabeth who was waiting to go with me to the laundry mat. Despite the heat, I wore a sweater to cover the bruises on my wrist. I didn't want Elizabeth in my business. The two of us talked around the noises that she heard coming from my house. Elizabeth took one look at me wearing a sweater on a ninety-degree day and I could tell from the look in her eye that she knew.

Larry was waiting for me on the sofa when I came in. It was almost seven o'clock and he hadn't even bothered to see about acquainting his stink with water and soap.

"Where you been?" he grumped.

"The Laundromat," I answered, putting down my basket. "I went with Elizabeth"

He looked out of the front window and saw Elizabeth across the street putting her key in the door.

"Mmph," he muttered. Larry turned to look at me. He stood rubbing his afternoon shadow, looking like he wanted to say something.

"You better get dressed, companies coming."

I was in the kitchen getting the food ready to set out when his guests arrived. Larry came out the bedroom as Dr. Jekyl to greet them.

I put the food out on the kitchen cabinet, and set out plates, silverware, glasses, and beverages—even though they'd brought plenty of liquor of their own.

"The food is in the kitchen fellas. Help yourselves. I'll just retire to my room."

I went into the bedroom and turned up the radio. I didn't really care to hear the things that a group of men discussed while playing cards. Mother always claimed that card playing was a devilish endeavor, and I believed her. I was dozing off when Larry called me.

"Bea!"

"Yes," I said, stepping out of the bedroom. The smell from

their cigars upset my stomach.

"We out of ribs."

"I cooked plenty…"

"We out."

"I'm sorry, maybe I could put together a small salad or…"

"Fry us up some chicken?"

One of his friends spoke up. Of the group of them, he was always the most reserved. "Ahh, she don't have to bother with cooking, we done had plenty."

"Oh yeah we fine." the other men agreed.

"I couldn't eat any more if I tried."

Larry spoke slow and deliberately. "She my wife. And she'll do what I tell her."

The tension in the room grew. I left the room and went into the kitchen to fry the chicken. My head was spinning from the smoke and standing over a hot frying pan wasn't helping it any. I placed the chicken on a platter and set it out on a cabinet.

"The chicken's done," I called over my shoulder as I headed to the bathroom to splash cold water on my face.

"Serve it to us," Larry commanded as he passed out the cards.

I stopped in my tracks and turned to look at him. He was the puppet master, and I was the puppet. I hated him for treating me like shit in front of his friends. They didn't know how to behave as I went around the card table passing out chicken. I got to the second person and the smell of the cigar smoke, food, and cologne combined was more than I could handle. I dropped the platter of chicken on the table and ran to the bathroom.

I could hear everyone making their apologies for leaving early as I heaved over the toilet bowl. After the last person left, Larry came and stood in the bathroom doorway. He was drunk. Lord, I was going to have to deal with Mr. Hyde.

"Excuse me," I said, half begging. Maybe I could make it to the bedroom and into bed without his interference.

"I'll move when I'm good and God damned ready."

I inhaled deeply.

"So you Miss high and mighty?" Larry said, waving a whiskey bottle in the air before taking a sip.

I didn't say a word, not that he was in the mind to hear me anyway.

"You flouncing round my friends telling me what you gone do."

I would have preferred not to go near his friends.

"Now you standing here lookin' at me like you the queen and I'm the, the, … Hell, woman Im'ma tell you right now, you ain't the queen of shit. I'm the queen of this castle."

I swallowed a laugh. "If you say so," I answered and made to go past him again.

Larry shoved me. "I tell you when to go, I run this," he said punching me in the stomach so hard I fell to my knees.

"Please," I begged.

"Oh, so now you want to get humble. Any other time you walkin' round with your head in the air like you better then the president."

I stared up at him thinking, God I hate him.

"Who the hell you think you lookin' at?" Larry screamed, and kicked me in the stomach.

I lay curled into a ball on the bathroom floor, holding my stomach and rocking back in forth in pain. I wasn't going to give him the satisfaction of my tears and prayed instead. "Saint Mary Magdalene, woman of many sins, who by conversion became the beloved of Jesus, thank you for your witness that Jesus Forgives through the miracle of love. You already possess eternal happiness in his glorious presence, please intercede for me, so that some day I may share in the same everlasting joy…"

Larry stood over me sneering. "What you calling Jesus for? He can't hear you!" Larry kicked me again then turned to leave.

I don't know what happened after that, I passed out and when I came to, Elizabeth was standing over me. "Dear Lord, we got to get you to the hospital."

"Oh no," Rachael said with her hand covering her mouth. She crawled over to me and laid her head on my knee. "I am so, so, sorry."

Thinking of that day set my heart on fire. "Can you believe Larry shuffled into my hospital room a day later acting humble with fifty-proof still on his breath," I said through gritted teeth. "Baby, I am so sorry. Im'ma change, you'll see. No more drinkin' no more card playing…Oh, baby, I'm so sorry," I said, imitating Larry. "I couldn't stand to even look at his ole raggely behind. Dirty rascal laid across my bed carrying on so the nurses were afraid to come in. Didn't matter to me though.

"Lying in that hospital bed, I didn't want to hear anything he had to say. Fool me once shame on you; fool me twice I'll be damned. I would have humped a tree before I let that man touch me again."

Vee came over to the couch and put her head on my other knee. I patted her head absent-mindedly. "He was only interested in his military career anyway. The military doesn't put up with any wife beaters. They will lock'em up or throw'em out. Of course it goes on all of the time, but they believe in Clinton's policy of don't ask, don't tell. And you damn sure better not get caught doing it. Yeah he might have felt bad about making me lose my baby. He felt worse about what the army would do to him."

Rachael sat up and took Vee in her lap. "So what did you do?"

I started rocking the baby, who was fast asleep in my arms. "I came home. I gotta give it to Virginia. She stood by my side. She was back in Albany by then and had been married for about five or six years and already had one baby. Her husband, Richard, was just starting his own practice as a family doctor. I was full of pride, too full to go to Mother with my sob story. She told me not to go back to him in the first place. 'Tell me Bea, how stupid do you have to go back to a man who drinks like he does? He was no good from the very beginning. Your father never ran around on me that way; you were not raised that way. My daughter's were brought up to lead respectable lives,' she said. I didn't want to admit it then, but she was right"

"I don't even want to think about all the stupid things I did just to spite my mother."

I guess that is how children behave with parents. I shrugged. "As soon as Richard found out what happened, he sent for me. He and Virginia had the money wired to Elizabeth, my next-door neighbor. The whole time I lived next door to Elizabeth, we never talked about my situation with Larry. The walls in our place were so thin she had to hear all the ruckus Larry kept up. She probably felt sorry for me, especially after taking me to the hospital.

She stayed with me the entire time I was there, since I didn't have any family in town."

"At least you didn't have to go through something that awful by yourself."

"That's true. Elizabeth took the money and bought my ticket. I didn't bother with packing up my things. I left with the clothes on my back. Larry could burn trash or give away the rest of my things. I didn't want it if it had anything to do with him. I don't know what made me think that I could keep Mother from finding out what happened. She had me signing divorce papers as soon as I stepped off that bus. She didn't play. She got me one of those quickie Mexican divorces. There had been more than enough bad blood between the two of us, but she was there for me that time. I can at least be grateful for that. When I left this time, Larry knew where to find me. I got a job at my Daddy's bank and tried to live my life as best I could. Wasn't no point in getting remarried. Thanks to Larry, I couldn't have any babies, and besides, once was enough. I never did like to play roulette; with love, I want some guarantees. Besides, in the eyes of the Church, we were still man and wife."

Rachael eyes rose up in surprise. "Still married. What do you mean, still married? You got a divorce."

I stopped rocking. "Yes I got a divorce in the eyes of the law. But in the eyes of the church, I am still married. That's why I never got remarried, it would be adultery."

"Wait, I don't get it, why would it be adultery. The Church allows you to get divorced."

"Not in my case. In the eyes of the church I am still his wife."

"And that's why you never got remarried."

"Yes." Talking to Rachael about my religion was like talking to a goose about a chicken. "Of course, Larry begged me to come back to him. I didn't even bother coming to the phone when he started calling me. When he saw that begging didn't wark, he started threatening. I had Richard, Sr. speak to him about all of his threatening. I don't know what he said, but whatever it was, it put an end to it."

"Well I'm glad to hear that. But didn't you ever have boyfriends that you got serious with after that."

"Of course I did."

"None of them ever wanted to get married."

"I already told you, I didn't want to get remarried. But Larry did. Years later, Larry moved back to Albany with his wife, and they had a daughter. He made a comfortable life for his new family. They had a nice house and his daughter went on to graduate from college, but the whole time he beat his wife. He never did stop drinking either. His wife and me got to be friends. At first, Maureen couldn't stand me. I would see her from time to time in passing at Ma Belle's house. I guess she finally realized that I didn't want her fool husband no more and let her guard down."

"What did the two of you talk about? I can't imagine that I would want to have anything to do with either of them."

That is the same thing that all of my friends said. "We talked about the problems she and Larry had and how he was always throwing my name up in her face. I don't know what for, he didn't have more than one good thing to say about me when we were married."

"Yes, well, you know what they say. The grass is always greener on the other side."

"I guess so. Believe it or not, the same things that he used to say to and about me, he said to her. Seems like all I ever heard was, 'Get your fat, black, lazy, ass here, shut your ugly face, you too triflin' to be alive.' Oh, he had a whole truckload of mean, low-down, rotten, dirty things to say to me. It was Maureen's turn to put up with his mess. I just shook my head when she told me about him taking her out in the night and whooping on her. I tried to tell her that, ain't no man going to beat my ass and rock my belly both. It's got to be one or the other."

"Did she leave him, too?"

"She certainly did not. After their daughter graduated from college, she died. Turns out she'd had sickle cell all along. Larry started coming by my house not too long after they put her in the ground. He went right back to saying how sorry he was for everything. Claimed he knew he was wrong, and what he didn't know was how to stop himself. Lord knows I wasn't the one to tell him how. Seems to me like it should be something you just do. By and by, we started seeing each other again. God's law said that we were still man and wife. Besides, I'm still a woman with needs. Nowadays, as soon as he get to talking and acting niggerish, I put him out. I don't let him come back around until he is ready to act like a person with some sense."

"Why would you even be bothered with him at all? It's pretty clear what kind of person he is. If I were you, I wouldn't even think about having anything to do with him period."

I looked down at the baby sleeping in my arms. It's so easy to say what you would and wouldn't do when you young and have choices. At my age, you have to take what you can, when you can. I would have never thought that I would have to borrow from a friend to get anything, most of my life I been the one doing the lending. After all these years, here I am almost right back where I started. Being used and abused by a man and starting over...at my age.

CHAPTER SEVENTEEN
RACHAEL

Walmart wouldn't accept my check. The clerk said my name was denied.

Aunt Flow arrived for her monthly visit. I was cramping and really needed my feminine products, so I could have choked the clerk on principle. The way she came at me with her home perm and dye job pants fit too tight outlining the crotch, I could have jumped across the counter.

I handed her my license and my check. Looking at it, she asked me what state it was in.

At first, I thought I hadn't heard her right so I asked her, "What?"

"I said, what state?" She popped her gum like I was the one that was stupid.

I shook my head to wake myself from the nightmare. "Like it says on the license, Georgia." Was it my imagination or didn't all Georgia licenses read Georgia. Hello! I shifted Elliot on my hip. My cramps weren't getting any better. I was ready to go.

This chic called her manager over. "Earl, I have a out of town check."

What was the friggin' deal? I had written off of the same account a thousand times at the very same Walmart. Why was having an Atlanta address such a big deal? I tried to ignore the people behind me that were growing impatient like the whole thing was my fault. One old lady in a motor cart kept rolling her eyes at me.

I turned my back to her.

Earl finally made his way over to the counter and took a look at my check, studying it and then comparing it to my license. Finally, he addressed me. "So you're from out of town?"

"Uh… yeah."

"And you're here for…" he said waving his hand in the air like he was waiting for an answer good enough to justify the reason why I might come into his store and write a check for my feminine needs.

I tried to shake some sense in my head to try and bring myself to reality. "Are you serious?"

He stared at me, not knowing what to say.

I shifted Elliot over to my other hip and stared right back at him.

"Well," he stammered, his face beet red. "This is an out of town check and our policy for out of state checks …"

I could see the light bulb going off over his head. The key word was "state." Georgia is Georgia all day long.

Instead of apologizing, he turned to the counter girl saying, "I'll let it go this time."

Before I could get into his shit, I felt something wet on my foot. Looking down, I saw Virginia standing in a growing puddle originating from a steady trickle down her leg. Ooh, damn those clothe diapers! I closed my eyes.

That's when counter chick told me that my check had been denied. Humiliated enough for one day, I grabbed Virginia's hand and left the store.

Thank God Richard bought a car; it was 1989 Datsun 210. He bought it dirt cheap at an auction. The car looked pretty sporty, but it smelled musty on the inside, like it had been stuffed to the gills with smoking clowns. The day I got it, I tried to erase the smell by super cleaning it with bleach and Pine-Sol. Instead of erasing the smell, the bleach and Pine-Sol sat on top of it. In addition to the smell, the check engine light stayed on accompanied by a dinging noise that started out quiet, but got louder, and louder. The longer you were in the car, the louder it seemed, kinda like Chinese water torture.

Despite the aggravating smell and irritating sound, the car drove fine. And I do like driving sticks. Anyway, Richard promised to get those things fixed. I zoomed up to the nearest ATM, praying that I remembered the code correctly as I punched in the numbers. That would have been too easy. Richard couldn't come up with a simple code that was easy to remember. He picked something asinine like the number of children his mother had, followed by the number of his birth, followed by how many children he had, plus the age of his oldest child; but not necessarily in that order. I tried different combinations of his dumb ass theory and was about to go a fourth round when the machine took my card! That really pissed me off. On the ride home, I tried to calm down, but that dinging noise in the car wouldn't let me.

Balancing a checkbook had never been my forte, but I'd been on the ball since I'd gotten my laptop. I made sure to record everything in the Excel file I'd created for our household budget. Spending money was a lot easier to control when you saw how every little item was deducted from a total. That is why I was so shocked in the store. It was so embarrassing standing at the checkout counter unable to pay for a pack of diapers, some tampons, and a bottle of Midol. Putting back cereal is one thing, but having to leave a box of tampons with Trailer Trash Barbie was more than a little embarrassing. Not to mention the fact that I had to go home, wad up some tissue, and stick it down my pants. Talk about reaching a new low.

After getting Vee and Elliot settled with a snack. I plugged in an episode of Veggie Tales and settled down next to them with my laptop. Praise the Lord for online banking. In the time it takes to write a check, I had all of my most recent account information sitting in front of me. I went down the list of transactions. I recognized the checks I'd written for Sherrill's tuition, the grocery store, AOL, but there was one strange transaction. Why would Richard write a $50 check without telling me? We were supposed to be on a budget. Here I was arguing with Virginia about treating us like adults, and he was out there spending money like nobodies business.

I had to disconnect the phone line from my laptop to call Richard. After three rings, the answering machine picked up. I left a message, "Richard, you wrote a check without telling me and now the account is over drawn. I can't even buy tampons. You need to take care of it, ASAP. Give me a call when you get this message." I hung up the phone and went to change my paper towel.

Knowing that I needed to do something to take my mind off everything, I took the kids upstairs for a, nap and then came back down to the den and settled down on the couch with my laptop. Opening it up, my eyes were drawn to the copy of *True Romance* that I'd picked up. I'd read all of the stories in it a good two or three times. Looking at that magazine, I decided, I was sick of reading other peoples stories. It was time for me to write my own.

I closed my eyes and took a deep breath. "Lord, please guide my words." I commenced to typing. The words started to flow out of me onto the keyboard. It was almost like having a conversation, or better still, telling a story to a group of friends. It was just that easy. I wrote a story loosely based on the time in my life when I was in college and Richard and I found out I was pregnant with Sherrill. While I was writing, it was like I was caught up in some kind of time continuum.

I had no choice but to come out of the zone when Vee tried to close the laptop on my fingers. "Mommy, he potty!" she screamed. I had to shake my head to bring myself fully back to the present.

"What?" I asked, getting up from the couch.

Vee took my hand and retraced her steps up the stairs, fussing at me all the way. "I call you and call you. Baby stinky, Mommy."

I stepped inside the bedroom and was hit full on by the smell coming from Elliot's diaper. I turned my head and sucked in air. I could see where Vee had climbed out of Elliot's portable crib. She'd piled a blanket and some stuffed animals on a corner of the crib and stepped onto the bed before making her way down the steps. I scooped Elliot out of his crib and grabbed the changing basket that I kept on the dresser. I can't even begin to explain the satisfaction I felt. It was like wow, I did. I finally did it. Thank you Lord.

I was still in a good mood later that afternoon after picking Sherril up from school. In celebration of my accomplishment, we were having everybody's favorite, we were cooking everybody's favorite: spaghetti. I had both Sherrill and Vee dancing around the kitchen singing "Celebrate" by Madonna into wooden spoons when the phone rang. "Hello, I sang into the phone."

"Rachael?" Richard asked.

"Tis I," I said and laughed at Sherril who was standing in front of the oven door and staring at her image as she sang into her microphone. She was flinging her little arms and switching her little hips, getting all into it.

"What are y'all doing?"

"Singing and cooking." I answered. I smiled at Vee who was doing more jumping up and down with her little blonde pigtails boinging on her head.

"Oh, well I'm sorry about the check. I put $200 in the checking account so you can go to the store now."

"No problemo."

"What's going on?"

"I wrote my first story. I don't know whether or not it's any good, but I wrote it. Zippaty doo da, zippity ay, my oh my what a wonderful day," I sang.

Richard laughed. "Well, good thing you aren't trying to be a singer. I'm proud of you, baby. Now all you have to do is keep at it. What did you write about?"

"When I got pregnant with Sherril." Sherril turned when she heard her name mentioned.

"Oh God," Richard groaned.

"Don't worry, the names have been changed to protect the

innocent," I assured him. "Besides, our lives aren't dramatic enough to fill a story for *True Romance.* They need more drama. Anyway, I have to go, my garlic bread is starting to burn. I'm going to let you speak to Sherrill.

Later that night after the dishes were done and the kids were in bed, I left Virginia in the den and took my laptop into the dining room to go back over my story. Aside from the den and the kitchen, I really didn't go into the other rooms on the first floor of the house. But as I sat in the dining room amongst all of Virginia fine things, I realized how truly blessed I was. I'd wasted so much time asking God to bless me with things that I already had. I realized that I'd had it confused. I was so worried about gathering possessions of my own, I completely overlooked the fact that God was blessing me through Virginia and her willingness to open up her home and share her possessions with me. So what if she got on my nerves from time to time. I'm sure that I got on hers, too.

I felt kind of like the Jews wandering the dessert and complaining to God for giving them manna day after day. He could have let them starve. The same held true with me, I wasn't starving, my family was in good health and, I had everything that I needed at my disposal. I started thinking about a verse in the bible, Mark 1:15 which says, The time is fulfilled, and the kingdom of God is at hand: repent ye, and believe the gospel.

CHAPTER EIGHTEEN
BEA

Same as I did every day, I was laying in bed thinking of that business with Eunique. True enough, I'd gotten three of my properties back, and I did have a tad bit of money left over after paying my monthly bills. All the same, I wanted all of what was mine not just some. When I finally got sick and tired of worrying myself bout half to death, I climbed up out the bed and pulled on my denim skirt and a blouse and went on over to Virginia's to see what Rachael was up to.

Rachael was in the den with the kids. She had the baby sitting in the middle of a mess of toys while she was trying to do her yoga. She had on some of those exercise pants that the women her age like to wear. You know the kind, they have to put elastic in them so that you can wiggle yourself inside, but if you not skinny in the first place, you end up looking like a stuffed sausage. I personally think that folks should stick to plain ole sweat suits when working out. they don't show your flaws, but that's me. Lucky for Rachael she didn't have any lumps and bumps to begin with. I'm not much for exercise in the first place, and I really can't understand what good it does anybody to try and stand with their feet flat to the floor, bent at the waist, and trying to put the palms of their hands behind their legs. It all looks kind of peculiar if you ask me. To make matters worse, Vee was dressed like her momma and trying to do everything that she did, but the poor little thing kept toppling over.

When it comes to dumb shit, people can come up with more than a little bit. Lately Rachael had been doing all of this meditation mess, writing things down on a little note pad. I picked up the baby and took a seat in the recliner. "I'm almost afraid to say anything to you," I said, "for fear that you'll write it down. I don't care what she wants to call it, it seems to me like a bunch of Voodoo mess."

"You are being ridiculous, Bea," she said, with her head poking through the opening in her legs. "Besides, you shouldn't be saying anything that you can't stand behind."

I rolled my eyes. "Do you mind not talking to me with your behind tootin' in my face?" I asked her. "You can meditate on whatever. Just don't be writing down nothing that I say 'cause I don't want no parts of Voodoo."

Rachael got down on the ground and sat on the floor Indian style. Only, she put her feet on her knees and Vee had a heck of a time trying to do the same until Rachael reached out to help her. Then, she looked up at me and grinned like I was a little child. If I didn't like her so much, I would have slapped her right then and there. If you going to treat somebody like they dumb, don't do it while you sittin' right there in they face.

"What you know about Voodoo other than Tarzan?"

Some people too damn smart ass for there own good. "More than you, thank you very much," I said, lifting the baby up in the air and shaking my head from side to side like him, before bringing him back down to my lap. I could only do it once though because he was heavy. "I know enough about it to know that it ain't nothing to play with."

"Uh huh," she said with that darn grin still on her face. "And how do you know all of this?"

More with the tired questions, I swear, half the time I felt like I was talking to a reporter on the afternoon news. I don't know why I put up with that child. She could get on my nerves so bad my toes curled up when she talked. She ain't the only one that got on my nerves like that either. "Cuz I tried it myself," I snapped. I bent to pick up one of the baby's toys that was close to my chair and handed it to him.

Rachael stared at me with her mouth hanging open like I was slow. Since I caught her attention, I explained myself. "It ain't like Voodoo my religion or nothing, but I tried it, and it works."

Rachael looked at me, still half bug eyed like she didn't know what to say. "You what?"

Trying to explain something to a fool can make you more than tired. "Yes I tried it. I ain't ashamed cause of what was done to me!"

She had her eyebrows raised to the top of her head and her eyes all big looking at me like I was a loon fresh released. "Uh huh." She kept blinking.

I don't know why I even bothered, ain't no use trying to explain nothing to somebody who figures they already got all the answers, even if you can see that they ain't got a clue. "Evil exists and I know it. When I left Larry for good, I thought that everything was over and done with. I lost another child, and I was glad to be rid of him. But when I got back home, Richard, Sr. told me it was important that I get myself checked out to make sure everything was okay. I did. Went to Dr. Evans, he did an exam and told me that I needed to have a hysterectomy. I had developed scar tissue in my womb, and my time of the month would be worse than what it already was. Without the hysterectomy, I would have female problems for the rest of my life."

Rachael bent over at the waist and started stretching out her arms until her waist and back were stretched out on the floor, but she was still sitting. Vee just crawled and flopped down with her head next to Rachael's and her arms stretched out. "Bea, as hard and horrible as all of that was, it still doesn't make Voodoo real."

Hearing her say that really got my goat. What did she know about the pits of hell? When Dr. Evans told me that, I felt like the bottom dropped out from under me. I gave up on any hopes or dreams I had about ever having a child of my own. "Don't you tell nobody," I demanded. "I ain't never told nobody this but you. Everybody knows who to go to for fortune telling, so I went. I wasn't interested in no fortune telling. What I wanted was a spell."

Rachael held up her hand. "Wait a minute. You mean to tell me that you actually paid your good hard earned money for a so called spell?"

"Yes, I most certainly did," I snapped. "You can think what you want. But, honey, I'm telling you, ever since then, Larry ain't had nothing but bad luck."

"Yeah right"

"I'm serious," I sniffed. "It wasn't hardly a year went by before he got discharged."

"He drank," Rachael said, raising her voice. "He was bound to get discharged."

"Well that don't account for his wife dying and getting sick."

"Bea, people die."

"Yeah, well now his daughter can't stand him. She talk to me more than she do her own daddy."

She looked at me with her face all scrunched up. "Hello, the man is an alcoholic that beat her mother. Don't you think that might have something to do with why she can't stand him. But then again," she said raising both hands in defeat. "Have it your way, Voodoo lady. You can believe whatever you want."

She was getting on my nerves so bad. "Everything ain't a joke. I ain't no Devil worshipper. I only did it that one time!" I shouted.

"Dang," she said, laughing. "Calm down. You're serious about this aren't you?"

I tried to control myself, this was the second time that I been accused of being a devil worshipper. "You better believe I'm serious. The devil is alive and well. That's what I'm trying to tell you. Be careful of that mess you fooling with."

"Uh huh. When I was four, I backed Aunt Della's car out the drive way. I told my dad that the devil made me do it. That's what you sound like now—a four year old, blaming her mistakes on the devil."

I wanted to choke her. "Now you telling me not to believe in the devil. You think everything is my fault!" I screamed on the verge of tears.

"Bea, calm down," Rachael urged, coming up off the floor and sitting like a normal person. "I didn't tell you to believe in anything one way or the other. You can believe what you want. But for a person who believes in God, why give the devil so much power over your life? If you're going to believe in God, then believe in him. You the one keeping secrets, hiding stuff from people, always worried about people up in your business. Instead of worrying about the devil, look at the people like Virginia, Red, and Dr. Evans that God has placed around you as a blessing."

This time I was the one with nothing to say. I had never thought of it that way before. But she had it worked out too simple. "The devil is tricky. He has a way of getting you to do things."

"So you're telling me that an evil little man with a pitch fork and tail been whispering in your ear and the ears of the people around trying to ensure that bad things happen to you?"

"You just trying to be funny. I ain't saying all that. The devil is alive and well. I suggest you know it."

"Whatever! I get sick of people talking about some kind of devil. I'm trying to do my concentrating on God wherever or whoever he is. Way I figure it, if I focus on the one the other will disappear."

"I heard you talk foolishness before, but now you telling me that you don't believe in the devil."

"Why should I?" I asked.

"How can you believe in God if you don't?"

Vee finally got tired of all that yoga nonsense. She got up from the floor, came over to my chair, and started playing with the baby.

"I guess it all depends on how you look at it. It's because I believe in God that it doesn't matter. With God on my side, what can the devil do to me? It's called faith. You walk around like the only reason you believe in God in the first place is to get away from the devil."

"So what's wrong with that? The important thing is that I

believe!"

"Yeah, but the question is what you believe in. You go to mass two and three times a week sometimes and ask for forgiveness, but you can't even forgive yourself. If you believe in God like you say you do, what is the problem?"

"Now see here," I said, putting the baby back down on the floor with his toys. "I don't play around with my religion! You know I believe in God. Look at all the time I spend in confession and at Mass."

Rachael stopped pressing her knees with her elbows and looked at me. "So what good has it done you if you doing all this believing? You still depressed, walking around mad at the world. At what point is all this religion going to come in and save you? Where does your faith really lie? At some point you have to stop being the victim. Bad things do happen to good people. When you realize that, you can become a survivor."

I stood up from my chair and lost it for real. "You ole yellow bitch."

"So now you want to cuss me out? I'm sorry. I forgot, the devil made you do it!"

I walked over to the door leading into the mudroom, with my hand on my hips. I knew I shouldn't have cussed like that in front of the children, so I tried to control myself. "You got some nerve telling me what I need to know and what I need to do. Since when did you learn everything?"

Rachael bent at the waist and pulled her head toward her tops of her toes. "I don't know everything. I don't know hardly anything at all, except that at the very least you deserve to be happy."

It shouldn't have made me no never mind what she believed

one way or the other. I still couldn't help but think about what she had said. People kill me who always wanna pick out the parts in the bible they like and forget about the rest. It ain't like I got it all figured out either. That's the main reason why I do go to mass and take my confession. But I do know this, the bible clearly says that there is a devil and that there is a war between good and evil. My whole life feels like I have been caught up right in the middle of that war.

Thinkin' about it gave me a good mind to call Eunique and give him what for! Course he hung up as soon as he heard my voice. That made me even madder. I don't know what I expected him to do. Lord knows he wasn't about to come in apologizing. Sittin' in that lawyer's office, he was spittin' out lies like a professional. If it had been a movie, he'd a got an Academy Award. It wasn't no sense crying over spilt milk. I tried to get my mind off of him, but I couldn't!

I started thinking to hell with everybody. All of 'em could go to hell: Virginia, Rachael, Red, Father Donahue, and everybody else that came to mind. I was sick of all of 'em telling me what I should do, could do, and wouldn't do. I was a grown damn woman and my daddy didn't raise no fool.

Life for me would have been so different if Daddy had lived. The more I thought about that, the more I thought about how much I missed him. I started remembering how he'd take us out on Sunday afternoon bike rides, and how he always got me two scoops of ice cream instead of one, even though Mother was standing there giving him the evil eye. Next thing you know, I was missing R. Thomas. Nobody could have fun like him and me. He was one of a kind. Why did he have to go and get sick?

Folks never did want to believe that it wasn't his fault. People are funny that way, if you have cancer they send cards and flowers of sympathy, but when it comes to mental illness, they want to act like somehow you caused your own self to get sick. It's a shame some of the things they said behind our backs.

Maybe Mother tried to keep him close to home because she didn't want him to get hurt. I don't know, for so long I been used to the idea that she was a mean, evil, old thing. Maybe she wasn't. What if I missed out on her love because she was right all along, and I just didn't want to listen. Everything seemed so sad and hopeless. How was I going to start over again at my age? I was too old to learn a trade, and my carpel tunnel stopped me from doing the one I knew. I was barely making ends meet with the rent I collected from all six of my properties. How was I going to live off of the rent of three?

I got up to go look in my medicine cabinet for something to help me get to sleep. Sleep seemed like the only way to stop my heart from feelin' so heavy. I needed to ease some of that weight that was layin' on my heart. Course wasn't nothing in there, the last thing I had money for was some sleepin' pills. I would have even swallowed a bottle of that nasty Nyquil to get me some relief. If I'd had a car, I would have drove myself over to Kroger. My damn car wasn't worth a shit, so I called somebody. I don't even know who I called. My fingers took over and did the dialin for me.

CHAPTER NINETEEN
RACHAEL

Something serious was going on with Bea. I mean, something outside of her normal drama. She always had a dark cloud hanging overhead. Lately, it was like the cloud had started thundering and lightening. Anything you mentioned to her brought on a tirade.

I asked her to come with me to pick up the kids Easter dresses from the cleaners, and she spent the entire ride going on about how the cleaner was no good.

"I don't know why Virginia insists on using this cleaners."

"Why do you say that?" I asked, pulling the car up to the cleaners drive through window.

"Because," Bea said in a huff as we waited for the little old lady who was working the window, "they messed up one of Mother's best dinner jackets."

I stared at her incredulous. "Did you say one of your mother's jackets?"

"Yes, I did."

I handed the lady my items and waited for her to write up the ticket. As we were leaving the cleaners, I turned to Bea. "How long ago was that?"

"Fifteen years ago, if that makes any difference. All they had to do was take out a little bitty stain. Instead, they made a hole in it. Virginia said it was a mistake, but I believe they did it on purpose."

I agreed with Virginia, it probably was an accident. Either way, you would have thought that it had happened just the day before the way she was carrying on; never mind that the person who did the damage was probably long gone by now.

Bea finally stopped raving about that when she saw Henrietta's old pastor in the drug store. "You see him?" she asked, pointing to man so old he needed the help of a nurse to get around.

I closed my eyes. "Yes," I muttered, begging her silently not to make a scene.

Bea proclaimed in a voice loud enough for everyone in the store to hear. "He refused to come out to the house and give Mother communion."

Damn, why didn't I have powers of invisibility? I realized there were a lot of people who would have been upset by his refusal. But the more she got into telling me what had happened, the louder she got. People were beginning to look at us. The poor man had to know that she was talking about him. Everybody standing around the counter did.

She turned to the man standing beside her. "Now mister, would your pastor do that to you?"

The poor man, he looked like a trapped mouse. "I, I, I don't know."

Not satisfied with his answer, she turned to the lady behind him. "What about you?" she said, pointing to the woman. "Would your pastor do that?

"You know ministers now a days ain't worth the cloth in their choir robes!" the lady answered.

"Yes, ma'am. You right about that, too. I want every body to know because I'm still alive to tell it. Mother was a charter member and faithful all her life. Im'ma tell you something else too. Pastor Edwards—and I said his name cause I want all of you here to repeat it—didn't have no trouble visiting her when she was alive and writing checks. Oh no," she said, pointing at the minister and his nurse who was helping him to shuffle away from Bea's line of fire. "He was her best friend in the world then."

I was so embarrassed I left her at the counter and pretended to shop for makeup. Out of the corner of my eye, I could see the pastor trying his best to ignore her. The more she ranted, the straighter he stood, which must have been hard. The man was only as old as Methuselah.

Finally, as Bea's conversation with the woman grew louder, the pastor turned to leave. He didn't bother waiting on his prescription.

Bea followed the poor man out of the store. He walked faster trying to escape her, but his feeble legs and cane could only go so fast. When he got inside his car, he said something to the woman at the wheel. The woman took off, burning rubber in the process. Bea was still going at it, and she moved only a little bit faster than the Pastor. She almost got run over which only called more attention to the entire scene.

Humiliated, I watched the whole thing from inside the drugstore. Not daring to come out until the Pastor was gone. Pulling out of the parking lot, I shrunk down in my seat so low I could barley see over the steering wheel. I hoped no one saw me. I was fuming.

"Do you really think all of that was necessary?" I asked

through clenched teeth fastening my grip on the steering wheel in an attempt to control my temper.

Bea didn't say a word. She remained quiet the entire trip home.

After putting the kids to bed, I went downstairs to the den where Virginia was watching television. I know that I promised to keep Bea's confidence, but, I felt like I'd done all that I could do. No matter how much we talked it over, or what advice I gave, she didn't seem to be doing any better. I was hoping that she'd feel better once she took legal action against the con man. Instead, she seemed to be getting worse. Her hair was a mess, she barley left the house, and she didn't seem to care. All she wanted to do was lay in bed, watch her stories, and fuss. Virginia really needed to know what was going on with her sister. I was worried about Bea.

I spent the first few minutes trying to decide how to initiate the conversation. Months had passed, and I still hadn't decided what to call Virginia. I could have called her by her first name, but that didn't seem respectful enough. Calling her by her last name felt too impersonal. There was something weird about referring to someone as Mrs. Roberts when you are Mrs. Roberts and related to her by marriage. I decided to jump right to the heart of things without calling her anything.

"I'm really worried about Bea," I said, sitting next to Virginia on the sofa.

It took her a minute to realize I was talking to her, but when she did, she turned off the television. Virginia put down the remote in her hand, turned to me and asked, "How is that?"

I started picking the fringe of one of the sofa pillows. "She is just so irritable lately, flying off the handle at the least little things. I dunno, I think that she's depressed."

Virginia eyes focused in on my hands, which were pulling at the fringe. "Yes. I noticed, but she can be so secretive I don't know what's happening with her. Asking her would only lead to a disagreement. Did she say anything to you in particular that led you to this conversation?"

I felt my face flush under Virginia's gaze and placed the pillow to the side. Putting my hands together in my lap, I thought for a second. "Well, I am not sure what you mean exactly but... She does seem to be focused on the loss of your parents and R. Thomas. It's almost like she wants to join them. She hasn't said that she wants to kill herself, but...she talks about death like it would be a relief."

Virginia let out another long sigh. Her shoulders dropped slightly, she seemed so tired. "A friend of Bea's called me a few days ago; she was also worried about her. Bea called her in the middle of the night, crying and rambling. Faye didn't know what to make of what Bea was saying. The next morning she went to see her. Bea told her that her legs were bothering her, and she wasn't in the mood for company. She was still worried and felt it best to inform me," Virginia said.

"Now what?"

Virginia drew herself up, set her shoulders back, and lifted her head. "I'll make a few phone calls."

I felt both relief and guilt. I was relieved that the situation would be taken care of but at the same time, I felt that I had betrayed Bea's confidence. Loyalty was a real sticking point with Bea. She would drop me in a heartbeat if she felt betrayed in any way.

"So do the children have anything to wear on Easter Sunday?"

"Yes."

"Both girls have dresses?"

"Yes."

"Are you sure that they fit correctly?"

I was sure that they didn't fit wrong if that is what she meant. "Yes I'm sure."

"Well you might want to try them on again. You know how quickly children grow."

My stomach started to get queasy. I saw where this was heading. I rose from the couch and headed toward the stairs.

My back was to the bedroom door when Virginia knocked. I rolled my eyes and gritted my teeth.

"Do you have all of their accessories ready: socks, shoes, ribbons?"

She followed me up the stairs to ask me that, amazing! That's when it hit me, why not be proactive? I got up from the bed, went around to the closet, and pulled out the dresses. I took the dresses out of the cleaners' bags and threw the plastic away. I hated having that stuff around with little kids in the house. "Here are the dresses that the girls are going to wear."

They really were pretty dresses. Sherril had a pale pink dress made of raw silk. It was a sailor dress with a creamy lace collar, and it stopped just short of the ankle. The dress also had a slip sewn in, which made the purchase of one unnecessary. It was a Martha Miniature. Normally, I couldn't afford to have bought such an expensive dress. I picked this one up from my girlfriend's garage sale last year. This was only one of the many dresses that her daughter had out grown. All of them were fabulous. My friend Serrita had great taste. With only one child; she was able to indulge it. The dress was perfect. The dry cleaner had done a wonderful job. It looked brand new.

Virginia took a long look at the dresses. "These dresses are really nice. We'll just send them to the cleaners," she said, taking the dresses out of the closet.

I showed her the ticket. "I already had them cleaned." I took the dresses back and returned them to the closet.

"Do you have a sweater, a cape, or something that the girls might wear over them? It is still cool in the mornings."

I hadn't thought of the cool mornings. As for the rest, I was speechless. Obviously, she didn't regard the cleaning job as highly as I did. The old me wouldn't have said anything, but this was the new me. "Virginia, they've already been cleaned at the cleaners you recommended. There is no sense in wasting the money to have them cleaned again."

Virginia looked at me for a second. "You're right," she agreed. "Why don't we all go out together to purchase accessories?"

Thank God, I prayed silently. "Good. I need to buy stockings and maybe a new pair of earrings. So, I'd love to."

The following day, Virginia left work early for our day of shopping. The sun was shining bright, and, fortunately, the weather hadn't turned unbearably hot yet. Everything was in full bloom. It turns out that Virginia was Ms. Horticulture. "That is cross vine," she said, describing a wild vine that was climbing with red flowers, climbing a billboard ahead of us.

"What's that, Grandma?" Sherril asked, pointing to another vine that was growing wild.

"Oh, honey, that is clematis. My mother, your great grandmother, used to love clematis. In the summer, the white flowers give off the most beautiful fragrance. It used to grow all over her courtyard."

"Grandma, can we plant some flowers?" Sherril asked.

Of course we can baby."

Virginia went straight to Belk's department store. Belk's wasn't a store that I would normally go to, but it was an institution to women Virginia's age. Most of their items were too conservative for me. They seemed to specialize in items for the southern belle there. It was the perfect place to go if you wanted your little girl to look like a little girl. Virginia insisted on buying everything for the kids. "It's what a grandmother is supposed to do. It's what we live for, spoiling our grandchildren." They got dress shoes, socks, slips, hair ribbons the whole kit and caboodle. They'd had such I good time, I found their mood infectious. What was the point in getting upset that Virginia wanted to buy her grandchildren a few things? Besides, the items she bought were nice. Virginia didn't believe in buying a lot of off brand junk.

I loved to go shopping with my grandmother when I was a little girl. We would go to all of the better malls in the Detroit area, and she'd buy up the stores! I swear, when we shopped in stores where the people worked commission, she became their friends for life. She bought me my first grown up Easter outfit. It was a cream colored, summer wool suit, from Saks Fifth Ave. That year she also bought me my first pair of nylons and a pair of cream-colored wedge heel shoes. Even though the heels were only ½ an inch, I walked around like they were three inches high. My mother wouldn't let me wear the outfit on Easter Sunday; I had to wear it to Good Friday service instead. For Easter, I wore this stupid lacey dress that came all the way to the floor. I looked like a twelve year old dweeb instead of the sophisticated young miss that I wanted to portray.

Virginia and I agreed that Elliot should get a suit. Going through the rack I started tearing up. My baby was almost one year old. Virginia held up a Mint green suit jacket and a pair of white short pants.

"I think that it would look best with a white shirt with a Peter Pan collar."

I was too choked up to speak, so I nodded.

Virginia smiled. "I remember when both of my boys got their first suits."

After picking out his suit, we headed to the shoe department. "Would you look at these," I said, picking up a pair of white patent leather high tops. Sherril had the exact same pair.

Virginia smiled. "I like it when children look like children, instead of like little adults."

So true so true," I agreed. Time was running out. Elliot was starting to get whiney and Vee was getting wound up. She kept pulling shoes down to try-on.I It didn't matter if they were for adults, kids or men. At first Sherril went running behind her trying to restrain her while Virginia and I picked out shoes. Finally, Sherrill gave up and came to sit beside me. I had to hold Vee on my lap while Virginia helped put on Elliot's new shoes.

"Oh, you look so pretty," I said to Vee who finally stopped wiggling when she had her new shoes on. She hopped down from my lap and went to stand in front of a full length mirror.

Virginia laughed. "I think we have a model in the family."

I didn't even bother taking Vee's shoes off of her little feet. It wasn't worth the hassle. Sherril was pleased when the sales clerk gave her a sucker. It wasn't until we were dragging ourselves out of the store that I remembered my stockings. Never mind, I decided. I'd rather get them from the gas station than deal with the kids.

Saturday morning when Richard arrived, we were all in a festive mood. Our bank account was benefiting from his hard work. He walked into my bedroom Saturday morning, picked up the baby and handed me a one hundred dollar bill.

"What's this for?"

"The kid's Easter," he said in between blowing raspberries on the baby's neck.

I wasn't about to spend that much money on Easter basket's for three kids under age six. But there wasn't any sense telling him that. "It's already April, and June is right around the corner. We need to actually start looking for a house." I thought I noticed Richard tense up.

"We are still planning on going back to Atlanta in June, right?'

He came over to my bed and sat down with the baby. "Of course."

"Then what's the plan?"

Richard lay back on the bed and started to throw the baby up in the air. Elliot loved it. The higher he flew up in the air, the more he laughed. My heart couldn't take it, I turned my head. "We need to start looking for a house," he answered finally.

A house. He made it sound like it was as easy as going to the store and buying a lollipop. "Well, I have been looking on-line, and I've picked out the ones in our price range. One is down-town," I said, taking the baby away from him.

Richard stared up at me from his position on my lap. "Downtown is too expensive and not enough yard for kids and a dog."

I put Elliot down so that he could cruise along the bed. He was going to be walking any day now. "We don't even have a dog," I said to Richard.

"Yeah," he agreed. "But, I want my kids to have one."

"Whatever," I said, shaking my head. We needed to deal with first things first. "We need to get a real estate agent. I mean, we know how much money we are going to put down, and how much house we want. But, a real estate agent can help make the whole process easier."

"Well, Rosalyn got a deal on her house."

I cringed at the sound of that woman's name. I mean, I know that I was trying to be a new and improved me, but Rome was-n't built in a day. "Oh, she did?"

Richard sat up. "Let me show you something," he said, walk-ing over to his bag in the corner. He pulled out a picture. "Did I ever show you this picture of Rosalyn?" He walked over to me and handed out the picture.

I couldn't see what a picture had to do with anything, but I took it anyway. My mouth dropped. The picture was of two women one in a wedding dress and the other in a pants suit. The two women were standing together in what looked like a sanctuary and they were kissing. "What is this?" I asked.

"That is a picture of Rosalyn and her wife," Richard answered, smiling.

My ears burned. "Wife?" I asked, taking another look at the picture. I felt so stupid. I know that it was stupid of me to think that she couldn't be gay just because she was so attractive. Like all gay women looked like a softer version of a man. But, what can I say, I am human.

"Yes, wife," Richard answered, laughing. "So you can stop being jealous."

"I am not jealous," I protested. I busied myself with changing Elliot's diaper so that I wouldn't have to face Richard. He wasn't about to let me off that easy.

"Of course you weren't," he said, pressing up against my back. "That is why your face is so red. So you want to talk about buying a house or what?"

"Yeah, we can talk about it, but I would love to see how you would behave if I started driving another man's car."

Richard put his hands on my shoulders, and turned me around so that we were standing face to face. Lifting my chin, his eyes searched mine. I smelled the coffee on his breath. "Have I ever given you reason to believe that I would cheat on you?"

I tried to look away, but he wouldn't let me. "No."

"Then I am not going to start now."

"I wanted to believe you but…"

"There is no but," he said kissing me. "How do you think it made me feel? All this time I have been working my ass off, and you've been acting like a straight…"

I cut him off with a kiss.

"So where do we start?" I asked as I pulled Elliot out of the closet. That boy was going to be worse than Vee.

"I already talked to Arnold." Richard said, laying back on the bed.

I was busy looking into Elliot's mouth. He was chewing on something.

"Baby, did you hear me?"

"Huh? Oh yeah." I pulled a Barbie shoe out of Elliot's mouth. I hated all of those little Barbie things, between the baby and the vacuum, they seemed to turn up everywhere, that and Brite Lite pegs.

Arnold was Richard's friend who owned a mortgage company. "What did he say?"

"He said that all we had to do was place an article in the real estate section of the paper saying that we wanted to buy a house, no money down no credit check. Arnold said we could forgo all of the saving and waiting and skip straight to purchasing."

I thought about what he'd said as I pulled one of Elliot's favorite toys from his crib. What he was proposing seemed rather circumspect to me. Who would want to sell a house that way? Not me, not unless something was wrong, and I was in a hurry to get rid of it "I don't know Richard. What if it doesn't work?" I waved the toy in Elliot's face trying to grab his attention with it.

"If it doesn't work, all you have to lose is the money that you spent on the ad."

"But then I don't get to pick what kind of house I get. I'll be limited to where I have to move and to the size and condition of the house. I don't want to buy somebody else's junk."

Richard rubbed his eyes like what I was saying irritated his brain. "Look," he said, taking a deep breath, "it doesn't have to be someone else's junk."

"Then why would someone sell their house that way?"

"There are a lot of reasons why, maybe the person is getting a divorce and they can't afford the house anymore, maybe they got a job transfer. Whatever the reason, it's not our problem. We just want a good deal on a house."

I was getting frustrated. This whole idea of placing an ad seemed so speculative, too speculative for me. The sense of excitement that I had about purchasing my brand new house downtown started to fade.

"Why does it have to be junk? Remember the townhouse Arnold had? That's how he bought it."

Arnold lucked out and bought a nice townhouse, but that didn't mean that I would have the same luck. Besides, I had my heart set on a custom built home downtown. I saw my dream house fading away.

"Maybe we won't be that lucky."

"It's not about luck, there's more than one way to buy a house." From the tone of his voice, I could see that he was agitated. That was when he suggested that we compromise. "Okay, I can see how uncomfortable you are. Let's just do both. We can place the ad and go the traditional route. That way if we find a house, cool, and if we don't we'll still be able to buy one your way."

Easter morning, the kids looked picture perfect. The bows that Virginia bought for the girls in addition to their lace socks and coordinating purses really topped off their beautiful dresses. We did that entire sweater searching for nothing; the morning sun was fully shining.

Virginia cooked a traditional Easter breakfast complete with cross buns. I'd never even heard of cross buns but Virginia explained that they were special on Easter Morning because the icing was put on in the shape of a cross. She also decorated the table with Easter Lilies. Instead of beginning breakfast with the usual prayer, Virginia told the story of the Easter lily.

Often called the "white-robed apostles of hope" lilies were found growing in the garden of Gethsemane after Christ's agony. Tradition has it that the beautiful white lilies spring up where drops of Christ's sweat fell to the ground in his final hours of sorrow and distress. Christian churches continue this tradition at Easter by banking their altars and surrounding their crosses with masses of Easter lilies to commemorate the Resurrection and hope of life everlasting.

The fact that she took the time and interest to go to that trouble really touched my heart. Instead of being a day that kids get dressed up and look for Easter eggs and baskets, Virginia turned it into a special family holiday. I made a mental note to continue the tradition.

CHAPTER TWENTY
BEA

I should have known something was going on when Virginia called me about an appointment she scheduled with my therapist. I didn't say nothing at the time. I was smoking in bed and my cigarette fell out my mouth. I was too busy putting out the cigarette before it set my bed on fire to bother with what Virginia was saying. I didn't get curious until she called to remind me to be ready, but she hung up the phone before I could get into it with her. I really got suspicious when she picked me up on time.

"Your therapist tells me that you haven't been keeping your appointments."

"When did it become your job to keep up with me and my therapist?" I was being nasty, but I didn't give a damn. At sixty-four, I figured I didn't have to account to nobody.

"She called me and asked me to attend the session. Care to tell me why?"

If my therapist was calling her, she had all of the information she needed. What was she asking me for? It didn't matter one way or the other what I had to say. But knowin' Virginia, she had to hear it from me. Since she started the game, I decided to play. "I look like a fool old as I am telling some young white lady, barely out of pampers, my problems. Besides, I don't have money to waste on a bunch of nonsense."

Virginia looked at me like I was the dumbest thing on the

planet. "Bea, you're being ridiculous. The woman's race has nothing to do with anything. She is a professional and you're in need of professional assistance. Anyway, I put in a few phone calls to some people that I know at the Department of Human Resources. Your disability should be finalized by the end of the week."

"It's about time." I put my hand on my head and massaged my temple.

"Darling, the employees at DHS are understaffed and overworked. It usually takes a lot longer than a few months to get Disability started."

Virginia thought she knew every darn thing. Once she got on a roll, it was hard getting around her. "I talk to my priest. You can't get no more professional than God."

That ought to shut her mouth.

"Then what is this I hear about you and sleeping pills?"

My mouth fell open. What ever happened to trust and friendship? I was half out of my mind when I asked for the sleeping pills. Even so, I expected confidence. That goes to show, folks don't know what true friendship is no more. "So there is a law against sleeping pills?"

"Huh." She sighed. "You know as well as I do that you haven't been doing well as of late."

As of late, I get sick of her talking to me like I'm one of them girls that she counsels at that college of hers. I was tired of her treating me like a child. "You the one started it. You had no business calling my therapist in the first place"

Virginia gave another long sigh. When she sighs like that, you didn't know what she was thinking. It got on my nerves.

I looked right back at her and said, "What?"

"How many people do I have to lose?"

Even though she had children, grandchildren, and plenty of friends, she felt the same way I did. The two of us were all that was left of Daddy and Mother. All we had was each other. We rode the rest of the way in silence.

I hardly heard a word that Miss Jacobs said, had too much on my mind. Mostly, I was trying to figure out if it really was a sin to commit suicide. That is what the Church said, but maybe Rachael was right. Maybe the Church don't know everything. I was a good Catholic, doing what I'm supposed to do. I said my prayers and went to mass on a regular basis. Ain't no denying the fact that I am a charitable person? I had a healthy fear of God, what more could he want from me. Then I started thinking about the devil. What if he was trying to trick me that suicide wasn't a sin just so that I would go to hell? That is what the devil does, trick people so that he can win their souls. As miserable as life was for me, I didn't want to spend eternity in a lake of fire.

Miss Jacobs put her hand on mine, interrupting my thoughts. "Would you care to tell me why you are being so non-communicative?"

I looked at her in disgust. Why couldn't she talk plain some-time? Everyone that came into her office saw that she had a degree. If I wasn't communicating, it was because I was tired. Bone tired. Shrugging my shoulders, I told her, "I been in this ongoing battle otherwise known as my life for over fifty years, and everyday is looking like a better day to surrender. That is exactly what I feel like doing."

I looked over to Virginia, trying to read the expression on her face. I couldn't tell what she was thinking. She sat up straight in her chair, adjusting her blazer and patting her hair. She was fidgeting in that chair, trying to do everything but look at me.

Ms. Jacobs looked back and forth between the two of us. "So surrender. I asked your sister here so that you can share your experience with her. Sometimes it helps to talk about our feelings with our loved ones."

I ran my fingers through my hair. Wasn't no sense in fighting. I gave up all my feelings of anger and the secrets that I been keeping for the better part of my life sitting right there in that office. I told Virginia everything. I could barely look her in the face when I told her about my missing child, but I told her. True to herself, Virginia didn't say a word. She shifted around in her seat and sighed. But she didn't say not one single word, and I was grateful.

At the end of my session, Miss Jacobs asked if it was okay if she spoke freely in front of Virginia.

"Of course," I answered. She was the one who had invited Virginia there in the first place. Wasn't any point in keeping anything from her now?

"Well, I am diagnosing you for clinical depression."

"Oh lord." I slapped my hand against my forehead. I was worried because I was too old and broke to be getting what R. Thomas had.

Virginia finally spoke. "Wait a minute Bea, let her finish."

Ms. Jacobs explained, "Clinical depression is nothing like

manic depression. In fact, many women suffer from some form of depression in their life. You don't have anything to be ashamed of. Think of clinical depression as a prolonged sadness that you can't get over. I want to confer with Dr. Evans and get you a prescription for some medicine that will make you feel a whole lot better."

"Humph!" I said. "It must be a miracle drug."

CHAPTER TWENTY-ONE
RACHAEL

I tried to make daily entries into my journal and do the exercises in my Creative Visualizations workbook. While the kids were occupied with their cartoon, I took the opportunity to sit on the couch and try to make my entry. It wasn't easy because I had to fight with Elliot who was now mobile enough to cruise from one piece of furniture to the next. Of course, he loved nothing better than to interrupt whatever I was doing. I gently pushed his little chubby hand away as he grabbed for my journal and continued writing. It's no surprise that Vee was writing in her own journal. That girl was a sponge. She kept looking over to my paper to check and see what I was doing as if she could read and write.

It's amazing how much attention you pay to the ordinary things in life when you decide to write about it everyday. On the mundane days, you tend to make the ordinary extraordinary. Like you're afraid that someone is going to read your journal and think that you are a drone instead of this fascinating person. At least that is how it started out for me. At first, it was a chore thinking up all of those witty thoughts, and then I thought to hell with it. By the time someone got their hands on my journal, they should know me anyway, and if they didn't, so what. Besides, those were my private thoughts written for me and by me. Once I stopped faking the funk, the real me started to appear in my entries.

It took about a week for me to realize that I was not a woman of action. According to what I wrote in my journal, I spent more time thinking about what it was that I wanted than actually doing what it took to get it. I decided to make a list of all of my goals, starting with the short term and working toward long term. From that point on, I would do one thing every day that would move me toward my goal.

It felt good to start checking off things on my goal list. I looked at my list and realized that without even giving it much thought, I'd done half of the things on it. I'd submitted my article, we were well on the way to getting or own house, and all of the financial stuff was falling in place. I put away my journal and pulled out my laptop and checkbook.

Committing to a budget brought us a long way. Early in our marriage, Richard was always trying to get me to talk about budgeting, but I was resistant. First of all, we had two different ideas about what our budget should be. Instead of compromising, we always ended the discussion arguing. My wants and desires didn't have a space in his idea of what our budget should be. His did, or at least that is how it seemed to me. He claimed that once he got his thing off the ground, it would be my turn. Six years later, I was sick of waiting and pass the point of arguing. No, I was moved to the point of indifference; those little budgets didn't mean a damn thing to me. The other thing that made our budgets useless—at least in my opinion—was the fact that they always projected what we needed to make as opposed to what we actually brought in. Till this point, I had developed the attitude of, "Whatever just get the bills paid."

Budgeting used to scare me; it was definitely not my deal. I used to think that committing to one was too restraining. What if I was in the mall and saw a pair of shoes that I liked that were not in my budget? Buying them would give me same guilty feeling that I have the first time I break my New Year's Resolution. It was an endless cycle of trying it again then breaking it again, and nobody wants to do that year-round.

But, since I'd arranged all of our bills according to the amount we owed. Which was another little trick that I learned on Oprah. I found that I loved to watch the amount dwindle in the column marked amount owed, each time I paid a bill. At the rate we were going, all of our bills would be paid off at the end of April. Man that felt good.

After making my entries, I was surprised to see that we were officially out of the red. "Woo hoo!" I screamed so loud I startled Elliot and he started crying. Praise the Lord and thank you Jesus. I jumped up grabbed the baby off of the floor and started singing and started singing, "We won, we won." Vee bounced all around the den right along with me. I had to restrain myself because we almost knocked over my computer. Anybody watching would have thought that I'd just scored the winning basket in the championship game.

When Richard called to see how I was doing, he was tickled to death. "Girl, if I knew you were going to get this serious about keeping a budget, I would have moved you in with Mama a long time ago."

"Ha, ha, ha. I am proud to announce that we are now one of the few, the proud, the debtless." I bowed down, even though he couldn't see me through the phone.

"You been talking to Mama?"

"No. Mr. Funny Man, I saw it on Oprah."

"I should have guessed."

"Anyway, you wouldn't believe how much money we used to spend on fast foods. McDonald's fries, shakes and ice cream were costing us a fortune. By cutting out fast foods, I paid off our small bills in three months."

"You go, girl."

"Baby."

"Yeah."

"Thanks for not saying I told you so. Budgeting isn't so bad after all. Whereas before our finances were a dark cloud always looming overhead, now I can see the light at the end of the tunnel. Now that we are going to have a little extra cash, we can start buying small stuff for our house."

"Baby, let's get the house first."

Whatever. Think positive, that was my motto. It was my personal goal to become a paragon of positive thinking. I included in my monthly budget one hundred toward the purchase of things for my new home. No more scratchy sheets, cheap bath towels, and making toast from the broiler in the oven. "So you're still picking us up this Thursday so that we can start looking at houses."

"I'll be there Wednesday night and we can leave Thursday morning. But I gotta go. I want to get some sleep before I go to work tonight. "

"I love you," I said, hanging up the phone.

Thursday morning, we left with the kids and drove to Atlanta in a car that Richard bought at an auction. The car made a beeping noise all the way to Atlanta. In an attempt to drown out the beeping, we sang until they fell asleep. With the kids asleep, I tried my best to tune out the noise. I refused to let that constant high-pitched noise claw my brain like a pair of talons. The more I thought about what it was that we were planning to do, the less I heard the sound, until it finally became a white noise.

Earlier in the week, I got in touch with Rob, an old friend of mine. My cousin told me that he was becoming really active in the community, rehabbing houses. I found out that he was on the board of directors of an association working to revitalize inner city communities. Ta da! I was already on track to fulfilling my list, not even consciously might I add. He told me all of the rehab work his group was doing in town buying dilapidated housing, selling it and buying more housing. They had already completed ten houses and were just beginning on a new group of houses.

When we got to Atlanta, we only had forty five minutes before our appointment with Rob. Course we weren't taking the kids, so we dropped them off with Richard's intern at the studio. I was pleased to see improvements at the place, like the wall-to-wall carpeting. They also fixed up the lounge. I wasn't too happy that they were using my couch, but at least I could see that my stay at Virginia's wasn't in vain. I put a new couch on my list of things to get for the new house. There was no way I wanted a bunch of greasy, smoking musicians or who so nevers sitting on my stuff. Later for that, I was on a mission.

The houses that Rob showed us were very nice. The first house he took us inside was his. "Keeping in touch with the architecture of the neighborhood," Rob said motioning to the houses on the street, "this house is built along the bungalow style."

I could tell by the expression on Richard's face that he wasn't impressed with the size of the yard, but his face brightened when he saw the hardwood floors inside.

Rob walked to the middle of the front room. "This is the living room, you can see that it gets lots of sunlight." He turned and walked to the back of the room toward an open doorway. Stopping at the door he motioned inside. "This is the kitchen."

Richard and I followed him to the doorway. The kitchen was way too small for us. You couldn't even fit a small dinette in there.

"I know it's small," Rob explained, "but it comes with great amenities. All of the houses come with stainless steel appliances that includes, stove, refrigerator, and dishwasher. And all of the counter tops are marble."

As nice as the amenities were, it didn't make a bit of difference to me. This was a house for a single person or a couple just starting out together. Our family of five needed something bigger.

"Man, it looks great, but we definitely need something bigger," Richard said.

Rob walked with us back outside. Already, I was falling in love with the neighborhood. It didn't hurt that Rob was doing a great job of selling the community. He motioned to the ongoing construction up and down the street. "The houses that they are building next door are much larger. They are two stories. Unfortunately, there is a waiting list. But you can always put your name on the list. You never know."

I noticed Richard didn't have much to say, but my mind was racing. The more I saw, the more excited I became. "How much will the two stories go for?" I asked. My mind raced with questions.

"We're trying to keep them moderately priced. None will exceed $250,000, but we haven't received the final numbers."

"How many square feet did you say that they would be?" I asked.

"Somewhere in the neighborhood of 1500 to 2000 square feet. I can tell you that it will be 3 - 4 bedrooms, 2 ½ baths, with a great room, and eat in kitchen. Keep in mind, we haven't approved the final designs, and the layouts, but we are still in the planning phase."

"Hmmm," I said, looking at Richard who wasn't even pretending to pay attention.

"I knew you'd be interested. Yours is the type of family that we want in the neighborhood. We want to create a diverse community of families, professionals, and people that have been here for years and want to take their streets back. You feel what I'm saying, a place where people care about where they live and are willing to work to make it special. Some of the houses that you see now belong to law enforcement officers, artists, and people who work for the community organization."

Richard didn't object to my putting my name on the waiting list, but he didn't waste anytime getting out of there either. When we got back in the car, he finally spoke. "You know that those houses are way out of our price range."

"I know," I conceded. I guess I got a little excited. "Let's have lunch."

"Where do you want to go?"

"Thumbs Up Diner." Thumbs Up Diner was one of my favorite inner city lunch spots. They served southern dishes with quirky twists. Thank goodness we got there ahead of the lunch crowd so we didn't have to wait long for a table. I ordered the turkey chili, and Richard ordered vegetarian quesadillas.

"So where do we start?" I asked as we waited for the waitress to return with our food.

"I already put the ad in the paper, and I got a ton of phone calls," Richard said after taking a sip from his water.

Man, it was good to eat at a real restaurant. I watched as the waitress walked past me carrying the breakfast special to the booth behind us. The restaurant was filled with a mix of people. Some were in business suits, some looked like students, and there was an openly gay couple in the booth across from us. Man it was good to be back. I forgot that they served real maple syrup with their pancakes.

"Baby, did you hear me?"

"Huh? Oh yeah. You got a lot of responses."

"We can go and look at the ones that sound the most promising next week. Anyway, I wanted to talk to you about something else."

I sat back in my seat as the waitress served our food. Just like I remembered, my chili smelled and tasted delicious. I took another bite and tried to discern what the secret ingredient was. It tasted like it might be cinnamon. "What's up?" I asked after taking several more bites of chili.

"I want to take some of the money we saved and get come CDs pressed up."

I took a deep breath. I felt a ball forming in the pit of my stomach. "How much?" I asked.

"Just a thousand," he answered.

What did he mean just a thousand, we weren't millionaires, for us, a thousand dollars is more than, "Just a thousand."

"Aren't you going to say anything?" he asked before taking a bite of his food.

"I'm thinking," I answered. I was determined not to panic. I thought about my life over the past few months. It had taken me months to cajole myself into writing an article for a romance magazine that didn't cost me anything but the price of a stamp and a copy of the magazine itself, and here he was ready to invest a thousand on something I had no idea about. "Why do you need CDs?"

"I want to give them out to deejays so that they can start playing NOTE's music in the clubs. I really think that we are going to get a record deal, but creating a buzz can't hurt."

"So how close are you to getting a deal?"

Richard pushed his empty plate away. "Two labels have made offers."

"Then why do you need the buzz?" I asked. I picked up my spoon and pushed the food on my plate around. Everything about the music business was a gamble. Nothing was certain.

"Bargaining power," Richard answered and leaned into the table closer to me.

"Do you talk to God?" I asked and pushed my plate out of the way.

Richard leaned in closer. "Yes, but what has that got to do with anything."

I shrugged. "I don't know, it's just that...well. It always takes me so long to make up my mind because I'm afraid that things won't work out and you seem so...so, fearless."

Richard took both my hands in his. "I talk to God every day. I mean, I don't get on my knees in the traditional way, but we talk. Who do you think has been taking care of us this far?"

He was right. "Take the money," I said and squeezed his hand. I looked away for a second and looked back at Richard. "If I tell you something, will you promise not to throw it in my face when we're having an argument?"

Richard squeezed my hand. "I don't know why you always want me to promise stupid stuff, but yes, I promise."

"I think that I have been jealous of you all of this time. I know I've been a bitch, always afraid that this wouldn't work, or that wouldn't work. I am not going to be like that anymore."

"Baby, I'm just glad you recognized it."

CHAPTER TWENTY-TWO
BEA

I decided that it was time for me to stop avoiding Virginia. After we left my therapists office, she didn't know what to say any more than I did. So we talked about what most people talk about when they are trying to avoid something, the weather. The next morning, Virginia stopped by my house on her way to work to say she wanted to go out to lunch. I wasn't ready to talk to her then either. Virginia persisted though. She continued calling me every hour on the hour until finally I unplugged the phone. Avoiding her was no easy task.

Finally, she came by my house late one night and used her key to get in. I gave her that key in case of an emergency, not to come barging in my home whenever she chose. I was lying in my bed when I heard the key in the door and knew it had to be her. Fine, if she wanted to come barging in my house, I wasn't going to stop her. But, I didn't get out of my bed because I wasn't going to make it easy for her either. I turned off the television and pretended to be asleep, but I don't think she was fooled her.

"You aren't sleeping, Bea. I heard the television when I came in. You are going to have to talk to me sooner or later."

I decided to go ahead and give her a call after she left.

"Hello," Vee answered. She was a mess. I loved the sound of that baby giggling. Her voice is sweet as pure sugar.

"Who is this?" I was trying to be serious as a part of our game it was her job to convince me who she was.

"It's Virginia."

"Virginia who. You don't sound like my sister to me."

"This is Virginia Anderson."

"No, it couldn't be Virginia Anderson, she an old lady. You sound like a little girl."

We had a good laugh together before Virginia came to the phone. "Well, Bea, it's nice to hear from you," Virginia said, like she hadn't left my house minutes earlier.

"I didn't feel much like talking."

"You know, you could have come to me years ago. Why didn't you tell me?"

I reached for a cigarette, lit it, and inhaled before answering her. "I was too shamed to tell anyone."

I heard ice cubes tingling against a glass on her end. "What was there to be ashamed about? The man was a low life. He tried the same thing with me."

I choked on the smoke from my cigarette. "What do you mean he tried the same thing with you?"

"He made passes toward me all of the time. I managed to stay out of his way is all."

Now ain't that something? All these years I thought it was something about me in particular that attracted him to me, and all the while he was running around like a dog in heat.

"Have you thought about finding your son?" Virginia asked.

I stubbed out my cigarette and reached for another one. I wouldn't begin to know how to look for him.

"Bea, are you still there?"

"Yeah, I'm here. I don't know, Virginia. What if I find him

and he can't stand me?"

"What if he's been trying to find you? Things don't always have to have a bad outcome, Bea. You did what you did because you had too."

"I don't know."

"Well, you don't have to decide right away."

I licked my lips. All that smoking was making my mouth dry. I poured myself a glass of ice water. The cold water running down my throat felt good. It cleared my mind a little. "So you don't have anything to say about the con man."

"What is there to say? What's done is done. I talked to Edward about it. He did all that he could. It's time to move on. The next time you have to hide someone from me, I hope you think twice about it."

I rolled my eyes, but she was right. I knew things weren't exactly straight with Eunique from the very beginning. I wasn't going to admit that to Virginia though. "Well, I have to go now."

"Bea."

"Yes." I secretly hoped that she would let it go at that.

"Don't forget to think about it. It might not be easy, but I'm sure we can find your son."

"I will," I promised. "Well, I need to get to sleep."

"Okay, well you have a good night." She hung up the phone, and that was that. It's funny, right when I thought I knew her like the back of my hand, she had to go and surprise me.

I didn't know if it was the medicine the doctor gave me or not but I was feeling different. My dreaming got better, too. I was finished with the nightmares. These dreams were more like sleeping memories really. I kept dreaming about things that had already happened.

I had this dream about a Sunday afternoon when I was sitting on the porch with Daddy, eating egg custard. Both of us were cracking jokes on Jellico, the old junk man that used to come down our street in a horse drawn wagon. We used to tease him and call him Jelly Roll instead of Jellico, because he was so fat. Stupid stuff is funny when you happy. Those were good times. It was the weekend. Mother cancelled my birthday party because I stuck this fool girl Ella in the leg with a fork. She had to be the best at everything, and when she wasn't someone had to pay for it.

Ella couldn't stand me. Every time she came around me, she had a piece of candy or something and went on about how good it was. She wouldn't share unless you begged her. I never understood how she could do that. "Ohhh, this is the best chocolate." She would say licking her tongue around the cone, like it was chocolate imported from Paris France instead of your everyday kind. Every one else was standing around mouths drooling. The girl was just plain hateful!

I decided to ask Daddy if I could have some money so I could buy my friends and me a treat. I didn't even have to tell him about Ella, he would give me what I wanted just because I asked.

The day I bought everyone a piece of candy, Ella was too through. She tried acting her nasty self, but this time all the girls ignored her. We went through the same thing the next couple of days. By Friday, she'd had her feel. It was the day before my birthday and Daddy gave me some extra money so I could "do a little celebrating" with my friends at the Sweet Shoppe. I bought a burger, fries, and soda for all of my girlfriends. I could feel Ella standing behind us at the counter just burnin' up. Truth is, I would have bought some for her, too, 'cause I'm soft hearted, but she was so hateful. Even if I offered, she wouldn't take it. Ella sat in the booth right behind us all by herself. We acted like she wasn't there and talked about my party and who was coming. Ella tried to break in with her smart mouth and was getting hotter by the minute cuz we kept on ignoring her. When we got to who I liked she said, "Ain't no need in worrying about that cuz you too fat for anybody anyway. That's why you got to buy your friends."

She said it loud enough that the whole place got quiet and everyone was stared at me. Fire came up my body. I know the devil took me over. I was so mad I couldn't see straight. I know I didn't like the girl, but I had never done her wrong for her to front me like that. I didn't learn how to cuss people good until I got grown, so I said the first thing that popped in my head. "Sticks and stones can break my bones, but words will never hurt me." It was a lie, because she had hurt my feelings bad.

Ella bust out laughing and the chocolate in her mouth mixed with nuts and spit flew out hitting me in the face. Worse than that, she called me a fat fool. I was mad as a bull in the ring, I could barely see straight. The sour in her spit mixed with the sweet of the chocolate dripping from the tip of my nose. I can't recall thinking, but I saw myself sticking a fork in her thigh. I came back to myself when I heard a bunch of boys yelling "Fight! Fight!"

Meantime, Ella was screaming something about me trying to kill her and another girl was yelling, "She's bleeding, she's bleeding." I sat back down in my booth half in shock and half thinking about what Mother was going to say. She wouldn't stand for me acting alley. The last thing she tolerated was for any of her children to act common.

Ain't no secrets in a small town, and Mr. and Mrs. Owens, who owned the Sweet Shoppe, lived right next door to Mama Seal, Mother's mama. They had to tell her what happened, they been knowing Mother all her life; they were like a second set of parents to her. Mrs. Owens called her husband out from the back to help her calm things down. She went to pull the fork out of Ella's leg and the dumb face girl lost it. It was clear to me that the girl was a fake. Her leg might have been hurt, but not as bad as she was carrying on, "Ow, Ow, I can't move my leg!" I could see Mrs. Owens trying to hold back a smile. Looking at her, I realized that I wasn't going to be in too much trouble.

Mama Seal was the sweetest lady that every lived. Mrs. Owens told her all about what happened with Ella and she never said a word. Even though she didn't get after me, she was going to tell Mother what happened. That's the kind of woman she was. I was shocked a second time when it was Daddy, not Mother, who came to carry me back from Mama Seal's house. Like Mama Seal, he said nothing. When we got home, he went straight to Mother in the kitchen and closed the door. I went on upstairs to my room to wait for Mother. Instead of lighting into me like I expected, she stood in my doorway shaking her head and said, "You really do need to learn how to control yourself."

I'm sure that Daddy said something to her while they were in the kitchen; it just wasn't like her to let go of things easy like. Later on that evening, Ella's mama and daddy came to the house. They talked to Mother and Daddy for a while. R. Thomas wanted to listen in at the top of the stairs, but I wasn't interested. Who wants to know beforehand what kind of trouble is coming. I took my time going downstairs when Daddy called me. He took my hand when I came in the room and took me to stand in front of Mother who was sitting in an armchair across from Ella's parents.

I could see why Ella was such a snot. She had her mama to learn from. You would have thought that they were visiting with the Queen of England the way that they were carrying on. Her mother was sipping from a teacup with her pinky finger poked out sitting on the very same divan that is in my living room now. I bet she had never even drunk a cup of tea and here she was carrying on like a little girl at play. They were all dressed in their Sunday best. Ella's mama had been in our house plenty of times. She was the seamstress in a dress shop downtown, and she brought dresses from the store for Mother to try on. Mother figured that her money was as good as any white person, and she would be darned if she couldn't try her dresses on. As a compromise, the store let her shop from home so that their white customers wouldn't know. Mother and Ella's mama were in the habit of gossiping about the white folks in town while she tried on clothes. White folks are funny, in the store they will talk to the seamstress like she a psychiatrist, but pass her on the street, and they don't even know she there.

Ella sat on our divan just as ignorant as her mama. Judging by the two of them, a person would have thought that we were playing tea. Ella's father, on the other hand, looked like a man out of place. He kept fidgeting with his tie and clearing his throat.

His hands looked much too big to handle a delicate china teacup. Bringing the cup to his lips they were shaking so bad, he spilled it down the front of his shirt. Ella's mama looked like she wanted to choke him, and Ella rolled her eyes in disgust. I felt sorry for the man.

"Don't mind that." Daddy laughed. "A real man ain't meant to drink out of no tiny little cups."

Ella's daddy looked grateful. Ella and her mama looked not so mad but not happy either. Her daddy cleared his throat and said that it was time to leave, and her mama shot him a nasty look.

"Before you do," Daddy said, applying pressure to my shoulder. "Bea has something to say."

His hand passed me the strength I needed to apologize. Without it, I would have spit on the girl or at least left the room.

I looked down at the pattern on the carpet and rocked back and forth on my legs "I'm sorry I stuck a fork in your leg."

Ella's daddy jumped up, shook Daddy's hand, and walked out. Ella's mother looked at him with her mouth open. And Daddy got up to open the door. Reluctantly, she took Ella's hand and followed him. I squinted my eyes and looked twice and sure enough, Ella was limping out on the wrong leg.

My dream was all so clear, even down to what Daddy said on the porch that Sunday.

"Bea, I'm sorry that your Mama didn't have your party. What you did was wrong. I know that she said some low-down, mean, nasty things. You might as well learn it now that you can't control what other folks say, think or do. The only thing that you can control is you. A hot pot has to be taken care of before it boils over. The best way to stop folks from tromping all over you is to nip it in the bud."

At the time, I didn't pay much attention to what Daddy was

saying. I was happy enough to sit on the porch and eat my custard with him. I couldn't get that dream oughta my head; it was high time for me to stop myself from boilin' over.

CHAPTER TWENTY-THREE
RACHAEL

I used to imagine what it would be like to shop for a house. In my imagination, I'd romanticize the whole thing. My husband and I driving up to the perfect family abode, kids in tow, and everyone happy. We'd step inside the house that was painted the prefect shade of sunny yellow, and I'd go straight to the sun filled kitchen to look out of the window at the sink. Through the window, I could see my large perfectly manicured backyard, which included a swing set that the kids had, of course, found. I would step out the back door onto a deck equipped with a gas grill and discover that, wonder of wonders, the previous owner had a well-established herb garden. In my dream house, the electrical and plumbing systems worked perfectly. The previous owner spent tons redoing the house, mind readers that they were; they installed my spa bathroom retreat. The only reason they wanted to leave the dream home they created was a better job opportunity in another part of the country.

In reality, I was way off. With June only a month away we were taking a week to look for houses Richard's way. The kids started complaining before we even got to the first house. Due to the awful directions we had, we got lost. "You know, you can always stop at the nearest gas station and ask for directions."

True to his sex, Richard refused to stop. "I can find it," He pulled into an empty parking lot and turned the car around for the third time. Richard shot me a look that let me know that under no circumstances was I to suggest that he stop again.

When we passed a Tudor on the corner for the third time, I felt it necessary to speak up. "I think we are driving in circles."

"No, we're not."

Was he kidding me?

"Daddy," Sherril whined from the back seat, "why do we keep going around and around."

I looked out of my window with a satisfied smile despite the fact that he would take the word of a six year old over mine. By the time we finally got the house, we were all rather grumpy.

The exterior of the house did nothing to improve my mood. The first thing that greeted us as we pulled into the drive was a mad Doberman on a tie out chain. Apparently, the dog belonged to the owners of the house next door to the house we were viewing. I had long concluded that the owners of vicious dogs rarely appreciate the way others feel about their animals. If they did, they wouldn't place them in positions to frighten and harass their neighbors. No wonder why the people wanted to give this house away, I thought. The dog was chained right next to the drive of what might have been the future home of my children and me. As far as I was concerned, the dog in and of itself took the house out of the running. Not to be deterred by the smell of decaying dog poop, Richard wanted to have a look inside.

Time we stepped through the door I knew that Richard wouldn't be interested. I smelled cats, and not in a good way. Mrs. Smith, the owner, was a sharp looking woman who was dressed to the nines. She held up her hand as she led us inside. "I swear, the carpets have been shampooed."

The fact that she started out swearing to it didn't lend anything to her veracity, but I couldn't tell it from the smell. Vee started singing a P U song, as Mrs. Smith showed us through the house. Thank God for Richards' cat allergy. I would have been embarrassed by Vee's song but she was doing the owner a favor. They needed to know about the smell. There was no way I could live in a house that funky. I excused myself and took Vee outside to face the mad Doberman before the smell of cat piss made us vomit. Richard followed right behind me and we traveled on to house number two.

I couldn't decide if the second house that we visited was worse or better. The owner of the house died, and his son was in town to settle his affairs. After the burial, the first thing he should have done was clean up the place. From the looks of it, the man had never thrown anything away. Two broken down cars were parked in the yard. The rest of the yard was littered with junk, including a doghouse that was falling apart, an old wheelchair, and all kinds of gardening supplies and equipment. At one time, the yard had probably been well tended; it was full of flowers that had grown wild because of neglect.

"I know it's a mess," Mr. West said humbly. "My father had a hard time letting go of things. I'm in the process of clearing things out now."

Oh my God. If he'd already started cleaning up the mess, I couldn't imagine what the house looked like before he started. In his effort to clean, Mr. West created piles of like items. There were stacks of clothing, papers, and mess in general. The place was a firetrap. We followed Mr. West into the kitchen trying not to disturb any of his piles along the way.

"This was my mother's favorite room in the house," he declared proudly.

I was afraid of what it might hold but surprisingly it was normal. Apparently, his father didn't like to cook. Although the kitchen, was clean, everything about it was outdated. They even had plaster mushroom molds hanging on the wall. It looked like something off of the set of the Wonder Years.

We were walking down the hallway to look at the bedrooms when Sherril fell and exclaimed, "Mommy, this place is too junky!"

I turned around quickly and placed my fingers against my lips and gave her a stern look.

Things were going just as I'd envisioned. I kept my mouth shut. Things were tense enough as it was. I didn't want to say anything to cause an argument. Richards' phone rang as we pulled out of the driveway.

"Hello."

Please, I thought, not another crappy house.

"This is he. How many bedrooms?"

Ugh, it was.

"Okay if you can give me directions and the address, I can come by now. Would that be a problem?"

"Geeze," I said without thinking. "Not another one!"

Richard ignored me as he called out the address and directions. Ottawa, I recognized the street. I went to college with Trina Moore. She lived on Ottawa. We had to do a project for a sociology class together. From what I remembered, it was a nice house with a big yard and a finished basement. I kept my fingers crossed that this house was at least in the same range as Trina's.

It wasn't Trina's house, but, finally, we drove up to a house that we could work with. I sensed Richard's excitement. "Hi, my name is Richard, this is my wife Rachael. What size is the yard?"

"It's half an acre. I'm Bob Jordan, and this is my wife Karen."

I reached out my hand in greeting. "It's nice to meet you." Richard had already blown our cover. We were supposed to be playing good cop bad cop, and I was supposed to be the good cop. It was my job to act excited, and Richard's job to act like the hard ass.

Bob went on. "Yes, this is a big lot. You know that can be hard to find at an affordable price in the Atlanta market."

"Well," I said, stepping on Richard's toe trying to get him back on track. "The grass is half dead."

Richard failed to pick up on my signal. "We can work with that."

We followed behind the couple as they led the way inside. Richard took my hand, and said a prayer under his breath. "Lord, Please let this be the one."

The inside looked far better than the other fixer uppers we'd seen. The important thing was that it was clean, and I didn't sniff any neglected pet smells. "I know that the avocado shag carpeting has to be replaced. But, the hard wood underneath is in decent condition," Karen pointed out.

"Oh, don't worry about that," Richard said with a wave of dismissal, "that shouldn't be any problem at all."

"This is the great room," Bob said, walking over to the stone fireplace. Pointing to the ceiling, he continued. "This room is two stories. We use the upstairs as the den."

Karen walked over to a sliding door and opened it up to a

deck. "This deck unites the kitchen, dining, and living areas."

Richard and I held hands as we followed them into the kitchen.

"So, here's the kitchen." Bob smiled. "You see, it's a nice size," he said, turning in a circle. "Big enough to fit a table that seats five and still gives you room to move around."

I walked over to the cabinets, and opened them up. Remember, I said to myself, you are now playing the role of bad cop. "The cabinets look a little worn."

"Yes, but they are solid maple," Karen said, opening another cabinet door and showing me the inside. "You can always refinish them."

"So the stove is gas?" I asked.

Karen nodded. "I prefer gas."

I was happy to see that the kitchen would accommodate a gas stove, a dishwasher, and a sizeable refrigerator. These were all of the amenities that I'd gotten used to at Virginia's.

Richard walked over to the kitchen window. "Babe, look at all of the light coming in from the backyard."

He was like a kid at the playground. I had to admit, the kitchen had a lot of light coming in through the window over the sink, much like my imaginary house. There was a door leading to the backyard. There wasn't any play equipment, but the kids did discover the backyard, and they were enjoying it. I let them play as we toured the rest of the house

Once upstairs, Bob directed us to the first door off of the hallway. "Here is one of the bathrooms."

I looked inside. "It's a little small." The bathroom was perfect for two little girls.

Richard walked up behind me. "This can be the bathroom for the kids."

Karen walked across the hall and stepped inside the first bedroom. She walked over to the closet and slid open the door. "This room has nice size closet space."

I nodded. The two girls would have to share a bedroom but at least they had floor space and a reasonably sized closet. The next bedroom they showed us was smaller, but a one year old only needed so much space.

The last room they took us into was the master bedroom. I would have preferred a larger master bedroom—the one in our old apartment got me spoiled. But this was definitely something I could live with.

"You see how it's tucked away on its own landing, away from other parts of the house?" Bob asked.

Richard and I both nodded as we looked around the room. After living with Virginia, the idea of that kind of privacy made me giddy.

Karen continued the selling points. "It's only a few steps down from the other two rooms, plus, it has its own private bath."

She said the magic words. Every woman wants her own private bath. Well in this case, it would be almost my own. Richard didn't have that much stuff.

So far this was the best house that we'd seen. The neighborhood was good, and the price was right. I stood back and let Richard work out the financial agreement. "The price you quoted over the phone was eight hundred and fifty a month right?

"That's it," Bob agreed. "We would like to get the first month up front, and also one months rent, but we can put that in an escrow account. Now, we agreed to owner finance for one year, and then you can refinance."

Richard nodded his head. "Agreed."

"Well, just so that I know you're serious, we need two thousand dollars in earnest money, and of course I expect you to pay the closing cost."

"Not a problem," Richard said, offering his hand.

The two men shook on it and went out to Bob's car to draw up an agreement on Bob's laptop. I was so happy I practically floated out to the backyard to collect the kids. I came back around to the front in time to witness Richard handing over a check for the earnest money. After signing the agreement, we went out to dinner to celebrate.

CHAPTER TWENTY-FOUR
BEA

It will never cease to amaze me how much you can do on the Internet. Once I told Rachael that I might be interested in finding out about my son, she got right on it. She pulled that thing out on the coffee table, plugged in the phone line and started pulling up all kinds of information. I tried to give her all of the information I could remember for the birth record.

Virginia was sitting at the kitchen counter drinking a glass of tea. "You know, Bea," She said to me through the half wall, "I've been thinking. I think that it's probably most likely that Mother gave your son to someone that she knew."

"Well how is that going to help me now?" I asked from my seat in the recliner. "Most of the people Mother knew back then are long gone."

Virginia took her glass over to the sink and came into the den. She started straightening the books on the bookshelf. "Well," she said, pulling a book from the self. "We could look through some of these old albums and maybe they'll help us think of a likely suspect."

Rachael looked up from her computer. "You don't think that we could find the birth record?"

Virginia sat on the couch with a stack of photo albums. "It might. But back then things weren't as formal as they are now. Especially among black people. There might not even be a birth record."

I shuddered and they both looked over to me. "I can't take it," I said, pressing my hand to my chest. "Maybe we should leave the whole thing alone."

"Bea, it's okay," Rachael said, trying to assure me.

"We don't have to do it right now. Virginia said. She got up and put the albums back on the bookshelf. We can try again when you've had time to get used to the idea. My heart was racing a mile a minute. I was feeling so flustered my head was starting to itch.

I went home and put my feet up. I was happy for Richard and Rachael, but I hated to think about them leaving. Here she was trying to buy all this furniture for a new house, and I had given away furniture that she could have had free and clear. I got madder and madder thinking about it. It just wasn't fair that I no longer had what was mine. Daddy worked hard all his life to see to it that we were well taken care of. For the most part, I squandered everything. Instead of feeling like I didn't want to live, I wanted to do something about it. I asked Rachael to drop me off at home.

When I got home, I called Faye and asked her if she wanted to go out for some ice cream later on that night.

"Bea, you know it's time for Jeopardy." You would have sworn Faye was married to Alex Trebec as faithful as she was to his show.

"Just come by and get me when it goes off. I know we old,

but it's too hot to be stuck up in the house."

I was sittin' outside on my front porch waiting when she drove up thirty five minutes later. Faye pulled into the driveway and blew the horn.

"What did you blow for?" I asked, opening the door to her Cadillac. "I was sitting right there."

"I didn't see you. Make sure you straighten out that towel before you get in. I don't want you messing up my seat."

Lord, Jesus I swear. The car was only ten years old. Faye bought it when her husband died. I made sure to spread the towel on the seat out, and then I fix the one up over the head rest, before taking a seat in her precious white leather interior.

"Don't slam my door," Faye said before I even put my hand on the handle.

I tried to close the door as gently as I could and still make sure that it was closed good enough that I wouldn't fall out. I nearly choked to death from the smell of all the perfume that was floatin' through the air. I reached out to turn the vent toward me when I spied a homemade sachet attached to it. I cut my eyes at Faye. I should have known. In addition to Alex Trebec, the woman was addicted to Estée Lauder. Instead of foolin with the vent, I let the window down.

"You know you wasting good air conditioning," Faye fussed.

I nodded. I wasn't interested in Faye's fussing. I was on a mission. "You'll have to excuse me, but I feel a cold coming on, and that air conditioning aggravates my chest."

"Chile," Faye said, pulling up to the light. "It's always something."

"Tell me about it. Listen, instead of Dairy Queen, why don't we drive through town. I heard about this new place that serves malted milkshakes."

"That's fine," Faye answered. "My outfit is too good to waste on those young folks at the Dairy Queen anyway."

I looked over at Faye's matching outfit. She took the time to put on a pastel pink Bermuda short set with matching tennis shoes and a matching sun visor. For her, any occasion was an occasion to get dressed. As we got closer to downtown, I started to get nervous. "I think you need to turn right here." I pointed to the street that Eunique lived on.

Faye turned onto the street. "I hope you know where you going."

"I think Miss Mary from my water aerobics class lives on this street," I lied. I didn't even take water aerobics."

"Honey, I am telling you, every since that woman has started losing weight, you can't tell her nothing," Faye said.

"Uh, huh," I said, half listening. Faye never got too tired to tell other people's business. I was busy looking out the window for Eunique's car; I wanted to see if he was still parking it at his sister's house. Sure enough, there it was. Seeing it, I ducked down in my seat. I wished Faye would hurry up. She was so busy running her mouth she was driving too slow, and there was a car with music blasting following behind us. Just when I thought they would blow the horn, they turned in Eunique's driveway. I let out a sigh of relief once we reached the stop sign.

Glancing in the rear view mirror, I watched them climbing out of the car. Thank you Jesus. I wish I had thought of this whole thing sooner. Those boys looked like they were up to no good. Eunique was selling drugs out of his sister's house. I don't know why I hadn't recognized it before. The whole time we was friends, Eunique made these stops by his sister's house while we were out riding. On COPS, I saw people selling drugs out of a house. It put me in the mind of Eunique. It had to be what he was doing. The man didn't have a job, always had money, and always out riding getting paged. Why else would he be hanging out with a bunch of low lifes? Yeah, that had to be what it was.

I decided to give our local police department a call. Thanks to Faye's slow driving, I had just the information that I needed.

CHAPTER TWENTY-FIVE
RACHAEL

I woke up the morning we were leaving Virginia's with mixed emotions. I'd come to her house acting like I'd just been assigned a long jail term, and now that it was time to go, I was a little sad. I was happy that Virginia and I had gotten to know each other at least a little better. Virginia was definitely a person to be admired, even if she did have a tendency to be a little bossy. After checking to make sure that we had all of our things from upstairs, I went down to the kitchen to tell her good bye. "Well," I said, walking up to her. "I think that we have everything."

"Goodbye darling" Virginia said, and gave me a hug. "I was at the store and they were having a good sale, so I got you a few things." She motioned toward the mudroom.

A few things were more like several shopping bags.

"Thank you," I said. "Whatever it is, I'm sure that we will be able to use it."

The kids all ran inside and said their goodbyes. Elliot was walking now and doing his best to keep up to his sisters.

Sherril stopped in the middle of the floor and asked Virginia, "Grandma, are you sure you are going to be all right by yourself?"

"Oh, baby, I'll be fine." She stooped to give Sherrill a hug. "But it was so thoughtful of you to ask."

"Well, Daddy says you need to get a dog."

"We'll see. And how about you, Vee, may I have a hug?"

Virginia threw her whole body into hugging Virginia and bounced out of the door without looking back. She didn't understand the concept of space and time well enough to know that we weren't going to live with Virginia anymore.

I picked up the baby and watched as Sherrill followed Vee outside. "We still need to go and say goodbye to Bea. I thought that she would come over."

"You know she doesn't handle good byes very well."

"I'm not surprised. Umm, I still want to help in your search for her son."

"Well I made a few phone calls and I think I have a good possibility. I don't want to say anything to Bea until I know for sure."

I nodded. "I understand."

Richard finished packing the car and tried to come in through the mudroom. "Who put all these bags against the door?" he asked, sticking his head through the small opening in the door.

"I just thought I'd pick up a few things for you to take back to Atlanta."

"A few!" Richard commented.

I hugged Virginia one last time before going to the door and taking some of the bags out to the car.

Bea drove up while I was trying to find some space in the car for the bags in the mudroom. I put down the bags and waited for her to get out of the car. "I'm so glad you came," I said, hugging her.

She was already starting to cry. "I sure hate to see y'all leave."

"I know," I said, squeezing her tighter. "That is why you have to come visit our new house. Potty time," I called to the kids.

I picked up the baby, and took the girls inside. Vee wanted to use the potty by herself like a big girl, so I joined Bea who was watching her soaps in the den. Her soaps were interrupted by a news update. Mr. Eunique Johnson and a three other men were shown being hauled off in handcuffs. According to the reporter, they were being arrested for gambling and drug trafficking.

"We are here live on the scene," the female correspondent reported. "Hold on, we have the suspect's sister and the home owner right here."

"Ma'am, can you tell us how long your brother has been running this illegal operation…"

A woman with her hair all over her head and a child on her hip proclaimed, "My brother ain't done nothing. The police always come down here harrassin' us."

The camera cut to a shot of several bags of white powder that the police were collecting from a card table inside of a shack in the back of the sister's house.

The neighbors told a different story. All of the things that they were afraid to say while the men were unshackled came spilling forth. A woman in a floral housedress hair in rollers stepped up. "It be people comin' and goin' at all hours. They threatened my cousin when he said sumpin."

A little boy who was darting back and forth in front of the camera chimed in, "They always shootin'!"

The reporter regained control of her interview as the cameraman did a close up of a SWAT vehicle. SWAT team members were loading the truck with boxes. "This house of ill repute is the base for illegal gambling and drug sells. This may be the biggest bust of the past five years," the reporter said in closing.

I stepped closer to the television. "Isn't that your friend?" I asked Bea in amazement.

"Uh, no! He ain't no friend of mine! See what a snake that man is. A criminal through and through, he gonna get what he deserve." Bea looked like the cat that ate the canary.

Maybe he was, although his going to jail wouldn't give her property back. I hoped it would provide her with some relief. "I guess all things do come together for the greater good," I said giving her a hug.

Bea hugged me back. "I'm gonna miss you," she said, tears welling up in her eyes. You just like a daughter to me. I wish you wasn't leaving."

"Ahh," I said, hugging her again. "I am really going to miss you too. But you better come visit me. I have to take you all around the hot spots!"

"There you go talking your nonsense. I'm too old for hot spots."

We laughed together. Maybe Bea would find some peace after all.

AUTHOR BIOGRAPHY

Colette Tells it Like It Is!

Colette is a creative soul, who has been writing since childhood. From short stories as a child, to heading her high school newspaper, Colette went on to win several awards in both high school and college. It was during college that Colette began working in the entertainment industry as a script consultant, which led to her stint as a copy writer for a small advertising agency.

After years of fulfilling her role as a wife, and full time mother, the creative urge was consuming her. Colette had to write! Undaunted by the lack of enthusiasm she received from the publishing industry, Colette took the bull by the horns and jumped into the world of self-publishing. The reviews for *Peace Be Still*, Colette's first novel have been phenomenal! Always ready to take advantage of an opportunity, Colette negotiated with Borders books located in Stonecrest Mall, Lithonia, GA., to moderate a monthly writing workshop. In addition to her writer's group, she is the host of Colette's Coffeehouse, a one hour talk show all about books. Colette's Coffeehouse features one on one-vibe sessions connecting readers to writers. In connection with her talk show Colette also moderates, a women's lit channel at Bella Online, a site dedicated to and run by women. With her effervescent charm and unique style, Colette's list of avid readers is sure to continue to grow.

Colette continues to reside in Atlanta with her husband and three children.

Contact:
Colette
www.colettewrites.com
chaywood_99@yahoo.com

See her other titles at **www.genesis-press.com**

Excerpt from

I'LL PAINT THE SUN

BY

A.J. GARROTTO

Release Date March 2005

In the morning when I awake, I stretch my hands over my expanding belly, measuring the widening distance between my fingertips. I feel you move within me and I speak your name. Tobías. We'll call you Toby. How different your childhood will be than mine, lived in cramped quarters on heavily trafficked, windswept streets of one of the world's great commercial and tourist centers.

I've stepped back generations in time into an unfamiliar culture to live among a people I long to understand and become part of. I perch here free as a seabird, gazing out from the uneven flagstone terrace of our new home. My eyes feast on the South Caribbean's turquoise expanse while, at my feet, the serene Santa Magdalena shoreline stretches left and right. My lips taste the salty breeze which invites me to open my silk robe and let the mild, humid air slip across my swollen abdomen like your father's gentle hands in the night. My senses fine-tune to island sounds and tropical fragrances having no particular point of origin. The melodies and scents of happiness, I call them.

The waves await their turn to tumble shoreward with the rush of a première danseur leaping across a broad stage. Their sudsy fingers claw at the white-sand beach before returning to rest in deeper water before making another run at the shore.

With golden sunlight filtering through my closed eyelids, I marvel that healing and new life have replaced my vow of a year ago, never to trust another man as long as I possessed sound mental and emotional faculties. Healing. No other word describes our experience. I inhale...heal...caressing the silent sound and exhale...ing. My spirit breathes its gentle rhythm. The cadence anoints me with its sacred oil. You, Toby, are its fruit, its prize and celebration.

Your father's restoration during this time has been even more unlikely than my own. Scarred men and women—children too—make pilgrimage to the world's designated holy places praying for renewal of body and soul. Our miracle happened in the city of St. Francis. Quite by chance, if one believes in coincidence. I don't, not any more.

On the turbulent SFO-to-Miami flight, I read Message In a Bottle. Garrett Blake's love letters to his deceased wife brought such sadness to my heart that I exhausted my supply of tissues and soaked your father's handkerchief. When the book ended, I napped, head resting on his shoulder. I dreamed of sea-tossed bottles and sealed-in treasures. I remember saying to someone in my dream, "We're all corked bottles, each with our deepest truths sealed inside."

We devoted our first days on the island to patching the frayed cloth of your father's relationship with your grandparents. Amid tears and laughter, the principals of that divided trinity have let go of old hurts and reknit bonds of love like fragments of shattered bone. I've fallen in love with these good people who welcomed their prodigal home without question, if not without the lingering pain of his leaving them. They have drawn me, a stranger and foreigner not-yet fluent in their language, to their bosoms with such open-hearted hospitality that I have vowed to model my parenting after their example.

A local real estate broker found us this furnished beachfront mansion that belonged to international recording star Eduardo Colón, whose name is spoken with reverence on this island.

"The only item Señor Colón and his new bride took with them to Paris was the grand piano," the broker told us. Minus the massive instrument, the conservatory looks like a glassed-in ballroom. You'll love playing in it. Why the Colóns left everything is a mystery to me. Did some tragedy scar the tables, chairs, beds, and mirrors, sending the newlyweds in pursuit of fresh dreams far from home? If so, I identify with their need.

It will take me years to integrate the events that brought me to this place. I began this year in despair, facing bankruptcy. Can it now be true that every brick and nail and pane of glass in this villa estate belongs to us, paid for in cash? The deck I stand on? The spacious bedroom in which we sleep? The broad pool we swam in last evening and made love in the night before? If you've paid attention, you'll come into the world knowing all about the birds and bees. What a relief that will be to your father.

Okay, Toby. That was a certifiable kick.

I'm your bottle, aren't I? Impenetrable green, like a liter of rich red wine. You, the unreadable message. Are you running out of patience with the sealed safety of my womb? Are you ready to embark on the adventure we earthlings call Life? I want to know you, learn your deepest desires, discover what makes you happy and sad. How I'd love to fast-forward, to see how you'll fulfill your destiny.

Not true.

I'm an impatient woman but I'd rather walk that unpredictable road with you, each day marking a single step along your life-path. I'll thrill with your every new discovery, rejoice in the measured unfolding of your inner spirit. Will the stories you tell your children come close to matching the ones we'll tell you on nights when tropical storms lash at the windows testing the endurance of our house? I can't bear the thought of you suffering, of ever losing your way as we did.

Two mourning doves just landed on the fountain in the corner of the terrace. I wish you could see how the jacaranda trees have spread a soft lavender welcome mat for them. These loving creatures remind me of a TV show in the States about divine messengers with the mission to heal the wounded, restore sight to those blind in spirit. If there's one thing your mom knows about, Toby, it's angels. I have two of my own. Let me tell you the miracle story of how our little family came to be.

PEACE BE STILL

2005 Publication Schedule

January

A Heart's Awakening
Veronica Parker
$9.95
1-58571-143-9

Falling
Natalie Dunbar
$9.95
1-58571-121-7

February

Echoes of Yesterday
Beverly Clark
$9.95
1-58571-131-4

A Love of Her Own
Cheris F. Hodges
$9.95
1-58571-136-5

Higher Ground
Leah Latimer
$19.95
1-58571-157-8

March

Misconceptions
Pamela Leigh Starr
$9.95
1-58571-117-9

I'll Paint a Sun
A.J. Garrotto
$9.95
1-58571-165-9

Peace Be Still
Colette Haywood
$12.95
1-58571-129-2

April

Intentional Mistakes
Michele Sudler
$9.95
1-58571-152-7

Conquering Dr. Wexler's Heart
Kimberley White
$9.95
1-58571-126-8

Song in the Park
Martin Brant
$15.95
1-58571-125-X

May

The Color Line
Lizette Carter
$9.95
1-58571-163-2

Unconditional
A.C. Arthur
$9.95
1-58571-142-X

Last Train to Memphis
Elsa Cook
$12.95
1-58571-146-2

June

Angel's Paradise
Janice Angelique
$9.95
1-58571-107-1

Suddenly You
Crystal Hubbard
$9.95
1-58571-158-6

Matters of Life and
Death
Lesego Malepe, Ph.D.
$15.95
1-58571-124-1

2005 Publication Schedule (continued)

July

Pleasures All Mine
Belinda O. Steward
$9.95
1-58571-112-8

Wild Ravens
Altonya Washington
$9.95
1-58571-164-0

Class Reunion
Irma Jenkins/John
Brown
$12.95
1-58571-123-3

August

Path of Thorns
Annetta P. Lee
$9.95
1-58571-145-4

Timeless Devotion
Bella McFarland
$9.95
1-58571-148-9

Life Is Never As It Seems
June Michael
$12.95
1-58571-153-5

September

Beyond the Rapture
Beverly Clark
$9.95
1-58571-131-4

Blood Lust
J. M. Jeffries
$9.95
1-58571-138-1

Rough on Rats and
Tough on Cats
Chris Parker
$12.95
1-58571-154-3

October

A Will to Love
Angie Daniels
$9.95
1-58571-141-1

Taken by You
Dorothy Elizabeth Love
$9.95
1-58571-162-4

Soul Eyes
Wayne L. Wilson
$12.95
1-58571-147-0

November

A Drummer's Beat to
Mend
Kay Swanson
$9.95

Sweet Reprecussions
Kimberley White
$9.95
1-58571-159-4

Red Polka Dot in a
Worldof Plaid
Varian Johnson
$12.95
1-58571-140-3

December

Hand in Glove
Andrea Jackson
$9.95
1-58571-166-7

Blaze
Barbara Keaton
$9.95

Across
Carol Payne
$12.95
1-58571-149-7

Other Genesis Press, Inc. Titles

Erotic Anthology	Assorted	$8.95
Eve's Prescription	Edwina Martin Arnold	$8.95
Everlastin' Love	Gay G. Gunn	$8.95
Fate	Pamela Leigh Starr	$8.95
Forbidden Quest	Dar Tomlinson	$10.95
Fragment in the Sand	Annetta P. Lee	$8.95
From the Ashes	Kathleen Suzanne	$8.95
	Jeanne Sumerix	
Gentle Yearning	Rochelle Alers	$10.95
Glory of Love	Sinclair LeBeau	$10.95
Hart & Soul	Angie Daniels	$8.95
Heartbeat	Stephanie Bedwell-Grime	$8.95
I'll Be Your Shelter	Giselle Carmichael	$8.95
Illusions	Pamela Leigh Starr	$8.95
Indiscretions	Donna Hill	$8.95
Interlude	Donna Hill	$8.95
Intimate Intentions	Angie Daniels	$8.95
Just an Affair	Eugenia O'Neal	$8.95
Kiss or Keep	Debra Phillips	$8.95
Love Always	Mildred E. Riley	$10.95
Love Unveiled	Gloria Greene	$10.95
Love's Deception	Charlene Berry	$10.95
Mae's Promise	Melody Walcott	$8.95
Meant to Be	Jeanne Sumerix	$8.95
Midnight Clear	Leslie Esdaile	$10.95
(Anthology)	Gwynne Forster	
	Carmen Green	
	Monica Jackson	
Midnight Magic	Gwynne Forster	$8.95
Midnight Peril	Vicki Andrews	$10.95
My Buffalo Soldier	Barbara B. K. Reeves	$8.95
Naked Soul	Gwynne Forster	$8.95
No Regrets	Mildred E. Riley	$8.95
Nowhere to Run	Gay G. Gunn	$10.95

Object of His Desire	A. C. Arthur	$8.95
One Day at a Time	Bella McFarland	$8.95
Passion	T.T. Henderson	$10.95
Past Promises	Jahmel West	$8.95
Path of Fire	T.T. Henderson	$8.95
Picture Perfect	Reon Carter	$8.95
Pride & Joi	Gay G. Gunn	$8.95
Quiet Storm	Donna Hill	$8.95
Reckless Surrender	Rochelle Alers	$8.95
Rendezvous with Fate	Jeanne Sumerix	$8.95
Revelations	Cheris F. Hodges	$8.95
Rivers of the Soul	Leslie Esdaile	$8.95
Rooms of the Heart	Donna Hill	$8.95
Shades of Brown	Denise Becker	$8.95
Shades of Desire	Monica White	$8.95
Sin	Crystal Rhodes	$8.95
So Amazing	Sinclair LeBeau	$8.95
Somebody's Someone	Sinclair LeBeau	$8.95
Someone to Love	Alicia Wiggins	$8.95
Soul to Soul	Donna Hill	$8.95
Still Waters Run Deep	Leslie Esdaile	$8.95
Subtle Secrets	Wanda Y. Thomas	$8.95
Sweet Tomorrows	Kimberly White	$8.95
The Color of Trouble	Dyanne Davis	$8.95
The Price of Love	Sinclair LeBeau	$8.95
The Reluctant Captive	Joyce Jackson	$8.95
The Missing Link	Charlyne Dickerson	$8.95
Three Wishes	Seressia Glass	$8.95
Tomorrow's Promise	Leslie Esdaile	$8.95
Truly Inseperable	Wanda Y. Thomas	$8.95
Twist of Fate	Beverly Clark	$8.95
Unbreak My Heart	Dar Tomlinson	$8.95
Unconditional Love	Alicia Wiggins	$8.95
When Dreams A Float	Dorothy Elizabeth Love	$8.95

Whispers in the Night	Dorothy Elizabeth Love	$8.95
Whispers in the Sand	LaFlorya Gauthier	$10.95
Yesterday is Gone	Beverly Clark	$8.95
Yesterday's Dreams, Tomorrow's Promises	Reon Laudat	$8.95
Your Precious Love	Sinclair LeBeau	$8.95

ESCAPE WITH INDIGO !!!!

Join Indigo Book Club©
It's simple, easy and secure.

Sign up and receive the new releases
every month + Free shipping and
20% off the cover price.

Go online to www.genesis-press.com and
click on Bookclub or
call 1-888-INDIGO-1

Order Form

Mail to: Genesis Press, Inc.

P.O. Box 101
Columbus, MS 39703

Name _____
Address _____
City/State _____ Zip _____
Telephone _____

Ship to (if different from above)
Name _____
Address _____
City/State _____ Zip _____
Telephone _____

Credit Card Information

Credit Card # _____ ☐ Visa   ☐ Mastercard

Expiration Date (mm/yy) _____ ☐ AmEx   ☐ Discover

Qty.	Author	Title	Price	Total

Use this order form, or call
1-888-INDIGO-1

Total for books _____
Shipping and handling:
$5 first two books,
$1 each additional book _____
Total S & H _____
Total amount enclosed _____
Mississippi residents add 7% sales tax

Visit www.genesis-press.com for latest releases and excerpts.